"You're in the wrong business."

She shook her head.

"Are you a pro?" John Eagle asked. She slid away from him and reached for the car keys. "No, I'm not a pro. But I'm not a prude either. With you it is something special. The moment I saw you in the hotel lobby, I knew what I wanted to do to you."

Eagle nodded. "And we don't want Helmuth to know?"

"Not if it can be avoided."

"I would just as soon not get involved," said Eagle. "And don't look now, but there is something in the bushes out there. . . . ."

HAVE YOU READ ALL THE
JOHN EAGLE—EXPEDITOR BOOKS?

#1—NEEDLES OF DEATH
#2—BRAIN SCAVENGERS
#3—THE LAUGHING DEATH
#4—THE FIST OF FATIMA

VALLEY
OF
VULTURES

by

PAUL EDWARDS

▲ PYRAMID BOOKS ● NEW YORK

VALLEY OF VULTURES
A Pyramid Book

Produced by Lyle Kenyon Engel

Copyright © 1973 by Lyle Kenyon Engel

First printing December, 1973

ISBN 0-515-03183-6

Library of Congress Catalog Card Number: 73-17975

Printed in the United States of America

Pyramid Books are published by Pyramid Communications, Inc. Its trademarks, consisting of the word "Pyramid" and the portrayal of a pyramid, are registered in the United States Patent Office.

Pyramid Communications, Inc., 919 Third Avenue, New York, N.Y. 10022

CONTENTS

ever spoke of it in such fashion.
 at all. Often, as he dreamed in his
, an islet off the Maui coast, he
air to the great glass window over-
of Makaluha, and watching the
fireflies in the gloaming, would
ht answer his ancestors—they had
in Virginia in the seventeenth cen-
return and enquire: "How stands

give those ghosts an affirmative
ht be alive to answer, was Merlin's

years before he conceived the idea
and while John Eagle was still a
up as an Apache on an Arizona
eeting, and what was to ensue from
 adumbration. Not even a misty
sized crystal ball.
e dangers. He knew the enemies.
eral and ruthless, and largely from
ied men. He lived among them for
m well, studied their strengths and
an to make a list of men who were
cause of their money, but because
nough for them. Men for whom
 means to power. Men who loved
hings and who were sure that they,
t was best for the world. Paranoia

in fought these men in subtle and
on he realized it was not enough. He
and in New York, in 1943, an at-
n his life. It failed as murder but
ning. Merlin knew who had paid for
 settled the score, but immediately
 to a remote castle in Scotland. He
at he had learned his lesson. He

10

VALLEY OF VULTURES

Not that Mer
He rarely spoke
Hawaiian hideav
would power his
looking the crat
sparks like erra
ponder how he r
settled tobacco la
tury—were they
the Union?"

That he migl
answer, that he r
single ambition.

It began twent
of the Expeditor
stripling, growing
reservation. Their
it, was not yet
shadow in a plan

Merlin knew
They were many
his own class. M
a time, marked t
weaknesses. He t
dangerous. Not I
money was not
money was only
power beyond all
the elite, knew w
wears many mask

For a time M
secret ways. But
had many failure
tempt was made
succeeded as a w
the bullet, and I
afterward he reti
let it be known

IN THE BEGINN
ous parapherna
devices, though
and time, but tl
That it must be

Merlin knew
spine in the A
wheelchair, he f
than any ordina
plan.

His great edg
Soon to be billi
up to the minut
best accountant
timate his wealtl

Long before
began putting hi
work. It was sin
generation, outn

The protectio
elaborate plan 1
imperfections, a
face of the eartl
the people, and

retired from activity, from all strife, content in his wheelchair and in the Highland fastness of Caithness, to let the world go to hell in its own way.

Simultaneous to his retirement Merlin hired another man to live his life for him.

The man was an actor of little repute. He was of Merlin's age and very nearly his physical double. He had no living relatives and, of mean and acerbic disposition, no friends. His career, when Merlin found him, was at a dead end. He was only too pleased to die and be buried at sea. You can open a grave, but who can demand of the sea that it reveal a particular corpse?

The actor signed a contract with Merlin. Just as John Eagle had signed a contract. And just as Eagle lived up to the terms of the contract, so did the actor. For money. A quarter of a million a year for life. Play the role of a crippled recluse in a wheelchair; live a sequestered and lonely life in a castle perched high amidst desolate crags—live a lie that after many years came to seem truth. Live Merlin's life under his real name.

It was, Merlin often congratulated himself, a stroke of genius. Both men were content with the bargain. The actor was an introvert, a studious man content with his loneliness, and he aged as the real Merlin aged. Once or twice a year he made an appearance at some local social event, or was driven to the local market town, to give credence that he still lived.

And he was watched. In a desultory fashion, for the watchers were long convinced that the cripple, the man in the wheelchair they believed to be Merlin, had seen the error of his liberal ways. To aid them in this belief, and to forward his own rather devious ends, Merlin let the actor contribute some large sums to various reactionary schemes. When the schemes failed, fell into ruin and disaster, the participants never really understood what had destroyed them.

So it had been for years. Merlin lived in ease and

safety amid the splendor of Hawaii; his alter ego, the *Doppelgänger*, enjoyed his income and the solitude of his Pictish castle. Then came the note, the card of invitation, from the Demogorgon Society.

DEMOGORGON (dē′mə gôr′gən; dem′ə-), n. Myth. A mysterious, terrible, and evil divinity, commanding the spirits of the lower world, and appearing in medieval literature as a demon of magic or as a primordial creative power. In the Middle Ages it was believed the Demogorgon was confined in Hell, but managed to escape from time to time and reappear on earth.

Merlin replaced the big dictionary on its stand and spun his wheelchair back to an ornate and outsize desk, once the property of a 15th century Doge. In moments of reverie Merlin often stared at the inlaid surface and wondered how many death warrants had been signed thereon, how many men sent across the Bridge of Sighs to the garrote. He brushed the cool smooth surface with his hand, playing his long tapering fingers over the chryselephantine inlay. Old gold and ivory, the *elephas* now beiged with time. The real thing.

Just as the note and card from the Demogorgon Society was the real thing. Expensive. Imposing. Both were of vellum, lambskin, and the engraving had been done in real gold. Both had been analyzed in Merlin's laboratories buried deep in the guts of Makaluha.

The card was 8 x 5 and of golden cream texture.

Chaste gold script, exactly centered, spelled out: THE BEARER IS ENTITLED TO ALL THE PRIVILEGES OF THE VALHALLA CLUB.

Simple. To the point. Merlin smiled. Not yet dead—certainly not in battle—yet he was entitled to Valhalla. How so?

The note explained. And yet did not explain. It teased and hinted. Merlin recognized the Madison Avenue touch. The note promised everything—and nothing. Nothing actionable. Nothing on which a lawsuit could be pegged.

Merlin read the note again. Thoughtfully. Coincidence was knocking on the limen of his consciousness, urging, soft-talking through the door, and he did not like coincidence. Random or otherwise. What then? Planned?

He reached into a humidor for a long dark Cuban cigar. His dislike of Castro did not extend to tobacco. He considered the weed to be neutral. He lit up, puffed, then brushed ash from his smoking jacket and stared at the gold phone on his desk. One of six phones, none the same color. From the gold phone his glance shifted to the gold engraving of the note and the card. Merlin sighed and tried to blow a smoke ring. No luck.

Coincidence. It pressed in, its whisper more urgent.

Yesterday, an hour or so before the mail from Scotland arrived, the gold phone buzzed. The President of the United States spoke briefly and to the point. He wanted a favor. An *ex officio* favor. Off the record. It was probably nothing. Another false trail. Bum steer. But he was trying to keep the Israelis happy and he had promised to look into it. All *sub rosa*. Will you do what you can, Merlin?

Merlin would try. After a few brief pleasantries they hung up and Merlin made a note to himself. Mere routine and beyond doubt another wild goose chase.

Why didn't the Jews give up—stop beating a dead horse? Merlin not only was convinced in his own mind, but he also had the files to back his contention that

14

Martin Bormann was dead. He had no intention of wasting any time, money, or manpower on the fools' obsession to unearth evidence to the contrary.

Then Polly Perkins brought in the mail and there it was—the card and note forwarded from Scotland. Sent to him there, addressed to his real name—a name worn by the actor alter ego for twenty years—and bearing an Ecuadorian stamp to the value of twenty *sucres*. Air mail. It had been sent on from Blacktower Castle, Caith, to a PO box in New York and then to another PO box in San Francisco.

At first Merlin wondered why his other *self* had bothered to forward the thing—for years they had had an understanding about mail—but when he read the note he understood. His *Doppelgänger* was having a little jest. Or perhaps he was interested, even if the real Merlin was not. For what the note hinted at—if it did not promise—was the discovery of a marvelous new way to make an old man young. Both Merlin, and his alter ego in Scotland, were old men.

Rejuvenation. A new set of gonads. Fresh flowing jets of testosterone. And not from bulls' testes, and not a synthetic—so the cautiously worded message implied—but from an *original source*.

An original source? What in hell did *that* mean? Were they saying they could give an old man a new set of balls and make him potent again? It was hard to say. The note was cleverly, and most ambiguously, worded.

That had been yesterday. Merlin had slept on it. Now, as purple dusk draped his islet and the calm sea, and his cigar burned out, he made up his mind. He punched the button that would bring Polly.

While he waited he pressed another button that set the glass-enclosed room in motion, revolving on its hydraulic swivel. The room could also be raised or lowered—as it pleased him—but at the moment he did not tamper with the elevation. He guided his chair to one of the great windows and watched the sea come into view. To the west, over Lanai, the sky was rose-scarlet and apple-green. A few last chords of sunset lingered, gilding the luminous dark water. The beacon at Lanai Airport swept around the dial of sky, ticking off cosmic time, and reminding Merlin of the fraudulent promise of the note from Ecuador. For fraudulent it must be. A brand new shiny pair of balls for old men! He smirked and was glad that Polly could not see him. They maintained decorum now—between them—though they had once been lovers. Long ago. His paraplegia had not incapacitated him sexually. Once in a great while, when an urge fostered by memories took over, he had a young woman sent in. Polly knew and did not resent it. It was not her affair. She had had his love once, and still had his affection and respect, and she wore them like a talisman. She knew this aging man to be unique, truly *sui generis*; and understood that it would be a long time before the world saw his like again.

Polly was late. Merlin punched the button again in mild irritation. He picked up the vellum card and note, studied them again and chuckled softly to himself. They would amuse Polly. As a rule he did not share his secrets with her—his vast staff worked on a strict need to know basis—but this was too good to keep to himself. And there was nothing here that needed discretion. No case. Yet.

The woman who entered, carrying a thin sheaf of papers and a spiral bound loose-leaf notebook, was in her middle forties. As usual she wore a flower-printed muumuu, but cut to show off a good, if study, figure. She was barefoot. Her breasts were good, large and firm—she never wore a bra—and a few strands of silver glinted in her dark shoulder length hair. Polly was one-eighth Hawaiian.

Merlin lit a fresh Havana and cocked an eye at her. "What kept you?"

"Major Kleinberg. He just this moment arrived."

With her Kamaaina glide, as though she balanced an imaginary basket on her head, Polly went to one of the

16

great windows. She was about to press a button that would close the glass louvres and draw the drapes when he stopped her.

"Leave them. And the drapes. I like the twilight."

Her stare was dark, her mouth twitching to show fine small teeth. "Your asthma? The air-conditioning is no good with the windows open. I've told you a thousand times."

He nodded and smiled. "I know, little mother. But to hell with my asthma. It isn't bad today. And air-conditioning—with fresh air like a baby's breath—is sheer stupidity. I don't know why I don't have it ripped out."

With a faint shrug of her shapely shoulders, Polly came to the desk. She handed him the sheaf of papers. "Samson's regular report." She kissed her finger and leaned to him, touching his forehead with the same finger.

He pushed the papers aside. Samson was his prime contact with John Eagle—his Expeditor Number One. Merlin knew what the boy was up to at the moment— campaigning, making speeches for his various Indian causes. AIPAC among them. American Indian Political Action Committee. Merlin, because he approved of the cause and to show his approval of John Eagle's work, had recently donated a million dollars to AIPAC. John, if he knew the source of the gift, had made no comment.

He handed her the card and note, along with the envelope in which they had come. "Just off the top of your head, Polly, what do you think?"

Polly settled into a chair to read. After a moment she glanced at him and said, "This was sent to a friend of yours?"

He smiled and inclined his head. He had taken to wearing his hair long. It was still thick and silver white and this, with his deep set amberous eyes, gave him a leonine appearance. An old lion in a wheelchair.

"You might say that," he admitted. "Yes. In a way,

17

a friend of mine." He had never told her about the man in Scotland.

Polly read the note again, fingering the rich paper. She looked at him and laughed. "Is your friend in the market for this sort of thing? For rejuvenation?"

"Could be." Merlin chuckled. "He is about my age."

She folded the note in neat halves. "My advice would be to tell him to save his money. It looks like a very high class and expensively set up con game. A new set of testicles! Where on earth would they get them?"

"I confess," said Merlin, "that part intrigues me. My guess is that they would have trouble finding donors. I doubt many men line up to donate their gonads. Or a woman for that matter, if the term is inclusive. Even granted the technique, which I suppose is possible in this day of surgical miracles, I definitely foresee a logistical problem."

Polly watched him. She always knew when he was being sly with her. He had many facets, this man she adored. Whom she still loved even though their physical fire had long turned to ashes.

"I don't understand," she told him. "I know you don't mean me to. But you asked for my reaction—it's a con game. A fake. The people are thinking big, whoever they are, but it's still some kind of fraud. Surely you're not thinking of—"

Merlin seldom laughed aloud. He did now. "You know me better than that, dear Polly. I have lived this long with my own testes and I shall continue to enjoy them. Weak they may be, but they still serve. Occasionally at least. But none of this is to the point."

She was puzzled. "Then what is to the point?"

"Two things. You note that the membership is very restricted. No one is considered for membership unless his private fortune is in excess of fifty million dollars."

Polly glanced again at the envelope. "Does your friend in Scotland qualify?"

He nodded. "I should think so."

18

"They're after big game," she said. "The very biggest. And I'll bet they find a few suckers. Even among men smart enough to have that kind of money."

Merlin agreed. "Yes. They will find some suckers. Hope springs eternal and there's no fool like an old fool. You know—all the tired clichés. A man can have a great many millions and still be a fool when it comes to sex. Or lack of it." And he laughed out loud again.

Polly regarded the sheet of notepaper again. "This letterhead—the Demogorgon Society. They operate this Valhalla Club? It's their venture? What does Demogorgon mean?"

Merlin shrugged. "I had to look it up. A fiend, a monster of some sort. A medieval superstition. The creature is supposedly locked up in Hell, but escapes every now and then and visits up here."

Polly looked doubtful. "I don't see the point in that. A Demogorgon doesn't seem like the best sort of publicity for what they're trying to sell."

Merlin held up a hand. "Maybe not, but if you look closely at the entire definition, as I did, it could make some sense. Presumably a Demogorgon is a demon who can work magic. And has creative powers. That fits."

Polly nodded but did not speak for a moment. She was staring at the stamp on the envelope. When she looked at him it was with quiet triumph. It was not often she could probe his brain, or come remotely close to what he was thinking. They had their intimate moments, but this was not one of them. Now he was, as he often did, using her as a sounding board.

"The stamp," she said. "The stamp and the postmark. Ecuadorian."

The man in the wheelchair nodded. "Yes. The Valhalla Club is on Isla de Pelo. Five miles off the coast of Ecuador between Punta Galera and Manta. A deserted stretch of coast. I had GEO check it out for me last night. They made a few phone calls to people both in Manta and Esmeraldas. The Valhalla Club exists. Owned by the Demogorgon Society, which is itself a financial consortium and quite legally registered in Quito. The Club is only one of their interests. They are also in oil and cacao, and beef and balsa. Some mining and light industry. All open and aboveboard. On paper at least. But I've got RESEARCH on it and I know what they'll find—all masked ownership. Holding companies and legal skulduggery. The usual thing."

He should know, Polly thought. Merlin was a wizard at hiding behind legal façades.

She sensed that he was wearying of their little game. He spun his chair about and glided to a window. The room was still turning, almost imperceptibly, on its hydraulic axis. It was dark now—a blue-black mist of night in which the small lights of fishing craft made spangles.

"I couldn't help noticing," she said, "when I was making arrangements for Major Kleinberg, that he had been routed through from Guayaquil."

He did not turn. "Yes. Major Kleinberg has spent the past two weeks in Ecuador."

The President had told him that. It was at the President's request that he was seeing Major Kleinberg. Not that it would come to anything. He was doing it as a courtesy for a man he respected. There was still the Martin Bormann obsession. They saw him in every airport and harbor, behind every neo-Nazi move. He haunted them. Their hatred he could understand, the mass hatred that clamored for vengeance on Bormann, a piece of filth, but they had let blind revenge take over. Lust for it warped their powers of reason and the fitness of things. Martin Bormann was dead.

Still, Kleinberg, the Israeli agent, was here and he had just come from Ecuador. He *might* have found something. He *might* know something not having to do with Bormann.

Merlin spun back across the room and took the note and card from Polly. He laid them carefully on his desk.

"Call Samson, Polly, and tell him to get in touch

20

with John Eagle. Eagle is to go on alert status at once. Better yet—Eagle is to return to his ranch in Arizona and wait for word from me. Get that out at once."

She left her chair. "This Major Kleinberg—when do you want to talk to him? And how? Personally or TV?"

Merlin glanced at his watch. "On closed circuit, I think. I don't feel like anything personal tonight. Put him in Eagle's room for now and I'll talk to him in a couple of hours. Of course you're taking good care of him? Every comfort?"

"Of course." She went to the door with her majestic glide and lingered a moment, hand on knob.

"He's fairly young. Late thirties, I would say. Good looking, too, but a very serious type. Tired looking. Beat. I don't think he's going to strain our hospitality."

Merlin nodded thoughtfully. "If he drinks see that he gets a few, as many as he wants, before I talk to him."

He liked to judge a man after a few drinks. Alcohol told a lot about a personality. How a man handled booze was a pretty good indicator—it helped you in coming to a decision about credibility. Or lack of it.

Polly knew the technique. As she left she said, "I wouldn't count too much on the whisky test with this one. He is pretty grim. Like he's got something on his mind."

Merlin turned off the lights and sat in the dark. The room turned counter to the earth's orbit. Makaluha coughed sparks into the night and he watched them die. Why not play the hunch, he thought. He had nothing to lose but time and money and he had plenty of the latter. It was a wild long shot, nothing much to go on, but he had seen wilder things come off and about this he had a feeling. A gut feeling.

It would be worth moving a lot of garbage to kill a rat. If there was a rat.

III

SAMSON CALLED FROM Prescott, a hundred miles north-east of John Eagle's ranch. The first time he called there was no answer. Eagle was visiting his foster mother, White Deer, on the Apache reservation. White Deer was of the Be-don-ko-he, Geronimo's tribe, and a great-granddaughter of that famous warrior. Her lustrous dark hair was streaked with snow now, but her walk was that of a nubile squaw and though Eagle searched for signs of decrepitude—without seeming to—he found none. Her mind was pellucid, bright edged, and she retained the dignity and poise he had known since he had been old enough to know anything.

White Deer still refused to leave the reservation—having lived with her people she was content to die with them—and she would not accept any large sum of money. What he did give her, Eagle knew, she gave away to the poorest in the tribe.

The evening before his departure they talked for a long time. Not as they usually spoke—with soft laughter and quiet affection, though these things were always present—but in a different vein. So subtle was White Deer, so lacking in self-pity or dramatics, that it took Eagle some time—as astute as he was—to realize she had shifted to a new vector.

When she spoke of the Spider Woman he came fully alert.

"I had a medicine dream last night," she said. "The Spider Woman came into my teepee and we did some weaving together. She selected the colors for me and taught me some new things."

There was silence in the room. Something stirred, moved, in the world, beyond the world. Eagle, all Apache for the moment, heard and understood and was afraid. Then the white man came back and he smiled at her.

"The Spider Woman is Hopi—what is she doing in your dreams?"

White Deer shrugged. "I cannot say. I had many Hopi friends when I was young. It is no matter why— the Spider Woman came to me and she taught me to weave and dye a death blanket."

Eagle found himself not wanting to hear this. Ridiculous. He was no longer a boy. He was a warrior. Death, from the time he had gone into the mountains for his own medicine dreams, had held no terrors for him. His personal death. But this was another matter—this was White Deer. Stubbornly he refused to accompany her to the point.

"I could understand a Navaho dream, but Hopi? It doesn't make sense. Hopi are snake dancers and cotton raisers. They've always been tame Indians, nothing to do with the Chiricahua." He grinned at her. "Old Hokwa-sikna would spin beneath his stones if he knew you were having Hopi dreams."

White Deer rocked gently in her chair and looked at him. He knew the look. When he had been a boy, and had done something particularly outrageous, she had given him that look.

"If you cannot be serious with me," she said, "we will not talk. Go back to Ruth Lame Wolf. She will joke and giggle with you. And spare me your anthropology, John. I know you are an educated man, but you do not need to impress me."

Eagle flushed and felt small and inadequate. Ten years old. White Deer was the only person in the world who could cut him down like this.

"You're right," he told her. "I'm sorry, Mother. Sometimes I am a damned fool and we both know it. Go ahead. Tell me."

White Deer smiled. Her teeth were still fine and white. "You are a good son and not a fool. But at times you make the mistake all warriors make—you confuse strength and courage with wisdom.

"I told you about the dream because it was a warning to me and so it should be to you. I did not see my death in the dream, and I do not think the time has come, but I think it is time *you* realize, John, that soon I must go. Years cannot be wished away, nor would I do so if I could. I have no wish to live too long."

Eagle nodded and was silent for a time. He paced, hearing the faint squeak of the rocker, glancing out the window at his new car parked before the house. The Apache in him knew, for Indians are realists, but he kept the white man ascendant. He turned to her, speaking crisply.

"Okay, Mother. No more about the old gods. How have you been feeling? Tell me the truth."

White Deer touched her left breast. "I have had pain. Here."

"What have you done about it?"

She smiled faintly. "I did not go to see a shaman, as you must know. I have been to the clinic."

Eagle swore mildly. He knew what the reservation clinic was. One of his dreams, through AIPAC, was to get decent medical attention for Indians.

"Forget the clinic," he told her. "You'll go to Prescott tomorrow. At least we can get a good preliminary there. After we hear what they have to say, after all the tests, we'll know better what to do. We may have to send you east or to the Coast."

To his surprise, White Deer did not argue the matter.

When he got back to the ranch he found a note from Ruth on the kitchen table.

Gone into village for groceries—a person called, urgent, left no name. Will call again. He asks you stay around to take his call — love,

Ruth

He glanced out at the barns and corral. Sooty knew he was home and was at the bars, his velvet nostrils quivering. The Ford pickup was there. Ruth had driven her Thunderbird. He took some sugar lumps and an apple out to Sooty, knowing that he overfed the damned black devil. Eagle was the only human being who could put a hand on that satin coat.

As he fed the colt he thought about Ruth Lame Wolf, visualizing the way it would be between them that night, and he felt a stir of white man's guilt. Stupid. And yet it existed—White Deer was in a Prescott hospital for a checkup and so was it wrong to think about Ruth's pale tan body? Stupid. Crazy. One thing had nothing to do with the other. He was a young man. His foster mother was an old woman. Old. He had to face that now—from now on. Old. Stop fooling himself—pushing it out of his mind. Stalling. Face it. Think about it. Prepare for it. Someday, White Deer was going to die.

He heard the kitchen extension phone ringing. That would be Samson, his contact with Merlin. Had to be. No way it could be anyone else. Eagle had the feeling and knew he was due. Only Samson would have left the sort of message Ruth had scrawled.

Eagle did not hurry. Samson wouldn't hang up in a

hurry. As he entered the kitchen he thought about death again. Not White Deer this time. Nor his own. Eagle thought about death in a general way as he picked up the receiver. Samson's calls usually meant death. For somebody.

IV

THEY DID NOT, thank God, send him to Camp Three for refresher training. Camp Three was a killer, a ballbuster, operating on the theory that if you survived Camp Three you could survive anything. Eagle had been twice through the Camp Three mill and, though he had not personally experienced Devil's Island, he had a feeling that the island was a pleasure resort compared to the camp.

But he was spared that cup. Instead he was flown to Hawaii and spent three days underground, in the volcanic tubes of Makaluha. Two of those days he spent in the South American Room. The walls were festooned with maps and charts and on an enormous table was a topographical mockup of the continent with plastic mountains and glass rivers, astroturf jungles, sandpaper deserts and fine gravel pampas. Flag pins carried information about elevation and weather.

Eagle was briefed by a platoon of experts, none of whom knew why they were briefing him. Any more than Eagle knew why. He listened patiently, asking questions, absorbing tons of information he would never use, yet knowing that somewhere concealed in this welter of overkill, in this flood of printed and spoken facts and statistics, there might be a word or a note or a figure that could save his life.

He studied the plastic Andes, all 4,500 miles of them to scale, from the tropical Caribbean to icy Cape Horn. And hoped to Christ he wasn't being assigned to Tierra del Fuego. He breathed easier when ordered to concentrate on Ecuador and its borders with Peru and Colombia. He did a close study of the Ecuadorian coast. Special attention was paid to a small island, the Isla de Pelo, between Punta Galera and Manta. Cool to cold, arid to semi-arid, transitional weather bridge from Peru below, with the governing Humboldt Current, to the jungle humidity of Colombia above.

Eagle's mind swam and his brain felt near to cracking. The South American Room, like all the scores of chambers hewn out of the volcanic fissures, was air-conditioned, but he imagined jungle sweat and Andean cold. He was relieved when the skull work was over and he was allowed access to the Target Room. He practiced for hours with the gas pistol, firing metal flechettes at man-sized targets that ran and leaped and presented themselves for a split second in side silhouette. He shot a 97 out of a possible hundred.

That evening he spent in the Secret Gear Room or, as Eagle privately thought of it, the Deadly Gimmick room. The purpose of his visit, so he was told by the pompous little prick who was in charge, was to "refamiliarize yourself with such weapons and gear you may have occasion to use in the near future."

The little man wore a white smock and thought of himself as a boss. Eagle thought of him more as a parts man, or a tool room clerk, but he smiled and nodded and got along with this self-appointed mentor who had never used any of the weapons he dispensed and never would.

It came as something of a shock to Eagle when, after several hours of this refamiliarization drill, he found that he was not to be issued any equipment. Nothing.

The white-smocked Cerberus, with a rodent smile, hid behind his wire grille and tapped a piece of paper.

"Nothing to be issued to you, sir."

Eagle rode the underground train back to his suite and rested. He had a magnificent dinner and all he wanted or needed to drink. When the question was popped on the scanner screen he eschewed female company for the night. He felt no desire. After talking to Samson, he and Ruth Lame Wolf had made love all night.

The screen was in the living room and a buzzer sounded to indicate that it was activated. Merlin did not intrude on the privacy of his guests. Or at least, as he pointed out to Polly, not any more than absolutely necessary. It was not yet 1984, he said, though some might think and act as though it were.

Eagle slept nude. He had turned in early and read for a time. When the buzzer sounded, he was about to doze off. He padded into the living room to watch a string of white letters crawl across the green eye of the scanner.

MR. MERLIN WILL INTERVIEW YOU TOMORROW AT TEN A.M. THE INTERVIEW WILL BE ON CLOSED CIRCUIT TELEVISION. THIS SCANNER WILL BE USED. IF YOU DESIRE ANYTHING DURING THE NIGHT PLEASE RING. GOOD NIGHT.

Eagle went back to bed and tried to get back into his book, but it eluded him. He thought of White Deer and wished he could call her, could talk to the doctors who had run the tests, but that was out of the question. He was under contract to Merlin. The contract still had three years to run. There was a million dollars at the end of the trail and Eagle wanted it. Plus all the juicy fringe benefits.

All he had to do was stay alive.

Ecuador. Just what in hell went on in Ecuador that required Merlin's attention? Eagle shrugged his big shoulders. He had no clue—not the faintest—and it did not bother him. Merlin must have his reasons for sending in an Expeditor. Eagle grinned and punched at his pillow. And he had his reasons for going. A hundred thousand reasons a year. Not bad for a former poor-ass Indian. For, as an Indian, he had been poor. As a white man he had been doing all right without Merlin. Most college graduates and Rhodes Scholars *did* do all right. But that had been as a white man. Eagle wanted to make it as an Indian, and never mind the blood. Born white and raised Indian, he thought as he drifted into sleep, had a lot of disadvantages. It was a schizo life in which he had to constantly adjust from red to white and from white to red.

There were compensations. His body, for one. It could survive under conditions that would kill any white man. And when he allowed the Apache to take over, as he did during a mission, the pressure and strain of white living dropped away. Eagle lived in the now, with an immediacy shared with nature and animals, with the genius for survival that savages have.

Next morning the interview began on the stroke of ten. Eagle lounged on a sofa in the living room, unbothered by the unseen television camera monitoring him, and listened to Merlin's voice. Pleasant, bland, giving nothing away.

"Good morning, John."

"Good morning, sir."

"You're looking very fit." Merlin chuckled. "But then you always do."

Eagle nodded. "Yes, sir."

Merlin cleared his throat. In the background Eagle could hear the hum of an air-conditioner. He felt relaxed and at ease. He was accustomed to these one-way interviews by now, to being seen and not being able to see.

Papers made a crinkling sound. "I observe," said Merlin, "that you have added four new dormers to your ranch house."

To let Eagle know he was watched. Eagle shrugged and nodded. He had learned to live with it. They

30

couldn't see into his mind and that was what mattered. His secret thoughts were his own.

"I took the liberty, John, since you have been incommunicado, of obtaining a report on your foster mother. She has a tumor in her left breast. A biopsy shows it to be benign. I thought you would like to know."

Eagle nodded and allowed white man's gratitude to show on his usually impassive features. Benign. A stone removed from his own breast. He smiled at the camera concealed in a fascia under the ornamental cornice.

"Thank you," he told the camera eye. "And thank you also for the million dollars. It will help a lot."

Pause. Cough. Then, slyly, "The million dollars?"

Eagle could be sly. He grinned. "Someone gave a million to AIPAC. I assumed—"

"It is dangerous to assume anything in our profession, John. Let it pass. Let us get down to business. You have, of course, the usual choice. You may refuse the mission if it in any way violates your conscience. I am sure you remember our agreement—three refusals and our contract is terminated, you to be paid to the end of the current year, the security clauses to remain in effect?"

Eagle nodded again. "I know."

He could always tell when the pleasantries were over. The voice altered subtly. The amenities were disposed of and they reached the point of no nonsense.

"This is a rather complicated matter," said Merlin, "and there are ambiguities. It is a delicate matter and could be more so in the future. I am, I confess, feeling my way at the moment. I am not really sure that there is a job for you. That is what you must go and find out. Once the need for your services is established, if it is indeed established, we will take it from there. This mission—I will call it that for convenience—will be identified as Operation Gaul. That is pure whimsy, of course, and of no import, but it *is* divided into two parts—not three—and the first part will be reconnaissance. A probing operation. You will travel as a businessman and you will be unarmed. You will carry no special equipment. If your person is searched, or your luggage, as they may well be, nothing must be found to raise suspicion. This is most important and you will heed it—you are to carry nothing more formidable than a penknife. If that.

"Your cover name will be Richard Brookson and you will, of course, be furnished with the necessary identification. That will be no problem. You know the quality of our work.

"Richard Brookson is companion and private secretary to a billionaire recluse now living in a wild part of Scotland. You will recognize his name."

Eagle did recognize the name. For a moment he was puzzled. "I thought the old man was dead."

Pause. Then a chuckle that was just a bit different. As if Merlin enjoyed some private joke.

"Yes. I suppose a lot of people think that. But they are mistaken. Our subject is still very much alive, haunting his castle and counting his money, but I don't think he is very happy. Let us say, for the sake of argument, that he is discontent with age. He is something of a fool, and is ripe for suckerdom. He is, in short, prepared to believe in the Fountain of Youth if the lie can be made palatable enough. Are you following me so far?"

Eagle smiled. "Just barely."

"Hah. I told you it was complicated. It gets more so. There are ramifications. Wheels within wheels and boxes within boxes. The plot—*if* there is a plot other than an international con game which is no concern of ours—moves back and forth in recent history. How do you feel about Martin Bormann?"

Eagle had not been struggling too hard to keep up. He knew he would get a final exhaustive briefing and it would all be in typescript for him to study at leisure. He did not even blink at the apparent *non sequitur*. That one he could answer without thought. Eagle felt very strongly about certain types of sub-humanity and Bormann—all the Bormanns—was one of the types.

He stared at the camera. "I'd like to get him in my sights. Or have him to myself in a small tight room for a few minutes."

Merlin said, "That is understandable. I very much doubt that you will get the pleasure. I will not explain that, for it is not germane, but what is germane is the name itself. Martin Bormann. The name is as deadly now as the man was. Five men have died in the past sixteen months. All were trying to find Martin Bormann. All five were Israeli agents. What do you make of that, John?"

Eagle considered for five seconds, then went straight as a war arrow to the point.

"They could be using Bormann as bait. The name. The man himself may be dead long ago. Probably is. But the name is all they need, that and the rumors that keep popping up about Bormann being seen in this place and that. Rumors which they probably start themselves. Sugar in the trap. To lure Israeli agents within killing distance."

There was a long pause. Eagle could not see the camera eye, but he imagined it staring, unblinking.

Merlin sounded pleased when he said, "That is pretty good thinking. No cause for kudos, because I expect it of you, but the point is very well taken." He chuckled. "It also conforms with a theory of mine, the details of which I will spare you. I have long thought the Martin Bormann thing was a hoax from the very beginning. Designed to lead the hunters astray, keep them off the scent of other war criminals, those who *are* still alive and flourishing. If so, it was a clever idea. And it worked. It may have been an important part of ODESSA all along."

Eagle nodded at the camera eye to show he understood. Yes, Virginia, there is an ODESSA! Mark the penultimate letters—SS. ODESSA was an acronym for *Organisation der ehemaligen SS Angehörigen*. When the murdering was over and the war lost, and rats both large and small squeaking and scurrying for cover, it was ODESSA that saved some of them. Too many. New names and new jobs in new lands. And, for many, new faces. Eagle knew. He kept up. Read and studied. It had not been his war—he was hardly more than a babe freshly weaned from squaw milk—but he knew a great deal about ODESSA. All part of his homework.

He caught the new tone in Merlin's voice. Subtle. Deadly. A Florentine dagger thrust into silk.

"We are digressing, John. None of this is immediately relevant. Not at this moment and in the context of Operation Gaul. However, there is such a thing as serendipity and who knows what you may encounter along the way. Should you encounter any former SS personnel I am sure you will know how to handle the situation."

Eagle nodded at the camera. "Yes, sir. I will."

Another long pause. Merlin appeared hesitant to leave the subject, though he had just acknowledged it a digression. Eagle heard the crackle of papers being shuffled.

"They have never really gotten over the shock of Eichmann," said Merlin. "When the Israelis hanged him the others were shaking and shivering in their holes. But it could be, now, after ten years, that some of the more valiant are venturing out. We will see. *You* will see.

"Our aging friend in Scotland, though something of a fool about youth and sex, is far from senile in a business way. I will quote one example—ten years ago, when gold was pegged at 35 dollars an ounce, he set out to buy up abandoned gold claims in Nevada and Colorado. He got most of them for a song. The owners, when he could find the owners, were glad to sell and thought they were taking advantage of a fool. Last week gold was selling for 145 an ounce. From this you may deduct that our old friend still knows what is going on and how to take advantage of it. I am not digressing again, John. All this is relevant. Extremely so.

"Our friend—your employer—also had many oil interests. Some of them happen to be in Ecuador. They are having an oil boom there and a new pipeline has just been completed to the port of Esmeraldas. Your friend and employer," Merlin's chuckle was again fraught with the obvious enjoyment of some arcane joke, "your employer has an agent in Esmeraldas. A Señor Chulde. He is a trustworthy man and is important as liaison with the National Planning Board of the country. All perfectly legitimate, of course, keeping in mind that when in Rome, etc., and that some transactions down there may seem a bit bizarre by Wall Street standards."

After a pause he added, dryly, "Maybe not so bizarre at that, by *present* Wall Street standards.

"Be that as it may, you will contact this Señor Chulde when you have finished the first part of the mission. The probe. You will report to him and he will report to me. You will ostensibly be on your way out of Ecuador, but you will not actually leave until you get word from me. By that time I should know if there is to be a second part to the mission and I will notify you accordingly."

"This Señor Chulde, does he have a first name?" asked Eagle.

"He does. Enrique."

Merlin chuckled again. A different chuckle. Different from all the other chuckles. Eagle wondered. What the hell? He knew by now that Merlin had a rather offbeat sense of humor, he liked to play little games within little games, but so far Eagle could make no sense of this particular little game. If, indeed, it was that.

The no-nonsense tone was back. "So you will have a double cover," Merlin said. "Most of it legitimate and what is not can be made to look so. Remember—no weapons of any kind. Before you leave here you will strip naked and be given a new wardrobe. Along with your credentials. You will not return to the mainland. I

35

will arrange for explanations to be sent to your foster mother and to the girl, Miss Lame Wolf. They will be plausible, as they always are.

"You are friend, secretary, and companion to our recluse in Scotland. He has received an invitation—it will be among your new papers—to visit an island off the coast of Ecuador. He has been invited because he is very old and very rich and—so the inviters must think—very soft in the head. But, though he is definitely interested in regaining his virility, and adding years to his life, he is not ready for the yo-yo academy yet. That is where you come in. Richard Brookson. Trusted right arm of our old Croesus in Scotland."

Again the secret-joke chuckle. Eagle kept his own smile secret. The old man was high on something today.

"This is where your double cover comes in. You are probably the only real friend the old man has. I fear that he is not really a very likable person, but you are loyal. He has been good to you and you are lovingly grateful."

Eagle interrupted. "Loyalty and gratitude have nothing to do with love, sir."

Pause. Merlin did not much care for the interruption. But after a moment he said, "You're right, of course. It would be stretching it too far. Okay. No matter. You are loyal to him, you admire him, you try hard to have a certain affection for the old curmudgeon. Above all you are aware of what he can do for you, has in fact done, and how much he may leave you when he falls off the limb. Better?"

"Yes, sir. Better. People understand self-interest. We all consider ourselves first. I am presuming that my cover—the story—will be checked out."

"Very likely it will. I will see to it that the answers are right. Very well, you have been sent by our financier to do a little checking out yourself. He is avid for new youth, if it can be purchased, but at the moment he is a cripple in a wheelchair. A trip from Scotland to Ecuador, in search of something as improbable

36

as a Fountain of Youth, is not to be considered. At the moment. But if there is a miracle our old gentleman wants to be in on it. So he does not entirely scoff—he sends you to see what is going on. Your attitude, by the way, is to be one of extreme skepticism. You will be hard to convince. You will demand proof that this miracle can indeed be worked. And while you are at it you will find out all you can about this Demogorgon Society and about the Valhalla Club. About the island itself. About any related matters, no matter how trivial or inconsequential they may appear."

"It shouldn't be hard to act skeptical about a Fountain of Youth," said Eagle. "I really am skeptical."

No chuckle. Eagle felt an odd sense of disappointment. Merlin was finished chuckling for the day.

"Your stopover, your enquiries about the island and the rejuvenation treatment, will be secondary. That is what *they* are to think. You have to be in Ecuador anyway and you are giving a passing glance to what you consider a con game. As a favor to your boss, an old man you admire and respect. You are in Ecuador to take care of his oil interests, and you are *really* there to scout for some gold diggings that can be bought up cheaply. You have it? Oil is your first cover, gold your second. Only incidentally are you looking into the youth scheme."

"It should work," Eagle assented.

He knew it would. Merlin planned well and never left anything to chance.

After a few more minutes of talk Merlin said, "You will receive a final briefing and additional material. Memorize it and destroy it. I suggest you pay particular attention to the memo on the Vilcabamba valley in Ecuador. That has received world-wide publicity and has been written up in leading medical journals— several men and women in that region are reported to have lived over a century. Some as much as 145 years. I do not believe this, lacking better proof than has been advanced, but you may be able to use it as a technique of disinformation. Mention it. Ask questions about Vil-cabamba. Admit that your employer has read the stories and they may have tilted the scale. It will make him look a bit less of a fool—crooks are always suspicious of someone they take in too easily—and allay some suspicions before they hatch. It's worth a try.

"How you enter Ecuador is your concern. This time. If you have to return we will plan for that when it occurs. I and my staff have done all we can for you. For the moment. If the operation develops, becomes ongoing, we will take it from there. My staff and I will do contingency planning meantime. As always, when you leave this island you will be on your own. I am sure you have not forgotten the terms of your contract."

Eagle shook his head. "No, sir. I haven't forgotten."

... the Expeditor signs this document with the full knowledge that his employment may be extremely hazardous to life and limb, and in so signing he relieves both Mr. Merlin and the United States Government of any responsibility whatsoever ... the Expeditor, fully cognizant of the military and diplomatic realities in the world today, agrees by his signature to forfeit all claims against Mr. Merlin and the United States Government in the event of his capture, torture, or execution by an unfriendly power ... he waives all right to claims of amnesty, succor, diplomatic immunity, recognition as an American citizen, or any aid and comfort whatsoever from any United States agency, foreign or domestic ... he is a stateless person with no valid claims upon the United States Government or Mr. Merlin ...

"Then I wish you well, John. Goodbye."

Eagle stared at the camera with a half smile. "Goodbye, sir. For now. Be seeing you."

V

THAT NIGHT, LONG after Polly had gone to bed, Merlin
sat in the revolving glass room, in the dark, and
watched the diamond studded heavens spin past. His
mood was fretful and uneasy as he smoked cigar after
cigar and regarded the celestial globe. There were black
holes out there, the astronomers now told him, through
which one day the cosmos would be sucked to an end
and a new beginning. Eternity became a misnomer and
time would have a stop.

He shook his head and spilled a cascade of cigar ash
down his front. Too much for him. He was something
of a theoretical physicist, and indeed had a modicum of
skills in many disciplines, but the bright young men
were getting beyond him in astronomy.

Merlin wheeled to his desk for a fresh cigar. Theories
were like fashions, they came and went, and what was
truth today would be discredited tomorrow. They were
after Einstein now—had been for years—but now a
new tribe of young brains was howling along his trail,
trying to prove him a metaphysical liar.

He went back to watch the stars wheel past. What
did they care? The light he saw now had left its source
millions of years before there were men to imagine a

cosmos. Light that would still be there when there were no men to see it.

Men. They dreamed the universe. And some of the dreams were evil. Nightmares.

His hunch, his forebodings, had grown stronger with each passing day. There was, he thought, deliberately mixing his metaphors, something rotten in the woodpile. A strong odor of rat. Nazi rat.

The time was ripe and the place appropriate. Democracy, never very strong in South America, was at the moment in parlous plight indeed. Allende had pushed Chile into Communism—though called by another name—and been crushed by his efforts. Uruguay had given up the democratic ghost to go Fascist. Also called by another name. Pern was back in Argentina and strong as ever. The colonels and generals ruled in Brazil.

And Ecuador? A military regime. The same old story? Just another *coup* in a country with a notorious history of political instability? Very likely. And yet perhaps not. There was a new element.

Oil.

Merlin watched the stars for a few minutes longer, then wheeled to his desk and turned on the lamp. Oil. He should know. He owned a lot of it. Or—and he riffled his papers and chuckled—the old codger in Scotland owned a lot of it. It was mostly his—their—money that had built the new pipeline to Esmeraldas. The oil moving in that pipeline had been sold months before. There was a world-wide energy shortage, some of it artificially induced but nevertheless existing, and the price of oil would remain high for months—years—to come. Ecuador was just coming into the market in a big way. There would be billions in the future. Trillions. The human race was busy polluting itself into extinction and it would take a lot of oil to do it. A lot of that oil was in Ecuador.

Merlin stopped writing, reading, and did nothing but sit in his wheelchair and stare at the desk. For a long

41

time, unmoving, he stared. Where was it? The nexus? The connection? The hidden corpse that was beginning to stink and had alerted him?

What linked these strange components of a weird puzzle? Oil? A con game? New balls for old? A smell of Nazi and no proof? Valhalla Club and Demogorgon Society. Five Israeli agents dead in sixteen months. All pursuing the ghost of Martin Bormann.

Merlin pressed a button, activating the tape made of his interview with Major Kleinberg. He did not need the video to remind him how tired and tense Kleinberg had been, a man nearly beaten but still defiant. A slim dark man, exhausted and underweight, with enormous brown eyes and a nose like a hooked blade. Merlin, who was seeing the man only as a favor to the President, had taken to him, liked him while disagreeing with his theories. Major Kleinberg, for his part, had not agreed with Merlin's theory that Martin Bormann was long dead, that the neo-Nazis were using the myth to lure Israeli agents within killing distance.

"The bastard is alive," Kleinberg insisted stubbornly. "Old, probably sick, but alive. We want him."

Merlin reached to turn up the gain. Kleinberg's voice came louder into the otherwise silent room. The voice recreated the tense dark visage, the weary blade of a face, the bagged eyes. Merlin lit a fresh cigar and settled back in his wheelchair to listen to the replay. The Major himself had returned to Washington a day before the arrival of John Eagle, and was now attached temporarily to the Israeli Embassy.

The tape spun.

"We'll never give up on the Bormann thing, sir. Not until we see his bones. Or at least his teeth. We've got his dental records. Or until we hang him."

"That is your government's privilege, Major. Personally, I think you are wasting your time. Unfortunately I cannot offer you proof positive that Bormann is dead. If I could do so I would, if only to cut down your casualty rate. But all that aside, Major, what is it that you think I can do for you? I cannot help you with the Bormann matter, as you must have known before you came, so if we could get immediately to the point?"

Merlin's cigar glowed red in the gloom. He watched the stars swing past and remembered the way Major Kleinberg had stared at the concealed television camera. Still defiant, yet puzzled. Hopeful, but prepared for disappointment. Merlin could understand and sympathize. The Major was a man pursuing a phantom, a will-o'-the-wisp, and it must have been most confusing to fly five thousand miles, on a prayer and a promise with no certainty, only to be subjected to a one way television interview with a man he had never seen and never would. The Major, Merlin thought at the time, must be wondering. Wondering indeed. Wondering how he had strayed through the looking-glass and into Alice land.

"There is something nasty going on in South America, sir. Especially in Ecuador. We're losing agents, of course, and three attempts were made to kill me. I managed to—"

The tape blurred and squealed where Merlin had made an excision.

"Careful, Major. No mention of your successes, if any, no matter how satisfying."

"I did have one or two, sir, but I understand. You're right, of course. Very well— I had to get out of South America. Things were too hot, too dangerous. I had to leave an agent behind, a woman, and I have no idea where she is, or if she is still alive. I made my report to our embassy in Washington and was there for a few days on standby. During this time—and this I did not know at the time—our Ambassador managed a secret audience with the President. I don't know all of it, sir. I wasn't told. I *was* told to come here, to see you and tell you what I knew, answer your questions, with the understanding that you might be able to help in some way."

The MEMCON tape hummed. Merlin puffed his

cigar into a glowing coal. He remembered the moment. He had been thinking hard. Thinking about coincidence and stray bits of puzzle that at the moment formed no recognizable picture. And wondering what—really—the Major knew that might be of any value.

"Just tell me all of it, Major. As you remember it, as it comes to you. Let me draw my own conclusions. Something you know may fit in with something I know."

"This is sort of a one-sided deal, isn't it, sir?"

"For the moment, Major, I am afraid so. I must insist on it. If you do not like the terms, of course, you are free to terminate this discussion at any time."

Merlin remembered Kleinberg's shrug. Fatalistic. Resigned. The man was weary. Perhaps still scared. He had been through a bad time and was living on his nerves.

"We have to accept help wherever we find it, sir. Beggars can't be choosers."

A moment of silence but for an electronic hum. Merlin had felt a bit guilty. He liked the Major, had in fact made a memo to himself to find out, in some future time, if Kleinberg would come to work for him. Merlin was always in need of good men for his staff.

"I seldom make promises, Major, but I will promise you this—if anything comes of this interview, if I act on information received from you and there are results, I will see that you are informed. That is the best I can do."

"That's the trouble, sir. Information. Hard fact. As opposed to rumor and guesses and half-truths. I had to get out before I could track down anything specific. I suppose the truth is that I chickened out, as the Americans say. I admit I was running scared. I had lost already too many people and they were closing in fast."

"They?"

"Nazis. A new breed to be sure, sir. Not just a vague

rumor—unfounded talk about a neo-Nazi movement—but real Nazis. Young ones. In their twenties
and thirties. Strong. Virile. Stupid, of course, but cun-
ning. And evil. As evil as the old gang."

Merlin stopped the tape for a moment. He turned off
the desk lamp and sat in darkness. Outside the glass
walls the stars continued to swing past, unheeding.

He thought back to that moment on the tape,
remembering his own reactions. Not favorable. Major
Kleinberg sounded like a man losing his cool—an
emotional man prey to wild fancies. Full of melo-
dramatic talk with no hard core facts to back it up. At
that point Merlin had been on the verge of terminating
the interview as quickly and as politely as possible and
writing it off. He would drop a note to the President, or
call, and say that nothing could be done. Nothing
added to nothing equals nothing. The Major's superiors
might do well to see that he spent a few weeks in
the hospital.

Merlin smiled in the dark. Now, with the advantage
of hindsight, he knew what he would have missed. He
started the tape again.

"I know you're not interested in rumors and wild
stories, sir, and I can't make you understand the
feeling, the climate, the atmosphere that I felt while I
was down there. But I was there, I felt it, and I know
something nasty is cooking. And before I lost my nerve
and ran for it, I came by one hard piece of information. It was a phone call from one of my agents. I
talked with him for only a minute—it was not a safe
phone—and I never saw him again. I read about him
in the papers next day. His body was found under a
culvert. Throat cut."

The tape hummed. Merlin heard Kleinberg clear his
throat, heard his own voice asking, "And what was the
hard fact, Major? What was the phone call about?"

"I'll repeat some of it verbatim, sir. My man told
me, 'I've found the rat's nest. But these are smart rats.

45

They know how to set traps for people. The Isla de Pelo.' "

Merlin stopped the tape again. What a long arm you have, coincidence! He felt again—nearly as cold—the *frisson* that rippled down his spine when he heard the name. Isla de Pelo. As Kleinberg spoke the words Merlin had only to reach across his desk to touch the rich vellum of the note and card. The Valhalla Club cordially invites you to invest in a new set of testicles. Sponsor and owner—the Demogorgon Society. A demon on leave from Hell.

Merlin did not immediately turn on the tape again. He thought back, remembering his amazement that such a long shot had come home. Then, acknowledging that it was only fitting punishment for his previous skepticism—no matter how courteously he disguised it—he let Major Kleinberg talk at will. And he listened, intently, to every word.

He started the tape again and the Major's words hummed into the room.

"Did your man tell you anything more about Isla de Pelo?"

"Not much. There was no time. We made a date to meet, but as I told you he was killed. Murdered."

"You then made your own investigation, Major?"

"I did. But as I have admitted, sir, I was at the moment very hot. They cut his throat and I was next. I got out of Ecuador the next night. Before I left I found out all I could about Isla de Pelo."

"And that was?"

"Not much on the face of it. There are a lot of islands off the coast of Ecuador. The Isla de Pelo is five miles out, between Punta Galera and Manta. There is some kind of health club or sanitarium on it, there does not seem to be any secret about this, and I found that you must be very rich to belong. I did not have much time to inquire, as I told you, but it must be well guarded and hard to get to. Unless you are invited, of course. I was not. I came up with one lead which I did not have time to run down—the health club, or spa, whatever, is called the Valhalla Club and it is owned by something called the Demogorgon Society. I got the impression that this society is legal and aboveboard. By Ecuadorian standards, at least."

"Judging by your tone, Major, I would guess that your opinion of Ecuadorian standards is not high?"

Remembering now—visualizing the TV screen—Merlin saw again in his mind the way Kleinberg had flashed at the question. For a moment the tired man was an exploding firecracker of anger.

"Not just Ecuador, sir. All South America, or most of it. The same damned dirty story—they give aid and comfort to the Nazis. The old ones and the new ones. They give shelter and protection to thieves and murderers. Oh, there is a lot of lip service paid to international law, and to democracy, but that is a lie, too. The Germans are solidly entrenched in South America, financially and more and more politically. They get stronger every day. The old ones are getting bolder and the new ones—the young ones—who have never known defeat, are dangerously arrogant. I tell you, sir, you literally can feel the underground swell, especially in Ecuador. And they're singing the same old song: tomorrow the world. I'm not imagining it, sir. I swear that. By all that's sacred I swear it!"

"Privately—very privately—I am inclined to agree with you, Major Kleinberg. Democracy has been a failure in South America, aided and abetted by some very stupid diplomatic and economic policies. And when a power structure fails it leaves a vacuum which must be filled, usually in a most distasteful manner. Two of the more recent examples, of course, are Pern in Argentina and Allende and his successors in Chile. Uruguay also. All this is regrettable. There is the ever present possibility of contagion. Democracy is in enough trouble as it is throughout the world—even in the United States. I believe that even in Israel you sometimes have difficulty making it work."

Merlin stopped the tape. At that point Major Kleinberg had laughed. And admitted that the Jews did a lot
of quarreling in the Knesset, even to the verge of
blows. Then he said something that stuck in Merlin's
mind. He started the tape to hear the words again.

"Jews can be just as stupid and evil as anyone in the
world, sir. We have our share of fools and rogues,
believe me. But we *believe* in democracy. We have to.
It is our only salvation. If we are to be saved, to continue to exist, it is because we are allied with the great
democracies of the world. If they go down we go with
them. And it is my very firm conviction, sir, that
democracy is in trouble today. Deep trouble. A lot of
people, and not only fools and weaklings, have stopped
believing in it. But they are not the dangerous ones.
The danger comes from those who never did believe in
it. They see their chance now, and they are coming out
of the woodwork."

"Again, and again most privately, I agree with you,
Major. These are perilous times. You may be right
about South America, even about Ecuador in particular. It may well be a focal point for the disease,
the new Fascism or whatever they will choose to call it.
There is little we can do about it in the large scale—we
are hoist by our own petard of democracy and can
hardly send in an expeditionary force to enforce
democracy on those who do not want it. But on a
smaller scale, ah, there we may be able to take some
action when and wherever it is feasible."

Once again Merlin stopped the tape. He lit a new
cigar and smiled at himself. He had sounded admittedly a bit pompous in that last bit. But the voice was
good, round and deep. Orotund. Yes, that was the
word. Which also, he recalled, had a connotation of
pomposity. Bombast.

It had not, of course, been bombast. He fully intended to take measures. Even then, while talking to
Kleinberg, when he had very few bits of the puzzle to
go on. Not that he had much even now. There was a

48

decided lack of major components. But there was a puzzle. The outline *was* there. And in time, as it always did, it would emerge. Patience. When you've spent most of your life in a wheelchair you can be *very* patient.

He flipped on the tape again and listened to himself saying: "We have been digressing, Major. Your one hard fact, I take it, is that your now deceased agent told you that Isla de Pelo is some sort of a Nazi setup?"

"He was a good agent, sir. Knew his job. I trusted him absolutely. His only meaning could have been that the neo-Nazis are using the Isla for something or other—maybe some kind of a staging area—and that is all I know. All he knew, I think. He died to find that much out."

"Very well, Major. Now, you mentioned that you had to leave an agent behind when you got out of Ecuador?"

"Yes, sir. A girl—a woman."

"Which is it, Major?"

"I think she is twenty-six. Woman, I suppose."

"You lost all contact with her?"

"Yes, sir. I suppose I can tell you about that."

"It would be a great waste of time and expense, Major, if you did not. You did, after all, come to me. Through very high channels. I did not send for you."

"I'm sorry, sir. Her name is Stella Helpern. At least I suppose that is her real name. It is the one we have on file. She is a very highly trained agent. Very dependable. A lot of guts, too. Too much for her own safety. I told her that many times."

"Just how did you lose contact with her, Major?"

"When it became clear they were after me, I broke trail. I deliberately broke all contact with her and left her on her own. I hated doing it, but it was all I could think of to protect her. They were that close to me. My nerves were shot and I was afraid if they took me alive they would make me talk about Stella. I'm not sure I would have talked but in the state I was in I couldn't risk it."

"Nothing to be ashamed of, Major. All men have a breaking point. No one stands up to torture forever. But you know that—did you give her an assignment before you left Ecuador?"

Merlin remembered the expression on the Major's face as he answered. Bitterness. Reluctance. Not so much at the question but having to think about the answer. Self-hate was writ large on the Israeli's sharp features.

"I made a suggestion to Stella—not an order. I did not think they were on to her yet, and as I was breaking the trail then and there I thought she might be safe for a time. I suggested that she might try to get near the Isla de Pelo, or even get on it, to see what was going on. She said she would try, or at least look into the possibilities. I warned her not to take any wild chances."

"She—this Stella—she was given to taking wild chances?"

"I told you, sir. Sometimes I thought she was a little crazy. Too much zeal. She lost all her people during the war—her father and mother survived, but all her other relatives died in the gas chambers. Stella was born in a camp for displaced persons. I think her father died of tuberculosis soon afterward. Stella and her mother moved to Israel soon after we became a state. Her mother died a few years ago. Stella has been an agent since she was nineteen. Her one interest in life is in finding and killing old Nazis. She has been invaluable to us. But as I said, she is sometimes over-zealous. I can't see how she has stayed alive this long."

"In her case the zeal can be forgiven, Major. But I can see why you worry. You have, of course, not heard from her?"

"Nothing. She knows how to get through to the resident at the Embassy in Washington, but I have heard nothing. And I don't expect I will hear anything. For that I have to blame myself. I should have stayed in Ecuador, stuck it out, remained with her."

"Had you done that, Major, you would probably both be dead now. There is no use wasting time on what might have been. Did this girl—Stella—have a code name? Something to which she would respond— would recognize as a friendly signal? This might be important for me to know."

"Yes, sir. Her code name was Sleeper. There is a Nazi organization known as the Seven Sleepers. They work all through South America—all killers, a sort of goon squad. We used the code Sleeper for Stella as sort of a joke."

"Rather a grim joke, Major."

"They're a grim lot, sir. They kill but they never get caught. A lot of people, my own superiors among them, think the Seven Sleepers are a myth, a nothing, a rumor started to spread terror. The Nazis are very good at terror."

At the time Merlin had indulged in a bit of duplicity. He knew the legend of the Seven Sleepers and he was inclined to believe, as Major Kleinberg obviously believed, that such a murder organization was functioning in South America. Yet, when he replied, he pitched his tone to indicate a shading of *arrière-pensée*. The Major caught it immediately.

"I can't prove the Sleepers exist, sir. They're never caught, or at least we've never identified any of them. The story I have, and I've heard it enough times to believe there must be some truth in it, is that the Sleepers take a blood oath when they are initiated not to be taken alive. If they fail on a mission they kill themselves. If I'd had the time and the men to run checks on a few suicides I could have come up with proof that the Sleepers exist."

"I do not entirely disbelieve you, Major. It boggles the mind, I admit, but the Nazis are romanticists at heart and with a romanticist anything is possible. And I am, of course, familiar with the legend of Barbarossa.

Yes. It is all quite possible—even plausible. The Germans are great worshipers of blood myths, more especially when they can turn them to some practical end. But we are getting off the track again, Major. Is there anything else I should know?"

There had not been much more of importance, at least to Merlin. He indulged the Major, who by talking—it was, Merlin thought, a sort of confessional—managed to purge himself of some of his guilt and fear. It was late when the interview concluded and the image of Major Kleinberg faded from the screen.

Now Merlin snapped off the machine and rolled his chair to a window. He touched a button and the glass room stopped revolving. He sat a long time staring at the eastern horizon. It would be dawn soon, but as yet the sky was folded in somber black. As dark as my thoughts, he told himself, and yet the analogy was not a true one. The sky to the east was an unrelieved pall of funereal color; only Merlin's thoughts were illuminated here and there by specks of light.

He had already come up with, and discarded, half a dozen theories. Several times he had been within an ace of realizing the noumenon—the purely rational—behind the apparent absurdities. What, for instance, did the promise of renewed youth have to do with a resurgent Nazi movement? Even if the latter existed outside of Major Kleinberg's tortured imagination?

Oil? Somewhere, somehow, he thought oil must come into the picture.

Money.

Oil *was* money. They were interchangeable.

Gold? Somehow he thought not. Gold was not an important counter in this game, other than what he chose to make it. Eagle, for instance, was using gold as a front.

A girl named Stella Helpern. Code name—Sleeper. The Seven Sleepers.

He knew the legend well. Barbarossa. Red-beard. Frederick I of Germany had never died. Still sleeps in a vasty dank cave in the Kyffhauser in Thuringia. He sits sleeping, this Barbarossa, at a stone table with six of his knights. Waiting. Waiting, so goes the legend, until Germany's need is dire. In the fullness of time, when his red beard has grown thrice around the table, Barbarossa will awaken and once again lead Germany to her place in the sun.

When the beard has grown.

From the ornate Venetian desk came a faint buzzing. A light was flashing. Merlin wheeled to the desk, flipped a switch and spoke into the intercom. He was not particularly surprised at the summons, nor would the caller be at his answer. COMMUNICATIONS was on 24-hour standby.

He listened, thanked the caller, and switched off the intercom.

Major Kleinberg was dead. Gunned down outside the Israeli Embassy by two unknown gunmen who had escaped. One of Merlin's contacts in Washington, alerted to keep a casual eye on Kleinberg, had called with the report.

Merlin sighed. I made a mistake there, he told himself. I should have put a protective watch on the little man. But no. Not really my province. He was a pro, after all, and he had his own people. No way I could have helped or prevented it.

He had liked the Major and did not try to shrug off the moment's pang. He wondered if the man had any people and who they were and how they would take it.

The Seven Sleepers? Who else? Certainly not a warring faction of the Knesset, or someone who did not like the shape of the man's nose. Arab terrorists? A possibility, but Merlin did not think so. The Seven Sleepers.

The beard was growing. They were getting bolder, pursuing Kleinberg to the States and killing him, and they had made a mistake. Kleinberg hadn't known all that much. His information, now stored on Merlin's tapes, had not been all that valuable. They could not know about Merlin, of course, or about the secret complex beneath the volcano. Merlin's security measures were the best, and the most expensive, in the world. The Russian leaders, the President himself, did not have the security Merlin provided for his guests.

A revenge killing? Possible. Kleinberg had hinted at some of his "successes." He may have killed a Sleeper or two. Merlin hoped so.

Yet would they pursue him all the way to Washington, with all the attendant risks, for revenge? No. But they might do it to keep him from talking. They might think Kleinberg knew more than he did.

No. Merlin was unhappy with his reasoning. He wheeled the chair around and around the room, ignoring the nacreous crack of dawn. No—no—no—the Major had spent time at the Embassy before his visit to Merlin. He must have reported fully. He would have told his superiors everything. It had been on the strength of that report that the meeting with Merlin had been arranged.

Why kill Kleinberg after the fact, as it were? If you discounted a revenge murder.

Merlin snapped his fingers. Not to shut his mouth. To open it! To make Kleinberg talk. They had not meant to kill him, not at the time. They must have been trying to kidnap him.

Merlin sped his chair for the desk. Easy enough to test the theory, to get a fuller report. The first flash had been nothing but bare bones.

Five minutes later he had it. He was right. At least the theory stood up. There had been a gunfight and Major Kleinberg had not died easily. Washington security was sitting on a lot of the facts, but Merlin paid fabulous salaries to efficient men. At least a dozen shots had been fired. One of the escaping gunmen was believed to be wounded. The Major had been riddled, five wounds. His marksmanship, Merlin thought as he shut off the intercom, had not been up to his courage.

They had wanted the Major for information. Merlin

pondered that. Indulged in a bit of prolepsis—suppose his girl agent, this Stella Helpern, code Sleeper, was somehow involved. Suppose, cut off and more or less on her own, she was indulging herself? Too much zeal, the Major had said. Suppose she was having herself a ball killing Nazis.

Merlin smiled at the dawn. It was all a little wild, but it made good supposing. Suppose the girl was leaving a bloody trail through Ecuador. Panic might ensue. They couldn't find her, stop her killing, not even the deadly Seven Sleepers, and *they* began to run scared.

Answer—find Kleinberg again and make him talk. That was not a difficult task, as events had proved. They had known about the Major, had been close to him, and he had slipped out of Ecuador just ahead of them. Leaving his girl agent on her own. To display zeal. Kill Nazis.

Merlin wondered how she did it. With her body? Sex. The oldest gambit in the world but it often worked. No man was really immune if the bait was tempting enough. Merlin had, on occasion, worried about John Eagle in that respect. Not really worried, perhaps, but the thought had occurred. Eagle on a job was made of ice, but you never really knew.

He broke his train of thought for a moment and smiled. One thing—if it did happen Eagle would never tell him about it. Eagle kept a large part of himself to himself. Merlin had no illusions about that—he purchased John Eagle's body, his brain and muscles, even his loyalty, but he had no claim to his soul. No Faustian deal could be made. Eagle wasn't selling.

But to get back—he would bet he was right. Stella Helpern was dealing death in Ecuador. They couldn't find her and they were angry and frightened. Possibly they didn't even know what she looked like. So they had gone to the risk and trouble and expense of picking up Kleinberg's trail and had tried to kidnap him to make him talk about Stella. No deal there. The Major

55

would have known instantly what they were after and had gone down fighting.

Ave atque vale, Kleinberg!

And to other matters: the beard was growing. Barbarossa was stirring. Merlin was sure of it now. The question was how to put Redbeard back to sleep before he fully awakened, before he began to lash out, before his six sleeping knights could awaken and help him? In short, how to nip this new Nazi plot in the bud? Kill it in infancy. If it were not already too late. Merlin had a dour feeling about that. It probably *was* too late. The times, the political climate, were ripe for a renascence of Fascism. It was even happening in the United States. Merlin did not concern himself overmuch with that. He had faith in the people of America. They would make it through. They would, in the interim, drive a sane man up the wall, but in the end they would make it through.

He was tired now. He should get to bed, snatch a few hours' sleep before Polly appeared with the day's schedule. Yet he lingered at the window, watching the sunrise. Pondering. Aware of decisions not yet upon him, at the moment only faintly outlined, but which would rise as surely as the sun had just risen over Makaluha.

Life or death.

Which for whom? Who would die and who live? Merlin had no illusions about his powers, the power of his billions, and he knew he played God. Polly told him often enough. If pressed, Merlin would have admitted that he enjoyed his power, liked playing the Deity. And accepted the responsibility.

John Eagle was on his way. In time, if he lived, Eagle would find the root cancer and report back. Ask for instructions.

Merlin's eyes closed. He could sleep now. He wheeled his chair toward the door. Let it go for now. He knew too little. It was all there but he had not yet the power of vision.

One thing he knew—a right decision at the right time was a thing of beauty, beatific, as sweet as a chorus of angels.

His last thought, as he fell into sleep, was of Eagle. Where was he at the moment? What was he doing? Had the blood begun to flow? If so, how? What engines of destruction unleashed? In the end it always came to that—knife or bullet, rope or poison, garrote or razor, car or spiked boot. There were so many ways.

VI

FROM THE FIRST it went slickly. Eagle went in through Cartegena. He lingered a day, making like a tourist, converting his dollars to pesos and loafing about, eating boiled iguana eggs from street carts and roaming the harbor. Checking his back trail. Nothing. As he had expected.

He stayed at the Hotel Caribe and spent Merlin's money with abandon. He turned down several high-class whores. He set traps in his suite and his baggage and they were not tampered with. He was Mr. Richard Brookson, traveling on legitimate business for ancient and eccentric Mr. F, of Scotland, and nobody appeared to suspect otherwise.

Next day he flew to Quito on Condor Flugdienst, a subsidiary of Lufthansa. He shared a seat with a cute little number who seemed not averse to a bit of knee rubbing. Eagle abstained. He was working and he had never been much for the sneaky little frivolities of sex.

They flew south along the spine of the Andes and he compared them to the mock-up in the South American Room. Not a bad facsimile. He spotted a solitary condor and thrilled to it. He had never seen one before. He craned to watch the majestic bird, wheeling in majesty over a fanged peak, until both were out of sight.

Eagle spent the rest of the trip mulling over what he had learned in his final briefing and from the mass of typescript he had read and then burned. There were some things he did not understand, some connections he did not make, and he knew he was not supposed to make them. He knew enough to do the job, as presently set forth. It might be, he thought, an easy mission. At least at first.

It was cold in Quito. Eagle shrugged into his topcoat and gazed for a moment at the snow-covered tit of Cotopaxi looming over the city. The volcano was still active and he hoped it would not wake up while he was around. He changed his money to *sucres* and made a phone call from the airport. To the offices of the Demogorgon Society. The name had been explained in his briefing. Eagle, who took extra pains when his life was on the line, had looked into the matter himself. Demogorgon—a demon. Medieval superstition. A demon who escapes from Hell periodically and returns to earth.

He wondered as he listened to the phone buzz. Someone was having a little joke with that name. A joke that might not be very funny.

Finally a woman answered the phone. Eagle gave his name, Richard Brookson, and explained why he was calling. The woman, who spoke English with a Spanish accent, said that he wanted Mr. Toller, Mr. Helmuth Toller, and she was sorry but Mr. Toller was not in at the moment. Could he leave a number or an address and Mr. Toller would get in touch.

Toller, Helmuth. German. Nothing too unusual about that. Many Quiteños were of German ancestry.

"I have business," he told the woman. "I will be at the Hotel Palacio, on the Avenida 24 de Mayo—"

The woman was amused. "Mr. Toller knows the Palacio, sir."

"Fine. I'll be there but I don't know exactly when. Tell him to keep trying until he gets me. You might also tell him that I cannot stay in Quito long and I would like to get this business over with as soon as possible. I am acting for Mr. Frobisher, not for myself, and, to be perfectly frank about it, I would just as soon not be involved. But I promised Mr. Frobisher I would look into the matter. Will you please try to impress that on Mr. Toller? I am in a hurry."

"I will tell him, sir. Be assured."

It was, Eagle thought as he left the booth, a good enough beginning. He had planted just the right note of skepticism. He was a youngish no-nonsense business type who humored the foibles of his elderly employer. Nobody was kidding *him* with a con game about new balls for old. That was a lot of horseshit. But he was loyal and true, and Mr. F paid his salary, so he was looking into this crap and not expecting anything but just that—crap.

Eagle went for a stroll to kill time and fill in his cover. He made no effort to check for a tail, doing so would be a giveaway in itself, and he did not think it possible anyone could be interested in him yet. As the day grew warmer he took off his topcoat and carried it over his arm. Quito has four seasons every day. The Indian part of Eagle never paid much attention to weather, it was something you accepted without question and lived with, but he found it hard to believe he was practically walking on the equator.

He made a few business calls, just in case, and left his card in various offices, among them a lawyer's and a British company licensed to explore old gold diggings in the Andes. His last stop was at an oil company where the manager handed him a sealed cable. Eagle put it in his pocket without comment.

After exploring the old city, centered around the Plaza de la Independencia, and gaping like a tourist at the presidential palace, he made his way on foot back through coach-wide streets to the hotel. He went into the bathroom and locked the door.

The cable had been sent from Scotland. It was in a

simple commercial code—Eagle was not carrying a one-time pad—and he worked it out in a matter of minutes.

```
Serendip -- if million one contact
Stella Helpern code Sleeper could be
friend in need -- K deceased hard
way --
```

Eagle held his lighter to the cable, then flushed the ashes down the toilet. He was slightly puzzled. So Kleinberg was dead, killed by violence, but why should Merlin think it important that Eagle knew? He had listened to Kleinberg's tape as a part of his own briefing, about the girl agent and the Seven Sleepers, and while it might be germane it was not likely to be of any real help. Eagle still had to get on Isla de Pelo and sort things out for himself. He was close to doing that now; he saw no obstacles unless he erred foolishly, which he wouldn't. The truth was that he had not paid a hell of a lot of attention to the Kleinberg tape. The man was telling the truth, or thought he was, but Eagle didn't like things to get too involved. He was a methodical man; one issue, one enemy, one killing at a time. Kleinberg had had the Bormann obsession; Merlin made it clear that Eagle was not to be sidetracked by that. If he found Martin Bormann tending bar at the hotel he was to ignore him, and if he decided to kill him he was to do it on his own time. Merlin had a deeper understanding of this matter than Kleinberg had, and was after bigger game. Eagle only wished he knew what it was.

He took a shower and put on a clean shirt. It had French cuffs, one of his affectations for this mission. He was fitting the links when the phone rang.

Helmuth Toller spoke Oxfordian English with a military crispness. "Sorry to be so late, Mr. Brookson, but I just got back to Quito. I hope you have not been inconvenienced?"

Friendly. Solicitous. And pressing a bit—trying to

establish that their meeting, their business, was important. Eagle would have to straighten him out on that.

"No inconvenience at all," he said. "I had business and I did a little sightseeing. I have never been in Quito."

"I hope you dressed for it," said Toller. "Our weather surprises strangers. We are two miles above sea level here."

Eagle did not want to prolong the amenities. He said, "I was very comfortable. Now, Mr. Toller, about this wild goose chase—I am a business man and I am accustomed to frankness. To be as succinct as possible, Mr. Toller, no bullshit and no beating around the bush."

Helmuth Toller laughed. Not quite genuine, Eagle thought, but adequate. It would have fooled most people.

"I believe in candor myself," said Toller. "We should get along. I know you are skeptical and I do not blame you. It does not bother me. I am used to it. But I think we are going a bit too fast—I know nothing of you, Mr. Brookson, other than the message you left with my secretary. And before we speak further let me warn you that I do not like to discuss business, *our* business, over the phone. We shall have to meet personally and talk, and not even that until we have established matters on, shall we say, a rather firmer footing?"

Eagle lay back on the bed and grinned at the phone. He had a character on the hook and a pretty cagey one at that.

He said, "All right. I agree. I represent a certain gentleman in Scotland who for the moment at least wants to be known as Mr. Frobisher. Mr. F would be even better. Do you follow me so far?"

"I do, Mr. Brookson."

Eagle glanced at his briefcase on the luggage stand. "Mr. F recently received a communication from you people, from a certain club and a certain society, in which you made, as far as I am concerned, some pretty goddamn wild promises—"

"We made no promises, Mr. Brookson. We are extremely careful about that. All we did was suggest certain possibilities, which we will not mention on the phone."

"Okay—okay. You made certain suggestions which I, frankly, do not believe. I also think you people are a bunch of jokers—con artists—trying to take advantage of an old man who is nearly senile."

The other man chuckled. "You will not succeed in making me angry, Mr. Brookson. I told you—I am accustomed to such skepticism. I expect it. I would be amazed, indeed suspicious, if I did not encounter it. But tell me—you have the card of invitation with you? The card that was sent to, er, Mr. F?"

"In my briefcase," said Eagle.

"Good." Eagle thought that Toller sounded relieved. "I see no point in discussing this matter on the phone, Mr. Brookson. I believe we understand each other. You are here because your employer ordered it and you are to take back a full, and truthful, report of what you see and hear. Correct?"

"Correct." Eagle was careful to sound grudging.

"Then it is all very simple, Mr. Brookson. Your own opinions, at least at this point, do not matter in the least. You are nothing but an emissary for Mr. F. We had hoped, of course, that the gentleman would come in person."

Eagle sneered. "Then you're out of your minds. Mr. F is nearly eighty and confined to a wheelchair. Come on, now, Mr. Toller. You didn't really think the old man was going to travel from Scotland to Ecuador just on the strength of a phony promise to make him young again?"

This time there was an edge in Toller's voice, but he did not break his cool. "No matter what we thought. You are here and that is all that matters at the moment. I will send a car for you, in say an hour. Would it be too inconvenient if we were to fly to Isla de Pelo tonight? We would go by helicopter, I do it all the time, and the trip is really not bad. A little over two hours."

"Fine with me," said Eagle. He nodded at the phone. That was why he was here—to get on Isla de Pelo.

"I'll be ready in an hour," he said. "Tell your man to have the desk call me."

"It will be a woman," said Toller. "Her name is Monika. I will see you, Mr. Brookson. And don't forget to bring the invitation. That is most important."

Of course. Eagle opened his briefcase and took out the card, glanced again at the golden gothic script— THE BEARER IS ENTITLED TO ALL THE PRIVILEGES OF THE VALHALLA CLUB. One of the privileges, he thought, might be to have your throat slit if you made a mistake.

At the moment he was not too concerned. He was clean. He was not even carrying the penknife Merlin had mentioned.

He put the card back in the briefcase. Merlin's lab had brought out the concealed number with ultraviolet. 69. Eagle frowned, then grinned. Probably coincidence.

He went down to the lobby to wait. As she approached the desk and spoke to the clerk he spotted her. She looked like a Monika. Obviously Aryan. Tall, slim-legged, and tight-assed in a skirt that showed the backs of her legs to advantage. Sensible shoes. Pale blonde hair drawn back from a high clear forehead. Wide-set eyes, a pale cool gray on him as he approached. Her nose was thin, faintly acquiline over a large red mouth. The mouth was too soft for the rest of her face, too moist, the lower lip that of a voluptuary. Her face, in turn, was too old for her body. She had faint wrinkles around her eyes and at the corners of her mouth, and her throat was a year or so short of crepy. For all that she was still a beautiful woman and knew it. Her appraising look and her greeting indicated that she thought Eagle was a beautiful man.

Her handshake was firm and warm. Her smile displayed a lot of good white teeth. "You're Mr. Richard Brookson? How nice to see you." Her smile changed and she squinted her eyes at him. "And how nice to find that *you* certainly don't need our services. I mean I didn't quite know what to expect. Most of our visitors are, well, rather on the geriatric side. Nice to know you're not. We've rather a shortage of virility on the island."

She held his hand a moment longer than was necessary and Eagle could not mistake the signal. Like that? Right off the bat. Come into my parlor and play. Genuine? Or part of the con?

She took his arm. "I'm Monika Altekruse. Welcome to Ecuador. No trouble, I hope? Customs or anything?"

Eagle let himself warm to the VIP treatment. It was what they expected. Just as they would expect him to respond to the sexual overtures she was exuding. Why not? Let them win him over. He was there to be convinced.

The bellman, a flat-nosed Indian with a skin like old leather, deposited Eagle's one suitcase in the back of a Rambler wagon drawn up to the curb. Eagle gave him money and heard him exchange comments on the weather with the doorman. *"¡Que feo invierno!"*

Monika Altekruse watched Eagle's face. "Everybody in Quito talks about the weather. All the time. Actually it has not been such a bad winter so far. Do you know Spanish, Mr. Brookson?"

He shook his head. "Very little." He smiled and stammered. *"Poco—poco."* He knew Mexican Spanish, and like most Apaches could get by in Indian Spanish.

The woman slid in behind the wheel, careless with her legs. They were fine legs in chocolate colored pantyhose. She leaned toward him and smiled and he could see the tiny golden vibrissa in her thin nostrils. She put a hand on his arm, a faint pressure of fingers on his hard biceps. "My," she said. "My. You certainly *are* in condition."

Eagle stared at her legs for a moment. If they were going to play it that way, from the very beginning, he might as well get the show on the road. They were rushing things, or she was, and he wondered why. Or maybe he was just playing his part well. Richard Brookson, businessman and skeptic. And sucker. They appeared to think so.

As they pulled out into traffic she tugged at her skirt, at the same time giving him another moist smile. Show over for the moment. To be resumed after intermission. After business.

As she made a left turn into Benalcazar Street she said, "Do you know Quito at all?"

Eagle shook his head. "I'm lost already."

"We're going to Hel's place—Helmuth Toller—you talked to him—for dinner. It's not far. Out by Sangolqui. Hel thought you would like that. I know you will, if you have any feeling for food at all. Hel is quite an amateur chef. We'll be dining Peruvian tonight. Seviche. Hel got the recipe from an old man, I think he's half Jivaro, who lives down in Piura." She giggled suddenly. "I hope you like raw fish, Mr. Brookson."

As a boy on the reservation he had often survived for days on raw fish. On those occasions when he ran away to Mexico with his friends to steal cattle, they lived off raw fish and roots and certain edible beetles.

But now he made the proper face. "Not one of my favorites, I'm afraid. Once I was in Korea on business and got trapped into eating octopus. It was like a rubber snake. Your friend, Mr. Toller, shouldn't have gone to all the trouble."

"No trouble. Hel loves to cook. That is just about the only feminine thing about him. But not to worry, Mr. Brookson. I was pulling your leg a bit. We are having seviche—an Ecuadorian Smorgasbord that is out of this world. I gain pounds just thinking about it."

Dusk was coming on. The woman chattered on about this and that. They got into the near suburbs and, after a brief run on the Pan American Highway, took a cloverleaf off to the southwest. The road turned narrow and became asphalt in bad repair, obstructed now and then by carts drawn by horses or oxen. Pig-tailed Indians, trudging along behind the carts, did not waste a glance on the Rambler.

Now that the menu had been given, the Altekruse woman seemed to have run out of small talk. Eagle smoked a rare cigarette—mindful of what was proba-bly the best pair of lungs in the world—taking it from a slim silver case with the letters R. B. He offered her one and she accepted. As he lit it for her she flicked her eyes over his body with obvious pleasure, then gave him the moist smile and got back to her driving. For a moment Eagle had the idea—absurd but he had it—that she was emitting heat, that her slim, well-cared-for forty-ish body was casting an oestrual warmth. Ridiculous. Or maybe not. Sex was where you found it. As the Rambler purred past fields of fire-colored gladiolus, he mused that the sex come-on might be part of the con or might be the real thing. If the latter case, he was not averse. If the offer was genuine and led to no complications, why not? This was not yet a serious mission. No hands had been declared. He was, in a way, only sightseeing. Probing.

It did occur to him that the lady might be combining business with pleasure. If there was anything to this mare's nest at all, if they really were servicing old gaf-fers things might still be a little dull for a not too old woman with a healthy sexual appetite. Putting new gonads on an old man didn't make him a young man. Maybe she was on the level. If so—Eagle remembered his Dickens—Barkis was willin'. He would not want to disappoint a lady, providing it did not interfere with the matter at hand.

"Not far now," Monika Altekruse said. "A mile or so. Could I have another cigarette, please."

He gave her one and lit it. Again her eyes strayed. He had the feeling that she wanted to touch him.

Instead she blew smoke and said, "Hel, Helmuth, tells me that you are a skeptic, Mr. Brookson."

Eagle grinned. So the foreplay was over. All the inviting conversation, the whimsical *savoir faire*, was *fini*. She had been sizing him up and they were, he was sure of it, about to get down to the nitty-gritty. The real test would come when he met Hel, who was such a precious amateur chef. She was going to lead into it, get him set up.

He nodded. "Yes. You might say that." The role of skeptic in this instance was not hard to play. A natural.

She eyed him sideways. "There is a saying in the States, no? Do not knock it until you have tried it?"

"I'm not looking for a new pair of nuts," he said. "Mr. F is. He's eighty and a little dotty about everything but business. I suppose it's been twenty years, maybe more, since he got laid."

She flushed and that surprised him. Rose color crept into the pale tan cheeks. The tan, and the legs, made him think for the first time that she must be a skier. Of course. A Monika like this would have to be a skier. He twisted in the seat to smile at her.

"I'm sorry if I offended you, Miss Altekruse. But I think we may as well have this thing right out in the open—I don't see much point in euphemism. I came here to do a job and to do it as quickly as possible. I have a lot of legitimate business to get on with. So, if you will again excuse a crude expression, I would like to cut out the shit and get down to it."

He watched her. For a moment she stared straight ahead, her mouth tight, then her moist red lips crinkled and she laughed. She put a hand on his thigh and squeezed.

"I am not offended, Richard. Not at all. And let us, as you say, cut the kidding. *Sans merde*. And you will call me Monika. Okay?"

"Okay."

A pretty prim pussy, he thought. Doesn't like to say *shit*.

"You are wrong," she said. "Very wrong to be a skeptic. We can do it—make old men virile again. Not in all cases, of course, but in many. We have had many successes."

"This I'll have to see."

She nodded. "Of course. That is why you are here, yes?"

"That is why I am here, Monika."

"I will not try to convince you, then. Not now. I will leave that to Helmuth. Look, just ahead. That driveway. We are almost there."

In the last of the twilight Eagle saw lights over an open iron gate. They left the narrow road, gone to gravel and dirt some miles back, and approached the gates over deep ruts. There was a high iron fence with bayonet spikes and a stone gatehouse that looked deserted. The lights of the Rambler picked out a plaque on the front of the gatehouse.

VILLA VILCABAMBA

Eagle thought of Merlin telling him about the valley of Vilcabamba, where everybody lived forever. Mention the valley as a technique of disinformation, Merlin said. So why not?

As they drove past the gatehouse he stared at the sign and said, "I've heard, or read, that name in connection with longevity. Vilcabamba? Anything to do with your swindle?"

Monika laughed. The laugh sounded a bit shrill and absent-minded, as if she were thinking of something else—like a Pavlovian reaction. She slowed the car as the drive twisted like a boa through a thick stand of corkwood. A bat fluttered through the tunnel of light and Eagle stared. It was the biggest bat he had ever seen.

"A vampire," Monika told him. "Bloodsuckers. It's unusual to see them so near the city, but we get one now and then. They don't bother us or the dogs. Sometimes the peasants complain about their cattle being attacked."

Still no sign of light ahead. The driveway climbed and twisted without apparent end. The woman drove slowly, cautiously, her eyes intent on the road. Her skirt had ridden up and he regarded her legs shining in chocolate nylon. Slim and well muscled. Definitely skier's legs.

They came to a long climbing straight and she relaxed. "I don't like to drive around curves in the dark. It's all right in the day, Hel's got his own beautiful little mountain, but I hate it at night. The worst is over now. To get back, Richard, Vilcabamba is *not* part of our 'swindle', as you so rudely put it. And so mistakenly, too. You are going to have a very red face when you see how badly you have misjudged us."

Eagle's teeth glinted in the dashlight. "I have been known to apologize."

"I will expect you to. But the Vilcabamba you are thinking of has nothing to do with us. It is in the south, near a little town of the same name. Close to Yangana. There has been a lot written about that region, and the people. In newspapers and medical journals. They do seem to live a long time down there, but I have no idea why. It does not matter. It has nothing to do with us."

"Mr. F thought it might," said Eagle. "That is where I heard it. I remember now. Mr. F read those reports and, when all the doctors seemed to go along with it, to verify the stories, I suppose it gave him hope that you people were not a hundred percent phonies. Funny, though, the name popping up on the villa if there's no connection."

Monika shrugged. "Helmuth bought the villa five years ago. From a man named Stresser. It was already the Villa Vilcabamba."

"So much for that," said Eagle.

"Yes, Richard. So much for that. You are an incredibly suspicious man, you know." She laughed. "One hundred percent phonies—von hundert—what a fool you are going to look by this time tomorrow. But before then I am going to take pity on you and do something you will not be so skeptical about."

She must have been waiting until they reached the graveled pullout, a crescent hacked out of trees and brush. She pulled the Rambler over and killed the engine. Eagle sat quietly, alert and waiting, watching her. He had some idea of what was coming.

Monika put her finger tips on his fly. She stroked the cloth, barely touching. "You will not think I am horrible and forward if I do this?"

Eagle grinned at her. "Right now I am not doing much thinking. But when I do I promise I will not think you horrible and forward. But I do have a question—is Helmuth going to like this?"

She did not seem to be wearing perfume. Her odor was that of a clean woman. He could not see her eyes in the gloom and in any case she was staring down at his fly. Shadows made her mouth appear redder, wider, moister than he remembered it.

She shook her head. "No. He will not like it. I do not want him to find out, but even if he does I do not much care. Helmuth and I have been lovers. It is over, for me at least. Helmuth does nothing for me now, gives me no excitement, and it is hard to find others. Young men—virile—you understand?"

"I understand. You're in the wrong business."

She bent over him. "Yes. But not the way you mean. You will see. We do make them virile. You will see proof of that. But an old man is still an old man."

Monika opened his fly. Eagle started to say something and she put up a hand and closed his lips. "Do not talk now. And do nothing. Do not touch me. I will do everything. Later it will be my turn."

Eagle enjoyed his turn. She was an amazing fellatrice. She did not release him until he was drained.

She raised her head to look at him. "You enjoyed that?"

Eagle nodded weakly. What he had just permitted was dangerous. She had distracted him to the point where a skillful man—a pro—could have approached the car and taken him.

Monika seemed to want praise. He gave it truthfully. "You're very good. Superb. Are you a pro?"

She shook her head. Her large red mouth glistened. "Of course not. What a thing to say! Are you trying to insult me?"

"Not at all. I'm just trying to find out if you are a pro. It makes a difference."

She slid away from him, behind the wheel, and reached for the key. "No. I am not a pro. But I am not a prude either. I like it that way sometimes, when I am in the mood. I like the taste. But with you it is something special, Richard. I hope you appreciate that. The moment I saw you in the hotel lobby I knew what I wanted to do to you."

Eagle nodded and zipped his fly. She had left it open. "And we don't want Helmuth to know?"

Monika shrugged again. "Not especially. Not if it can be avoided. I don't suppose it can. Hel is very sharp. And he is jealous of me, even though we are no longer lovers. But don't worry about it. I will handle him."

"With my permission," said Eagle. "I would just as soon not get involved. And don't look now, but there is something in the bushes out there."

The woman laughed. "Just the dogs. Hel has two big Alsatians. I said not to worry—the dogs won't tell him."

VII

THE HELICOPTER WAS American Army surplus, a reconditioned S-58 large enough for most jobs, with seats for four and cargo space, and mobile enough for jungle- and island-hopping. Eagle made no sign of recognition, Richard Brookson was not likely to know much about helicopters, but he knew the Army had used the S-58 to transport Littlejohn rockets in Nam. A sturdy workhorse chopper.

Monika was at the controls. This did not surprise Eagle. She was a capable woman in many ways. Her gifts were not exclusively sexual, as he had discovered during and after dinner. A charming hostess who looked stunning in an evening gown, braless, with the small uptilted breasts of a twenty-year-old. She was efficient and politely cold with a brigade of soft-footed Indian servants. Her manner at table had been only slightly less distant, courteous but cool. No one, Eagle thought with sly amusement, could have guessed that an hour earlier she had been sucking his cock.

"A million dollars down is the very least we can accept," said Helmuth Toller. He was speaking close to Eagle's ear, his voice raised against the beat of the rotors.

"A million," he repeated. "Some of our clients pay

73

more than that and do not complain. The money, naturally, will be no problem to your Mr. F."

Eagle nodded. He and Toller were in the two rear seats. He watched the woman's silhouette, the easy way she handled the helicopter as it skittered toward the coastal town of Pedernales. Toller had been, to this point, very courteous and correct. Miffed a bit, if unreasonably so, because Mr. F had not made the journey in person. "The invitation was sent to *him*," Toller pointed out. "We did not expect an emissary."

Eagle had grinned at him. "Sorry. Me or no deal."

Now, with scattered lights below and a gibbous moon hanging over the Andes, he listened to Helmuth Toller with only half an ear. Toller had said most of it before, at dinner and in the library afterward while Monika changed clothes and had the 'copter serviced on a pad behind the villa. Toller was a great talker, a big mouth, and Eagle wondered why. Toller did not look like a man who would be afflicted with logorrhea. A lot of things about Toller puzzled Eagle. Most of the things he did not think he would like, even if he understood them better. He did not want to jump to conclusions. He had a pretty good, if still dim, suspicion of what Toller was. Of what Monika was, for that matter, but so far he kept an open mind. His job was to probe and learn. Not to judge or execute. He concentrated on his role playing. So far he had not given himself away, that he knew of. He was still Richard Brookson, impatient young businessman doing a distasteful job for a crazy old employer.

Every now and then he had to answer Toller. He said now, "You don't have to worry about the million. That's pocket change to Mr. F. What you do have to worry about is selling me a bill of goods. I hope I've made that perfectly clear—if I'm convinced Mr. F will be convinced. If I take back a negative report, which I think I will, you're a bunch of dead con artists as far as Mr. F is concerned."

Toller smiled widely. His teeth were better than

74

Monika's, and hers were perfect. Toller nodded. "*Ja—ja*—I understand. You are a good courier, Mr. Brookson. You do your job. You guard your employer's money as if it were your own, no?"

Eagle inclined his head. "I guess I do. If I do a good job maybe a lot of it will be mine someday."

Let them think he had a little larceny in his heart. Crooks responded to that. Not that these people were ordinary crooks. If, indeed, they were crooks at all in the ordinary sense. Eagle didn't know much about them yet, but he knew *that*. There was more involved than a get-rich-quick scheme—a con game to milk nutty millionaires.

Monika shouted at them and pointed down. She reduced power and banked, the helicopter dropping like an express elevator. Eagle saw a spangle of lights below.

Toller pointed. "Pedernales. Not much. A fishing and tourist village only. Living is very cheap. Many artists and writers live there—most are alcoholics. We on Isla de Pelo have nothing much to do with the village, we use it only for provisions. And as a staging point for some of the old gentlemen who do not like to fly, or are perhaps afraid. We run a hydrofoil out to the island."

Eagle nodded and kept silent. Toller took the cue and, smiling and patting Eagle's knee, went to sit beside Monika. The helicopter passed over the village and swung out over surf.

Eagle had the feeling that Merlin would have recognized Toller's type, and properly niched it, long before. But Merlin had the advantage of a couple of generations.

He studied Toller's back. He and the woman were talking, Toller gesticulating now and then. No need to whisper with the blatting of the rotors.

Helmuth Toller was late fortyish. Prime condition. Tall, wide-shouldered, trim-waisted. A predatory nose and a wide loose mouth. Yellow hair, cut in close

75

military style and sprinkled with gray. The eyes were small and wide set and intensely blue. Eagle had been studying eyes all his life and he knew a fanatic when he saw one. Toller was a fanatic. But about what?

Eagle usually had a gut feeling about people, about what he could or could not do with them. He thought he could handle Monika Altekruse, either through sex or terror; about Toller he did not know. Toller was a marvelous physical specimen. Eagle had twenty years on him, yet he knew better than to underrate him.

Toller leaned to shout something at the woman. She shook her head. By freak, some one-in-a-million aberration of acoustics, Eagle heard Toller's question. Part of a question.

"Mordklub? *Das schlaferin*—"

Eagle had read German classics while at Oxford. He thought it a clumsy language, all hind to fore, and had never become adept. But there was no difficulty with the word and phrase he had just heard.

"Murder club? The sleepers—"

Eagle closed his eyes and appeared to doze. He decided to be grouchy as hell when they deplaned. Hungry, sleepy and in a bad mood all around. They might leave him alone. He glanced down at his watch. Not yet midnight. Plenty of time to snoop, given the opportunity, but he did not think highly of his chances. Grim. Going alone, cold, into a hostile environment—never mind the VIP crap he had been getting—it would be a damned hostile environment the moment they tumbled to him if he snooped and got caught at it.

But he had it. A clue. Hard fact, as Merlin would put it. It came as no surprise, but he *had* heard it. Murder club. "The sleepers" could only be an allusion to the Seven Sleepers. Killers.

Merlin's cable had been preambled with Serendip—meaning info just come to hand and may be of some bearing on present circumstance.

K deceased hard way

Eagle had never met Kleinberg. The man was just a name to him, an Israeli agent interviewed and sent on his way before Eagle arrived in Hawaii.

For the first time he felt a sense of kinship with the dead Kleinberg, He opened his eyes and watched them, the woman and Toller. The helicopter was falling, swooping down toward a lighted pad. Toller turned to look back and Eagle stared at him. Toller nodded and waved, shouting. "Here we are! Isla de Pelo!"

Eagle nodded and patted a yawn. The helicopter touched down lightly and the rotors flapped into silence. Eagle unstrapped, thinking that if he went it was also going to be the hard way. Goddamned hard. On them.

He was borrowing trouble, of course. Probably nothing was going to happen. As long as he played it cool, stuck to his role and didn't slip up there was no reason they should suspect him. The card of invitation had passed muster—Toller had taken it away and come back in ten minutes with a satisfied smile—and old 69 was in like Flynn.

And yet Eagle, as he climbed out of the helicopter and stretched, had a buzz in his belly. Trouble coming. Trouble which he would probably start. He could play it cozy and sit on his ass and not find out anything of importance. Any damned fool could do that.

The pad was on a strip of smooth brown beach. Powerful lights were rigged around a bull's-eye painted on a cement slab. Asphalt paths led away from the pad like wheel spokes. There was no moon now and the air was crisp and damp. There was no surf and he knew they were on the island side of the Isla de Pelo.

Toller joined him, grunting and stretching. The woman was doing something to the helicopter. Around the pad, back in the shadows, a ring of white-clad men watched them.

Toller jerked a hand at the silent men. "Servants. Mestizos, most of them. Good workers and they know how to keep quiet. Intelligent, too. The best of both bloods, Indian and Spanish. We need a very large staff

77

here, mechanics and chefs and maids, all things. You would be amazed at how much it all costs."

"You can afford it," said Eagle. "With your clientele—and the minimum deposit."

Toller's teeth glinted in the powerful lights. "Ah, yes. Quite correct, Richard. You see that I drop all formality. You will do the same and call me Helmuth, no?"

Eagle had noted that Toller spoke perfect English when he chose. On occasion he lapsed into the idiomatic, mixing American and English slang with equal ease. Mostly he used a stiff, half-Germanic form of speech. Very natural to him, as he had explained at the villa. He was Germanophile in most things. Both he and Monika had been born in Germany. They were good Germans but better Ecuadorians. The old Germany was finished. She had been evil, Germania, and deserved to die.

Eagle, at table in the Villa Vilcabamba, had silently finished the thought for his host. A better Germany would be born—in South America.

Toller shouted at the woman. "Come on, Monika. Don't be all night with that. Richard is tired and hungry and so am I. We will have some drinks and a bite and then he can see some of our films. What in hell are you doing?"

She came ducking out of the machine, smiling at Eagle and ignoring Toller. "A good pilot checks everything, before and after. And I want a drink also—I have been doing all the work while you two loafed—but how can you think of food? After that seviche? I cannot eat for hours yet."

The raw fish had been good, pickled in lime, though Eagle had pretended to dislike it. Tastier than speared trout from a canyon stream, sliced with a flint knife. He burped and the fish came back to haunt him. What in hell were they waiting for? Standing around like statues. The mestizos, working under the direction of a *honcho* who exchanged a spate of Spanish with Toller, were beginning to swab down the helicopter and

78

refuel it. They worked silently, ignoring the two men and the woman.

Monika took Eagle's arm and gave it a squeeze, at the same time glancing at Toller and frowning. "Where is your fabulous Doctor Six? You did radio him from the villa?"

If her obvious sexual interest in Eagle angered Toller he concealed it well. His smile tensed quickly and vanished, but he pointed and spoke calmly. "Here he comes now. With Klaus."

Eagle had already picked up the electric purring sound. Two golf carts glided out of the shadows, their rubber tires sibilant on the asphalt paths. Eagle was introduced to the drivers of the carts.

"Doctor Franz Six and Doctor Klaus Neidler, Mr. Richard Brookson. You may call him Richard, I think. He understands that we are not formal here. Richard is a surprise for us. He comes to investigate for number 69."

That was how they did it. Numbers on the cards of invitation. Concealed numbers brought out by ultraviolet. And code marks that Merlin's cryptologists were still studying.

When Toller finished the introductions only Klaus Neidler offered to shake hands. He was young, in his early thirties, a pinkish man already balding. His handshake was firm and dry.

Doctor Franz Six was an old man. Late seventies, Eagle guessed. He was thin almost to emaciation and would have been tall had he been able to stand erect. This he could not do. He stood with his spine hinged, his upper torso jutting forward at so severe an angle that he had to roll his eyes upward to see the person he was addressing. Eagle got the clue from the man's hands, large hands with the joints twisted and swollen. Arthritis. His spine was fused into chalk.

Most of Six's life was in his eyes. They studied Eagle coldly—muddy brown, penetrating intelligent eyes. They made Eagle think of a lizard.

It was a case of instant dislike. Disbelief and wariness on both sides. Eagle had never before met a man he disliked so intensely at first glance. He cautioned himself. This old bastard was trouble.

Six grunted something at Eagle, then turned to speak to Toller. His mouth was pursy and he dribbled when he spoke. He began to spray a torrent of German at Toller. Toller stopped him. "Speak English, Franz. Richard is not fluent in German."

Doctor Six gave Toller a look that condemned such courtesy, but he turned to dribble at Eagle in a thick accent. "You will excuse, I mean no offense, you understand, but this is not a good thing. Helmuth has broken one of our rules. We deal with the principals only. Only with the principals."

Eagle gave the old man stare for stare, decided to sock it to him a bit. He nodded and put a sneer in his tone. "I can understand that, Doctor. It's logical. Old men, hopeful old men praying for a miracle, are a lot easier to fool than young men."

Monika tugged at his arm. "Richard! You are not polite. And you must not mind Franz. He is not well. He is always in great pain."

Six gestured sharply with a swollen hand. He took a step toward Eagle. His shadow on the landing pad was dark and predatory.

"Do not speak of my pain, Monika. I am sure this young man, Richard Brookson, is not interested. Nor am I. I am interested only in my work. As you all know, but this young Richard does not. This is so, young Richard? You do not believe in the work we do here? You are a scoffer, a skeptical?"

Eagle, trying to be as infuriating as possible, said, "At the moment, yes. I've already told Helmuth and Monika where I stand. What I think. I haven't tried to fool anyone and I won't be fooled. I think you're a bunch of crooks trying to fleece wealthy old men."

To his surprise the old man smiled. He still had a few of his own teeth, brown and worn down to stumps.

"Ach," said Doctor Six. "You are a young *dummkopf* but at least you speak your mind. I do not dislike this. And I will make you change your song. You will see."

Toller, no *dummkopf* himself, saw the opening and leaped in. With a laugh he said, "You mean tune, Franz. He will change his tune. And speaking of changing, let's all go up to the big house and change into a dry martini."

He winked at Eagle. "Not very funny, I know, but I heard it once in New York and have never forgotten it. And it is the way I feel now—I need a drink. Come on, all of you. Franz, you and Klaus come with me. We can all crowd in. Monika will take Richard."

Eagle got into a golf cart with the woman. He looked back to see the mestizos pushing the helicopter off the pad. Off in the dark he saw what looked like a big Quonset hut. Probably a hangar.

Monika drove the cart. She pushed her knee against his. "You must not mind Franz. He is very old, nearly eighty, and as I said, in great pain. You saw his spine."

"Arthritis?"

"Yes. Terrible. He has not walked erect for years."

"I wonder what he did to earn a punishment like that."

Her glance was sharp. She took her knee away. "What do you mean? What he did? These things can happen to anybody. To you or even to me. Especially when we grow old."

Eagle decided to play the Monika angle for all he could get out of it. She might be conning him, probably was, but at least she was involved to a certain extent. She had appetites. She had not been faking back there in the car. She had liked what she did, and she did it because *she* wanted to. It was the only break he had gotten so far—meeting a genuine oral erotic.

He put his hand on her leg. "I didn't mean anything in particular. Just a thought. You've got to admit that he's a pretty repulsive looking old man. I'd be a liar if I said I took to him. He gives me the creeps."

She picked up his hand and toyed with his fingers. The cart whined quietly along the blacktop. They passed a light stanchion where moths as big as bats tried to electrocute themselves. There was no sign of the other cart. It had taken a different path.

Monika squeezed his hand. "I hope I am not making a mistake about you, Richard."

"How could you do that, or why should you? We're total strangers. You don't know anything about me. I don't know anything about you. It will probably stay that way. What difference does it make?"

"It might make a difference, Richard. If you wanted it to."

He pulled his hand away.

She slowed the cart. They came to a light where the asphalt paths forked. She took the left turning. He was silent until they went up a little rise, then down, and he heard surf pounding on a beach he could not see.

"I'll bet a few marks," he said then, "that this path does not go to the big house."

They passed another light and he saw her smile. "You would win. But why do you say marks? Why not dollars? Or pounds?"

He shrugged. "When in Rome, you know. It seemed appropriate. You and Helmuth. The good doctors— Klaus and Franz. I don't know, maybe I'm just getting in the mood. *Gemütlich*."

They came to the end of the path. The cart rolled onto smooth beach and stopped. Monika moved to press herself against him. Her mouth slid across his cheek and stopped at his ear. She nibbled at the lobe with her sharp teeth.

"There is something funny about you," she whispered.

Eagle had superb control of his body. She would learn nothing from any nervous reaction, if that was what she was after. He put his hand between her thighs and began to caress the soft flesh under the cloth. She expelled her breath. Eagle was satisfied. She was react-

82

ing, not him. If this was a trap she was more likely to be caught in it.

"Something funny," she repeated. "Not really funny, but peculiar. Strange. I sense it, I am almost sure of it, but somehow I cannot make myself care. One thing I am sure of—you are not a fool. And another—you are not a man to be trusted."

"Trusted with what?"

For a moment she did not answer. Then she whispered, "With secrets, perhaps. Perhaps with the secret of what is in my heart for you."

Since he was in this far, Eagle thought, why not go all the way? Explore this vein until he struck it rich or it petered out. Not a bad cover. It was amazing what some women would believe. And a jealous and angry man gives a lot away to his opponent. It might just give him a little edge on Helmuth.

He kissed her for a long time. Monika was not a passive kisser. She responded wildly, thrusting her tongue into his mouth. She moved her head back and forth frantically and moaned. She opened her breasts to his mouth. She dug her fingers into his hair and held his face close against her flesh.

"Mein Gott! Richard, *liebling."*

Her nipples were standing firm. He caressed each with his tongue.

"Liebling—liebling—liebling. That goes through me like a knife."

They were too cramped in the golf cart. Eagle pulled her out and they fell to the sand. She had flown the helicopter in breeches and riding boots and it was a damnable struggle to get them off. Eagle tugged and cursed, as aroused now as she was, knowing it was foolish and dangerous, but determined to have her. When at last he penetrated her he nearly lost control, iron man though he was sexually, and he was relieved when, after a very short interval, Monika climaxed in a paroxysm of screaming and moaning and thrashing

83

about. For the first time in his life he had nearly fallen short of satisfying a woman.

The fact was—as he lay gasping he tried to puzzle it out, the fact was that he had a sort of nympho on his hands—one who could achieve.—*Nympho*—probably wasn't the word. When she wriggled down and took his limpness into her mouth he thought of the word—*insatiable*. Better—*starved*.

Eagle thought he knew the truth about Helmuth Toller. He tried the idea on for size.

"Toller is impotent, isn't he?"

She stopped what she was doing. For a moment he thought she was not going to answer. Then she put him away and zipped him. "Yes. How clever of you to guess. Or perhaps not so clever. I have been acting like a sex-starved woman, no?"

"Yes. Toller is impotent?"

She got to her feet, pulled up her breeches, then sat down again to tug on the boots. "I said yes. But that is not the reason, not why I am like this. Oh, perhaps a little but not all. I have fallen in love with you, Richard. And I was out of love with Helmuth for a long time before he could no longer—"

They went back to the golf cart. She clung to his arm. "A woman who tells a man she loves him, and means it, is a fool."

"I've heard that," he agreed. "I don't think it is necessarily true. Tell me more about Helmuth—how does being impotent affect him? His character and disposition?"

Amazing that she would try the love bit, but things were getting more bizaare by the moment.

As they started back along the path she said, "You must not let Helmuth guess that you know. It will make him furious. I should not have told you."

"You didn't tell me. I guessed."

"I know that. But Helmuth will not. He will be certain that I told you and that we—you—are laughing at him. Helmuth has a great thing about maleness. Manliness. He has a good façade but there are many cracks behind it."

Rather well put, Eagle thought.

"There is much you do not understand," Monika said. "That no outsider can understand. Perhaps I will explain in time. Right now I do not wish a confrontation with Helmuth. Over you or, well, other things. So you must pretend that you do not know about him."

They were back at the fork in the paths. "I don't give a damn one way or the other, Monika. But for a woman who does not want a confrontation you sure go about it in a hell of an odd way. You don't try to conceal much. Right now, for instance. What do you think Helmuth is thinking—that we went down to the beach to gather seaweed?"

She did not glance at him, intent on steering the cart. "I said to leave Helmuth to me. We will talk again when there is more time. It is true that I like to tease Helmuth a little, taunt him. I am getting back for things he has done to me. But I am careful about it. There is the big house now. They will be waiting for us. Doctor Six will want to show you some of his films. I am tired and after a drink I am going straight to bed. So I will say goodnight now."

They were still in shadow. She reached over to give him a squeeze. "Poor thing. It is still exhausted, no?"

Eagle grinned. "Had a hard day and night. But it will come back."

"I hope so. One thing I hope you understand about me, Richard. I am a woman who must be gratified each day. Sometimes more than once, depending on my mood. I do not take excuses."

He nodded. "This I believe." It was, he thought, the one unqualified pure grain of truth that had emerged from the day's events. He had a uteromaniac on his hands. An oralist, too. Nazi business or not, con game or not, this lady was on the level about that. She was sexually obsessed and he should be able to make good use of the situation. The old joke popped into his head—about the man who was looking for the perfect wife, a rich nymphomaniac who owned a distillery. He laughed.

Monika cocked her head at him. "Something amuses you?"

Eagle raised a hand. "Nothing."

The black asphalt path curved into a circle of light. It lost itself in a tar-colored rondel centered by a splashing fountain and a flagpole. Amber spotlights played on the fountain. The flagpole was bare and Eagle wondered what they ran up at dawn—the Ecuadorian tricolor or the Nazi crooked cross?

Monika laughed throatily. "They are waiting for us. Play it, as the Americans say, cool."

"Never play it any other way. But if they think I'm going to stay up all night and talk business they're wrong. I'm as bushed as you are. I'll be sociable for two drinks and that is damned well it."

He discarded the idea of snooping tonight. Not intelligent and not in the cards. They were sure to be wary tonight. And he did not know the island. To go stumbling around strange terrain in the dark was asking for trouble. It was a fairly large island, about five miles by two. A lot of area to cover and there could be a lot of man-traps. Monika was right, if in another context. Play it cool. Wait.

The big house, as they called it, was indeed that. A four-storied mansion, a *palacio*, of pale tan stone. It had inner *galerias* on three sides, overlooking a central court, and tall *miradors* at each corner. A powerful light played from each turret. More of a *schloss*, Eagle thought, than a house. There were no trees or shrubbery close to the house and the lights had been planned to sweep the exterior walls and the grounds beyond. Somewhere a dog barked and he saw two gaunt figures slink into bushes as they approached. They vanished in an instant but he pegged them as Dobermans. For the first time he wished acutely that he had a weapon.

The great house represented money. Lots of money.

Business must be pretty good. Something was pretty good.

Monika parked the golf cart with a line of others and they walked a graveled path leading into the courtyard. Gravel, Eagle noted. It is impossible to walk silently on gravel.

He jerked a thumb at the golf carts. "They your only means of transportation?"

"No. We have cars. Quite a few. Cars and jeeps. We keep them garaged most of the time. The noise, you see. We like to keep it as quiet as possible for our patients. I suppose I should say clients."

Eagle smiled and nodded. "I bet you keep a good supply of straitjackets on hand, too." It was time to get back into his role as skeptic. He knew he could handle Monika, for now at least. He had something she needed. The purest luck, but there it was. Now he had to worry about the silent threesome waiting on the *terraza*.

Monika let go of his arm and moved away. "I will make my excuses after a drink. See you tomorrow, *leibling*."

"Sure."

Eagle heard the rockers squeaking as they climbed three stone steps. Old-fashioned, cane rocking chairs. Squeak—squeak—He caught a whiff of expensive cigar. The veranda was shadowy due to an overhang that baffled the lights. None of the three men rose to greet them. Old Six rocked in the middle, flanked by Toller and Klaus Neidler. For an instant Eagle allowed fantasy to take over—three vultures rocking. Young vulture, middle-aged vulture, and old vulture.

Helmuth Toller's voice was strained. He was furious and yet only a hint showed. He was back to his Oxfordian tones.

"Did you get lost, Monika? How very strange. I would have thought you knew the way by now."

"Don't be a fool," she told him snappishly. "Of course I did not get lost. It is a pleasant night and I took Richard across the island to the beach. You object?"

Toller had his control back. "Object, my dear Monika! Certainly not. I am only thinking of our guest. Richard must be fatigued. There is all of tomorrow to show him the island."

In a cold voice she said, "I am not going to quarrel with you, Hel. And do not tell me what to do. I am going to have a drink and then retire."

"Good idea," said Klaus Neidler. "Let's go in. We were only waiting for you, Monika." He stood up and bowed to Eagle. "And, of course, our guest."

Eagle nodded. "I could use a drink. Been a rough day."

Franz Six had not spoken. He sat in the cane rocker, knobby hands in his lap, his ruined spine jutting forward, and watched Eagle with his lizard eyes. Eagle watched back. He had noted Six's eyes as mud colored, but now he saw a glint in them. Eagle knew then, with certainty, that while he might be fooling the others he wasn't fooling the old doctor. The man was suspicious. To what extent Eagle could not guess. Nor could he guess why. He was sure he had not given himself away. Maybe Six was just naturally suspicious of everybody. Maybe he had more to lose than the others.

Six looked away first. He gave Eagle an odd smile, showing his remaining brown teeth, and extended one of his bumpy hands. "If you would be so kind, Richard? I need help to rise."

Monika moved away. Toller and Neidler watched. Doctor Six waited, still smiling.

"Of course," Eagle said. He took the hand and lifted the old man gently from the chair. Six smelled bad and his hand was like a dead toad. Eagle steadied him and stepped away. "Don't you use a cane, Doctor Six? I would think it would be easier."

"I don't need it," the doctor said. "Weakness. I don't need a cane."

Monika moved through a door. "Are we going to have that damned drink or not!"

Six followed her, a grotesque hobbling. Toller and Neidler followed Eagle. They went into a bar set off a black and white tessellated corridor. The bar room was long and richly decorated in crimson and gold. The elegant swan-neck chandelier alone must be worth a fortune. There were tables and booths, the latter covered in rich leather, and a row of goatskin-covered stools at the bar. A sleepy white-coated mestizo snapped awake as they entered.

Monika took a stool a little apart from the rest. "A glass of wine, Rosario. The *lacrima*. Be sure it's the Vesuvius, not the Piedmont." She gave them a sulky stare and then ignored them, her long fingers tapping on the bar.

Eagle had a Cutty Sark and water. Toller and Neidler had vodka. Six ordered a schnapps. He gulped it down and ordered another, keeping his brown stare fixed on Eagle.

Eagle decided to irritate them a little more. Gaucherie might do it. He gazed about at the sumptuous lounge and said, "Some saloon. All the pleasures of home. You must have to carry quite a stock of booze to satisfy your clientele."

Toller moved his glass on the bar, making circles. He said, "Everything. Ask and you shall receive."

Klaus Neidler had moved down the bar to speak to Monika. Eagle watched from a corner of his eye. Klaus asked a question and got a bad answer. Her mouth twitched angrily and Klaus flushed and turned from her. So much for that, Eagle thought. The lady isn't having any. Satiated for the night.

"Speaking of clientele," said Eagle, "where are they?" He looked up and down the bar. "All gone to bed, I suppose? Old men need their sleep?"

Doctor Six watched him. The old bastard was trying to make up his mind about something.

Toller said, "The truth, Richard, is that we only

have two people here at the moment. It is not a busy time just now. And they are both, as you say, old men."

Eagle nodded. "I thought they would be. Old and probably too sick to talk to me tomorrow?"

Neidler, after an angry glance down the bar at Monika, raised his glass. "Not at all, Richard. Quite the contrary. We want you to talk to them. Want you to see proof for yourself. Living proof. The fact is that we have an American gentleman here, a Senator or perhaps I mean ex-Senator, who should convince even you. I drink to you, Richard, as a skeptic who is about to be convinced. After you have talked with Senator Middlesworth—"

Six rapped his glass on the bar. "I will decide that, Klaus. You will stop talking now. Unless I permit. I have been thinking and I have decided. I will handle this."

Eagle had a feeling that the *gemütlichkeit* had just ended. He gave the old doctor a stare of innocence. "Handle what, Doctor Six? I don't understand. Is something the matter?"

Monika was watching in the bar mirror. The mestizo bartender was on his stool as far away as he could get. Klaus Neidler stared down into his glass.

Helmuth Toller said, "There has been a slight complication, Richard. At least the doctor thinks so. I do not agree with him." He turned to Six. "Please, Franz. This is not necessary. Not this way, not tonight. I assure you a thorough check is—"

Six waved a hand like a broken baton. "I give orders here, Helmuth. Only me. And I have decided that there will be no pretense, we will do things, as they say, on the right foot. I do not think our friend Richard will be offended with the truth. An understanding will make it easier for all of us."

Toller slapped a hand on the bar in anger. Before he could speak again Eagle said, "It's all right, Helmuth. I want to hear. What the hell is going on, doctor?"

"I am not entirely satisfied with your credentials, Richard. I have suggested to Helmuth that they be checked again. Perhaps more carefully this time. I am sure that if you are what you say you are you will have no objections?"

How to play this? Eagle held up a finger to the bartender. He needed a few seconds to think. He had absolute faith in Merlin. His cover was flawless. Wasn't it? They could check to hell and back and come up with nothing to discredit him. He decided to go with his strength and trust Merlin.

Eagle shrugged. "No objections at all, Doctor. Why should I have? But it is quite a twist. I'm the skeptic, remember. You people are supposed to convince me on behalf of Mr. F. Why this sudden change?"

"I will be frank, Richard. How do you say it—the candor. *Offen.* I must protect myself and perhaps certain people who are stupid."

Eagle raised his hands in despair. "I wish you would get to the point, Doctor Six. Just what in hell are you talking about? If you don't like my company, or if for some reason you distrust me, take me back to the mainland and cancel all offers. This trip was not my idea, you know. In fact, I was against it from the first. But Mr. F is my boss. He pays well and it's his money I'm spending—throwing away, rather—to satisfy the curiosity of a silly old man. Just say the word. I'm ready to leave now."

Toller tried again to intercede. He said, "You are doing this all wrong, Franz. This is not the time and certainly not the way. I—"

Klaus Neidler grunted and slid his glass at the bartender.

Doctor Six ignored Toller except to wave a silencing claw. "I said I would handle it. Let me try to explain, Richard."

Eagle sulked. "Do or don't. Frankly, it's of little concern to me."

Six tried to sweeten his brown smile with dire effect.

"But I care, Richard. We care. But it is true that we must take careful precautions in this business. There are many fools in the world. Well intentioned, perhaps, but still fools. We have had some small troubles before, you see. Not serious, for we are not frauds—crooks—and yet we do not like that sort of thing. A bad name is also bad for business. And, again I am frank, we are in business for profit. We have no wish to become involved with laws and courts. There are even hypocrites who wish to persecute us on moral grounds. It is a very delicate business, you understand, and that is why I speak as I do now. I am sure you will understand. It is only for a little time. Until your—what do they say—*bona fides* are completely proven. You will be patient and enjoy your stay with us, no?"

Eagle thought he had it. He feigned astonishment. "You think I'm a private investigator! Some kind of a law officer."

Toller made a fist and slammed the bar. "I tried to tell him, Richard. I checked you out myself."

Six looked at him, and Toller shut up. Six said, "Not exactly a policeman, Richard. Not Ecuadorian, at least, and who else would concern us? *Nein*. We are merely making sure that you are not a newspaperman. A sensation-monger who would write lies about us. The police in Ecuador are friendly. We have high connections. But we cannot trust journalists. Such men could ruin us."

Eagle's laugh was genuine. He did not show his relief. They were on a false trail, but for a moment he had begun to doubt. He played it for stupidity.

"A reporter? Oh, for God's sake! I distrust the press as much as you seem to. They're always badgering me about old Mr. F. But I don't quite see your objections. If you're on the level, and if your rejuvenation program really works, how come you don't want publicity? Why not tell the whole world about it?"

Both Toller and Neidler stared at him with disgust. Six shook his head and got off the stool with a muffled groan. He peered up at Eagle from his crouch. "I should think the reasons would be obvious. Our wealthy clients do not want any publicity. We are not charlatans. I admit to some failures, but not many. But such an operation is still not a thing that men, wealthy and important men, want talked about in the world press. So if you will just be patient, no? I am sure that Helmuth is right and there is no cause for suspicion. But I cannot accept chances. I have—we all have—too much to lose. In the meantime—"

"In the meantime," Eagle said brusquely, "I don't know that I want to hang around here and waste valuable time while you run another check. It might be better if I left first thing in the morning."

Six began to hobble painfully toward the door. "I am afraid that will not be possible. Helmuth will explain. *Guten abend*, Richard."

"*Guten abend*, Doctor."

He turned back to his drink. Only then did he notice that Monika was gone. There was a door back where the bar curved.

Eagle stared at the bar mirror. To Toller's reflection he said, "Why can't I leave in the morning? Or right now if I damned well please?"

Toller grinned and hunched his shoulders, but his eyes were narrow. Eagle realized that he had just been subjected to the old police routine—one hard and one soft. One aggressor and one, apparent, friend.

"I'm sorry," said Toller. "I know it's damnable and looks like a cheap game, but actually something has gone wrong with the helicopter. You do remember that Monika was fussing with it. Also—"

"Don't tell me," said Eagle. "Let me guess. Sheer coincidence, and as you say, damnable, but the hydrofoil has gone bad too. Right?"

"I *am* sorry," said Toller. "I know how it must look."

"That is exactly how it looks," said Eagle. "No other means of transportation?"

Klaus Neidler laughed and reached for the bottle of vodka. "Not unless you can swim five miles. And like sharks for company. But cheer up, Richard. It will only be for a day or so. It will be okay. The old man gets these crazy ideas."

Toller touched his arm. "You want to see those films. I don't think Franz will object. They're pretty hot stuff—for scientific studies."

Eagle gave him a hard look. "Stow the films. I'm going to bed."

VIII

DURING THE NIGHT Eagle was awakened by the sound of a big helicopter coming in. He padded in the dark to one of the barred windows and pulled back the drape. He was no expert but he had flown in enough choppers to know that this must be a big cargo job.

He was on the third floor and his view was blocked by one of the miradors, but he could see a penumbra around the turret. The pad lights were on. He wondered what they were bringing in. Or who?

Before he went back to bed he tried the door again. It was still locked from the outside. Eagle shrugged and got in bed. Before he dropped off he thought that it was a tempest in a teapot—nothing yet to get alarmed about. He believed that Doctor Six, the old horror, had been telling the exact truth. He *was* suspicious and running a double check. Fair enough. The man was a doctor, he was old, he was German, and he was deathly afraid of newspaper men. Other things being equal, assuming this was a neo-Nazi setup, it made a lot of sense from the doctor's viewpoint. His withered old ass was at stake. Eagle wondered just what atrocities the old boy *had* committed in the concentration camps. Whatever, he was running scared and he didn't trust the younger generation to cover *his* ass. Six was a do it yourself man.

He had left a drape open and sunlight awakened him. He tried the door. Unlocked.

Eagle bathed and shaved and went downstairs. He passed a mestizo servant on the broad staircase and another sweeping a terraza. He gave them a *Guten Morgen* and they stared.

He switched to Spanish. *"Buenas dias."* This got him a nod.

He slanted across the rondel and out of the courtyard. The flag was up. Ecuadorian. We are all good little Ecuadorians here. Heil Hitler.

No sign of the Dobermans. Probably locked up during the day. He passed an Indian working on a hedge of white deutzia, tried German again and got a sullen stare. He doubted that the help knew much of what went on. Or cared.

Everything looked different in the bright sunlight. Eagle took the path leading to the landing pad and found it deserted. He had been right about the Quonset hangars. Three of them. One large and two small. All locked and barred and without windows.

As he left the pad he glanced back at the house. Atop one of the miradors light shimmered and broke. Someone was watching him with binoculars.

He swung off the asphalt path onto one of gravel. The island had a network of paths. This one took him past tennis courts and an enormous swimming pool of red and yellow tile. Part of the pool apron was roofed with glass and an old man was lying on a deck chair. He was deeply tanned and naked except for a white jockstrap. On a round garden table were a thermos jug, a glass, and a bottle of whisky.

Eagle started to veer off, choosing another path that would take him across the island to the sea, when the old man raised his head and called to him. "Good morning."

96

Eagle raised a hand. "Good morning, sir."

The old man beckoned. "Come and bat the breeze for awhile, son. You American? English? You sure don't look Kraut."

As Eagle approached he saw that it was not a jock-strap. The old man's privates were bandaged.

Eagle extended his hand. "Senator Middlesworth, I presume?"

The old boy chuckled. He was scrawny and bowlegged, with a freckled bald head and a crepe-skinned potbelly that accordioned as he sat up to shake hands.

"Used to be Senator, son. Not anymore. Just plain Homer Middlesworth now. You gonna tell me your name's Stanley?"

"Brookson, sir. Richard Brookson. I got in last night."

The old man looked him up and down. Eagle was wearing slacks and blue sneakers and a tail-out sport shirt. The old man grimaced. He did not have his teeth in.

"What the hell for?"

Eagle begged his pardon.

"I said what the hell for? What are you doing here? A young specimen like you? Don't tell me you're having trouble getting it up at your age."

Eagle smiled. "No, sir. It isn't that. It's my employer that's having the trouble. I'm on sort of a scouting expedition for him."

The old man nodded. "Yeah. I get it. Some people don't like to come here until they're absolutely sure. Then they usually sneak in *incognito*. Not me, though. I came down here under my own steam and my own name. Homer P. Middlesworth. I don't give a good tinker's fuck what the folks back in Indianapolis think. It's my dick. Sit down, boy. Have a drink. Talk to an old man. This place ain't so bad, but I get lonely. Only one other patient here right now, some character from France, and I hardly ever see him."

97

Merlin, Eagle thought as he drew up a deck chair, would have preambled it Serendip. This old man was a fountain and he was dying to spout.

He refused the drink. "Too early for me, sir. But I'd like to talk to you. People sleep late around here." He glanced at his watch. A quarter after nine.

The old man poured himself half a glass of whisky and reached into the thermos jug for ice. "Never too early for me. Nothing for an old man to do but drink and screw. And don't call me sir. I had enough ass-kissing when I was a Senator from Indiana."

Eagle nodded. "What do I call you?"

The old man's eyes were red gimlets under white thatch. "Call me Homer, goddammit, that's my name."

"Okay, Homer." Eagle stared at the bandages. "Does it work? The operation or whatever it is? That's what I came here to find out. You might be able to save me a lot of time and trouble. If you don't mind talking about it."

The old man gulped half his whisky before he answered. "Don't mind at all. I don't like the people much, never did like Krauts much, and they're a bunch of highbinding thieves, but they do the job. I got me a new set of balls. Had the operation last week. Of course I haven't done any screwing yet, too early for that. Got to wait until I heal. But I believe that Krauthead Six—it's gonna work. My pecker sure wants to get up when it sees the right excitement."

Eagle considered that for a moment. The old man said, "You got a cigar on you?"

Eagle shook his head.

"I left mine back in the cottage," the old man said. "I been damned absent-minded lately. Probably because I got my mind on cock all the time."

"Let me get this straight, Homer. They did a transplant on you? A testicle transplant."

"They sure did. The whole bag, scrotum and all. I'd show you the stitches, show you my operation, but the doc says not to fool with the bandages. And what that

98

old creep says I do—this deal has already cost me over two million bucks."

Eagle considered *that* for a moment. He was fast becoming a believer. Just how it might change things, if at all, he had no idea at the moment.

He said, "Where do they get the testicles?"

The old man turned sly. "That's the sixty-four-million-dollar question. I didn't ask it. All they told me was that they came from an eighteen-year-old-kid. They said he was a professional donor and did it of his own free will."

Eagle eyed him. The old guy was pretty drunk but he wasn't lying. Eagle said, "A professional donor? I suppose he grows new balls and parts with them regularly for a fee?"

Middlesworth splashed more whisky into his glass. "Does sound kind of unlikely, don't it. My own idea is that they get them off fresh corpses, only they don't want to tell the customers that. Wouldn't matter to me, though. I don't give a rat's ass where they get 'em as long as they work."

Eagle felt like having a drink. For perhaps the first time in his life he felt that he really needed a drink. He ignored the craving.

"And you think yours will work? That the operation will actually rejuvenate you sexually? That's what I'm here to find out—what I have to tell my principal when I get back."

The old man drank and wiped his mouth with a veined hand. "I guess they've had some failures. The doc, old crouchback Six, was pretty honest about that. Some old fogeys just can't make it back. But I can. I *know* I can—know how I feel down there. I can get a half hard right now and I still got the stitches in. Hurts like hell. But as soon as they get the stitches out I'm gonna give the girls hell."

"Girls?"

The old man pointed over the pool. "Over yonder by the golf course. See that house by the dogleg, seventh

99

hole? That's where the girls stay. The *casa de puta*, as the Spanish say. They got some beauties in there, too. Some real dollies. I already picked mine out."

Eagle's glance followed the trembling old finger. The house was large, villa type, its soft pastels washed by morning sun. It figured. If they really *could* do this operation they would need women to prove it out. And he believed now that they could do the operation, were doing it. And why not—they performed miracles these days with hearts and kidneys. Even liver transplants. Why not testicles? Prime specimens. From a kid in the sexual prime of life. Balls unscarred and unshrunken, producing a steady flow of testosterone. Not so much of a miracle after all. Just good surgical technique. In time it would probably become routine.

Fine. But one quibble. What eighteen-year-old in his right mind is going to give up his nuts? Willingly? Corpses? Possible. Eagle did not think so. What then? One possible answer was pretty nasty.

Homer Middlesworth was slouched in the deck chair, eyes closed and hands folded on his belly—old leather held together by fatty connective tissue. Midwest Fascist. Indiana type. How did a man like that make his millions and become a Senator? Certainly commerce of some type and payment for favors. Political payoff. Eagle shrugged, smiled, and stood up. No skin off his ass. He had his own problems.

The old man opened one eye. "You going?"

Eagle stretched. "Thought I would walk a little more. I'm beginning to think there are some very interesting things on this island. I don't want to miss anything."

Old Homer misunderstood him. He winked and said, "You better stay away from that whorehouse. That *casa de puta*. They got guards on it. I guess to keep the Indian servants away from the girls. Been nice talking to you, son. You ever get to Indiana you come see me. I got an office in the Circle Tower and a farm in Rushville. Just ask around for Homer Middlesworth.

100

Anybody worth knowing knows me. See you. I think I'll catch a little snooze right now and dream about young pussy."

Eagle laughed. "You're a dirty old man, Homer."

"You're so right, son."

"One more question, Homer, and I'll let you sleep. You said you'd already picked out your girl. What did you mean? And where do they get the girls?"

The old man grinned up at him. "That's two questions, son. But I don't mind. They show you movies of the girls. Just girls. Girls doing things to themselves and each other. They give you a lot of bullshit, too. The movies are experimental and scientific, to test your sexual powers before and after the operation. Stimuli. You know. But I'm not a mealy-mouth and I call 'em dirty pictures. Why not? Why horseshit around? They do the job. They sure stimulate the hell out of me now, after I had the operation. That's why I know I'm going to be fine. And that's how I picked my girl already. I saw her in a movie and told the doc I wanted her for my first test." He sighed. "That'll be a week yet. I hope I can make it without pulling off."

"I hope so too," Eagle said. "Good luck."

"As to where they get the girls, son, your guess is as good as mine. Mine is out of whorehouses, *casas*, or maybe off the streets. Where else? I was sort of concerned about that myself, because of disease, you know. I'm eighty-two and the last thing I need is a dose of clap. Or syph. Anyway I thought old fartface Six was gonna have a convulsion when I asked him. He did a lot of swearing in Kraut and then told me that all his girls, *his* girls, were practically virgins and as antiseptic as an operating room. Now beat it, son, and let me sleep. I got to conserve my strength. This deal has cost me two million already and I don't want to pop off before I get my money's worth."

Eagle skirted the nine-hole golf course. Mestizos were tending the greens and one was running a power

101

mower up and down a fairway. As he passed the pastel villa he saw no sign of women, but saw two guards talking together near the door. They wore light khaki shirts and pants and peaked caps without insignia. Black belts and holsters with lanyarded revolvers. Eagle waved as he passed fifty yards away. One man raised a tentative hand. Both watched him out of sight. The first sign of real muscle he had seen. There would be others.

IX

THE WOMAN WATCHED Eagle until he was out of sight. At first sight of him she had begun to hope, knowing it was foolish and dangerous, but hoping all the same. Not for herself. She was sure she would not leave the island alive. It no longer mattered. Not if she could kill *him* first. At least him. And as many of the others as she could manage.

It could be, she thought as she turned away from the window and went into the bathroom, that Kleinberg had made it out. He had been badly frightened when last she talked to him. He was running, breaking trail, and leaving her on her own. Fine with her. K had always been too cautious. And he did not like killing them. To him it was a distasteful duty. To her it was a joy.

She sat on the toilet and thrust her fingers into her vagina. K had said, during the last hurried conversation, that if he made it to the Embassy in Washington he would try to send a man in to help her. He would not return himself. He was blown with the Seven Sleepers. She was not. They did not, so far as she knew, know what she looked like, her age, or her name. Not that a name mattered. She had many names.

She brought the slim aluminum tube from her vagina

and looked at it. Coiled in it were many sheets of thin rice paper covered with micro-writing. She had put down the story as best she could, as she had heard it from Hans Rascher. Before she cut his throat.

She washed the tube in the lavatory bowl and replaced it in her vagina. The tube, the micro-writing in it, represented her dilemma. She had to get it out. Get it to someone who would not dismiss it as an idiot's dream, who would at least look into the matter. Admittedly the story was a wild one. A lonely secret valley hidden on the eastern slopes of the Andes, a Nazi village hanging above the jungles of Oriente where there lived a man, a young man, who was the avatar of Adolf Hitler.

A wild and impossible tale. Told by an idiot. Stella Helpern gazed at herself in the mirror and laughed. Yes, an idiot. Hans had been that. But his story, wrung from him as she cut off his penis inch by inch, had had a ring of truth to it. At the last, when even stupid Hans realized that he must die, he spat at her, reviled her, and swore that the story was true and that one day his comrades would avenge him. This time the job would not be botched, not left half finished. All *Juden* would be swept from the earth like trash. Not one would survive.

Stella dropped her wrapper and got into the shower. She had not believed the story at first. Did not really believe it now. But she had written it down in micro-shorthand and secreted it in the safest place she knew.

A phone rang in the bedroom. She cursed and stepped out of the stall shower, not bothering to put on the wrapper.

The Kraut bitch was on the line, her voice cool and commanding. "Stella?"

Using her servile voice she said, "Yes, Miss Alte-kruse." Her subtlety had been double—using her given name and not concealing her Jewishness. She had, in fact, called attention to it. They were arrogant, these young ones, and sure of themselves. And careless. She did not look Jewish. When they found out it pleased them. She had counted on it. Having a Jewish whore around was more than they could resist.

This Monika was trying to be friendly in a superior way. She said, "I'm afraid you're going to have to start earning your keep, Stella. We're going to make some films. You can pick your own companions if you like—I would suggest Marie and Conchita. They know the ropes and can help you."

"Yes, Miss Altekruse. I'll be ready. What time do you want to begin?"

"Right after lunch, I think. Say about two. Doctor Neidler and I will be doing the filming. How is everything, Stella? You are comfortable? You do not need anything?"

"No, Miss Altekruse. Nothing. The room is lovely. I have no complaints."

"That is fine, Stella. Good." The woman's voice changed a bit, became warmer. "Remember what I told you—if you have any difficulty adjusting you must come to me. To me personally. I will be glad always to help."

"I will, Miss Altekruse. Thank you."

She hung up and stood for a moment, thinking. She went to the window and peered out. No sign of the guards now. Or of the strange man, the tall stranger who had strolled past and started her hoping. Was it possible? Was he K's man? She shook her head. There was just no way of knowing. She had to find out. How? She had no idea. Certainly not during the day. After dark it might be possible. The guards were sleepy and lazy and she was an expert. Last night she had prowled for a time, in and out of the house like a ghost, and had seen the second helicopter come in. The big one. She watched it unload. Six rough-looking men in wide-brimmed jungle hats and bush jackets. All heavily armed. She had followed them for a time, seen them carry two white chests—they looked like ice or re-

105

frigerator chests—into the lab building. Where *he* worked.

Stella had not given the chests much thought. Not her affair. She could not be bothered. Her job was to get the tube out and to kill *him*. It was time to pass the torch. Long past time, she thought as she went back into the bathroom.

Face it. She was twenty-seven and looked forty. What beauty she'd had was long gone. Her figure was still good, and her teeth, but her hair was ruined by too much dyeing and her eyes had seen too much. She was adept at makeup and, in a pinch and with proper lighting, could pass as an old thirty if the customer was not too discriminating.

She brushed her teeth and stepped back into the shower. As the hot needles stung her she thought of Monika Altekruse. Fräulein Altekruse. Hah! The Altekruse had not been a Fräulein for a long time. The lines were there, the wrinkles coming. But still attractive. Give her that. And attracted—by anything in pants. Or skirts.

Stella had known at their first meeting, when the woman came to Madame Bobo's whorehouse to recruit. The cool and superior Nordic façade did not fool her. One glance and she knew. This one was obsessed by sex. A certain smile, a kind of look and touch, and they would have been in bed together. As casual as having a drink, a pleasant fifteen minutes, and as quickly forgotten. Stella, hiding in a brothel from the Seven Sleepers, had hardly believed her ears. Go to the Isla de Pelo for special work in films! And other duties which would be explained later. Stella hardly heard the rest of it. She could scarcely contain herself. When Monika Altekruse left the room she flung herself on the stained bed and cried, then laughed so hard she had to stuff the corner of a pillow in her mouth. Try to find out about the Isla de Pelo, Kleinberg had said. Try to get on it if you can. See what goes on. Sort out and check the rumors.

106

The mountain had come to Mahomet. The best place in the world to hide is in the last place they will think of looking for you. Unless they were being as subtle as she was and this she did not believe. The Altekruse had hardly looked at her face, had been only interested in her body, and so K must have been right. They did not know what she looked like.

Stella dressed slowly, thinking about the tall stranger. He had looked somehow out of place on Isla de Pelo. Somehow different. She could not put her finger on it, and she did not trust inspiration or impulse thinking, but the thought would not go away. His pantherish walk—he moved as easily as an Indian in a jungle—the cast of his features, the set of his big shoulders, all these things meant nothing in themselves. If they *were* suspicious he could be a lure, a trap of some kind.

She pulled on beige pantyhose and smoothed them on her legs. She would have to take a chance, gamble. There was no other way. The trouble was, she thought with a sour smile, too much of a good thing. After a long dry spell, during which matters had gone all wrong and she had lost all the battles, she had suddenly come up with an excess of goodies. More than she could handle alone. One thing she swore—she would not leave this island while *he* was still alive.

Now, in 1973, he called himself Dr. Franz Six.

In 1943, when Stella's mother had been in Ravensbruck, his name had been Wolfgang Sechs. An SS doctor. One of the worst. *Standartenfuhrer Sechs*. Infamous even among the Nazis.

Stella put on a miniskirt and a low-cut blouse that showed her still firm breasts to advantage. She seated herself before a dressing table and began to brush her ruined hair. She could think about it quite calmly now—had been able to for years. She had hated so deeply, for so long, that nothing could really hurt her now. Not even thoughts of her mother. Or her father coughing up his lungs. Or her grandparents, cousins, uncles and aunts—all gassed or burnt or shot in the camps.

She had never believed in God, Jewish or otherwise, but during the past few days she had come to believe in Fate. *He* was here. Still alive. Still performing his filthy operations. When she first went into the lab, just after her arrival on the island, to have her physical examination, she had not been expecting any miracles. One had already happened—she was on Isla de Pelo—and you could not expect two.

A youngish doctor, balding and too free with his fingers, had given her a preliminary examination and taken swabs and slides. The Altekruse woman had been positive about that—any sign of VD and Stella would be sent back to the brothel. She had been told nothing about her work except that it would entail making films and being with older men. The movies would be made with other women, no men, and if she were lesbian so much the better. The job paid better than most such jobs and she would have a nice room to herself in a quiet villa.

It was sheer happenstance that she saw *him* at all. It was quite possible, she told herself now, trying to touch up the dark circles under her eyes, that she might have worked on the island for days, weeks, and never have encountered him face to face.

Fate. He had stuck his head into the examining room to ask the young doctor a question. Something technical that Stella did not understand. She did not hear anything after the first few words. She had gone faint. It had taken all her control, all her years of training, to avoid giving herself away. But she knew. Knew at once and with certainty. She had studied his file and photo a thousand times and she had listened, from childhood, to her mother's descriptions of the man.

Wolfgang Sechs. SS doctor. Butcher. Sexual experimentalist. Botcher of a thousand operations. No matter. Plenty of Jews available. If one dies, send in another. No anesthetic. It is too precious, too scarce, to

108

waste on Jewish excrement. Save it for the brave wounded supermen.

Stella's mother had told her. Weeping. Told her about the degradation far worse than any pain. Her mother had shown her—the scar where the famous SS doctor had tried to implant a penis, to make a man of her, and had failed.

He was gone. Vanished back into his lab. Stella somehow got through the rest of the examination and returned to the cubicle where she had left her clothes. The aluminum tube was still in a pocket of her skirt— why would they bother to search a whore's clothes?— and she slipped it back into her vagina. The tube, and the weird story it held, did not seem important now. It was, of course. Terribly important. If there was any truth in it. Far more important in the long run than killing Wolfgang Sechs. So her chiefs would say. So Kleinberg would think. But not to her. Not to Stella Helpern. Fate had come around. Fate loved her. Fate had delivered a monster into her hands.

And now to play it carefully, with utmost caution. Make no mistakes. Wait. Be patient. Strike only when she was sure of success. Scheme a way to get within killing distance of Sechs—or Six—and be very sure she did not botch it. If she had to die, so be it. She was prepared for that. A fair enough trade-off.

Stella went into the garden behind the villa and smoked a cigarette. Some of the other women were there, sunning themselves and chattering, and she exchanged a few words before she found a stone bench to herself. There were seven other women in the house, all whores like herself, and she had managed to be neither too friendly nor too distant. She had no interest in them and they none in her. Most of them were still young, pretty and brainless, and getting along with them was easy. None of them knew what really went on, anymore than Stella did. The real business of Isla de Pelo was not their business. Their business was whoring—to do as they were told.

Stella watched them as she sat apart on her stone bench and smoked. She felt that she could do with a drink, but she stifled the desire. She wondered again about the big cargo helicopter and the rough men and the white chests they had so carefully transferred to the labs. What did that mean?

She could not concentrate on it. Her thoughts kept coming back to the tall man she had seen passing the villa earlier. She was torn by indecision. If her hunch, her intuition, was wrong and she disclosed herself to him she would blow everything. They would have her and Wolfgang Sechs would escape. The mere thought crushed her heart like a steel hand. What to do? How could she play it safe?

Marie and Conchita, with whom she would be working after lunch, were chatting nearby. Marie was laughing. "Last night I had the Frenchman. *¡Por Dios! Poco juiciosas.* Four hours we try. Four! I do everything. Nothing happens. I say use the splint but the old frog he does not want—but then we do. *He* does. *¡Sin ayuda!*"

When they stopped giggling Conchita called over to Stella. "You have been told? We work today for the camera. We do a loop—*un circuito.* The three of us."

Stella nodded. "I know. She called me."

Marie laughed. "La Altekrusa? Si-si—I think that one would like to make a loop also if she had the nerve."

"That frozen-faced *perra?* That *ramera.*" Conchita made a grand gesture, mimicking Monika Altekruse. "You will be well treated as long as you behave, girls. You will strictly obey orders. You will ask no questions of things that do not concern you. You will be examined often by the good doctors. No disease is permitted. No letters or phone calls are permitted. No visits to the mainland are permitted. No drunkenness is permitted. No fun is permitted. Nothing is permitted. Verboten—Verboten—"

Stella had to smile. Conchita was a good mimic.

Marie said, "You are a fool, Conchita. We have it good here. Better than before in Esmeraldas where all the men stank of oil. I like it here and do not want it spoiled by your big mouth. Save the talk and use your tongue for what it is paid to do. And who are you to call anyone a whore?"

Conchita stuck out her tongue at her friend. They fell to laughing again. Soon a guard came into the garden to announce lunch.

Stella did not go into lunch. She remained on her bench, smoking and thinking. Knowing she was going to do something foolish. The tube in her vagina must have its chance. She could not judge such a story. Leave it to others more qualified. A valley where Hitler lived again! It made no sense.

A hidden valley, Hans had gasped out just before he died, a valley so remote and inaccessible that it was known to few men. A preserve set aside by the government where condors were permitted to nest and breed unmolested. They were worried, did not want the condor to become extinct. There were heavy fines and many years in prison for anyone caught invading the sanctuary.

A breeding ground for vultures.

Valle de Buitre. Valley of Vultures.

Geier das Tal.

The condor was a magnificent bird, but a vulture nonetheless.

She rose and went back into the villa. Drinks were permitted in the small bar after lunch and then she would go to the studio and take off her clothes and do as she was told—simulate love with another woman.

She decided. She would make every effort to get the tube out.

But the killing of Wolfgang Sechs came first.

X

THE NINTH GREEN was on a promontory overlooking the sea. Eagle took a breather. This was the highest point on the island, but for the miradors on the big house, and he studied the layout. There were plenty of bushes and gardens and scrub growth, but very few trees. Across the island he could see docking, piers and a ramshackle boathouse built over the water. There was no sign of the hydrofoil mentioned by Toller. Probably locked in the boathouse. Or on the mainland.

There was a high hanging haze, but by shielding his eyes he could see the dark line of the coast. No hint of Pedernales, the coastal village Toller had pointed out in the flight over. Eagle wondered if the village had a police force. Probably one cop.

He started back, taking a path that cut across the island on a long diagonal. A few minutes later he saw a husky bald figure jogging toward him. Klaus Neidler.

Neidler was sweating heavily. He collapsed on a bench and mopped his shiny head as Eagle approached, calling out a greeting.

Neidler acknowledged the greeting. He looked at Eagle's trim hard body with envy. "You're certainly in good shape, Richard. Lucky. I jog every day and I still can't keep the lard down. How did you sleep?"

Eagle joined him on the bench. "Well. Nothing disturbed me. It was thoughtful of you to lock the door so the bogeyman couldn't get me."

Neidler fished in the waistband of his sweat pants for cigarettes and a soggy packet of matches. "Not me, Richard. Dr. Six. You must understand about that—he is an old man and maybe a little eccentric. *Baufallig*. But a genius. Helmuth and I must humor him. As I trust you will. The thing about newspaper men I myself do not understand—he has such a fear and loathing of them. But we have assured him and now he makes his own investigation and all will be well. In the meantime if there is anything I can do?"

Eagle nodded. "I was just talking to one of your clients. He had some good words for you people."

Neidler inhaled and blew smoke from his broad nostrils. His face was porcine. Eagle had not noticed it before. A pig with blue smoke leaking from pushed-in nostrils.

"I saw you talking to Senator Middlesworth," Neidler said. "I am glad he gave us a good report. It is perhaps the first step to converting you, no? Of our honesty? Of the true worth of our work here? I hope so."

"The Senator seems to be sold," admitted Eagle. He grinned at Neidler. "That's a pretty good pair of binoculars you have."

It was a mistake. A business type like Brookson wouldn't be sharp enough to spot the binoculars. Or be looking for them.

Neidler did not comment. He smiled and said, "I will not lie and say I am a bird watcher. I am not."

Eagle nodded. "More of a people watcher?"

"I suppose so. I like to think it is only natural curiosity. I like to know what is going on. And I was wondering where you could be going so early, without breakfast. That is all. No harm, I think. I am not *ein piepen*."

"You wouldn't have had any luck at the women's

113

villa, anyway." Eagle stood up. "They keep the drapes closed. I took a look as I passed."

Neidler chuckled. "It is too far for the binoculars. And would be wasted effort. I see all of those women I wish. We use them to make films and to service our clients. In a scientific manner, of course."

"Of course." Eagle started to move off.

"Richard—a serious word, please."

Eagle turned back. "Yes?"

Neidler was either embarrassed or putting on a good act. He shrugged. "It may not be important, but I think perhaps it as well to warn you—Helmuth is in a very bad mood this morning. A vicious mood."

"That's his business," said Eagle. "Why tell me?"

Neidler actually wrung his fatty hands. "You do not understand. And perhaps I should not be telling you this—but when I say vicious I mean it literally. Helmuth can be terrible when he is crossed at times like this. *Verdammen*! How can I convince you? You do not know Helmuth well enough to understand. When he is in these moods he is, I think it is not too much to say, literally insane. You understand? Do not quarrel or even talk to him if you can help it. Not until he is over this mood."

Eagle raised a hand. "Okay. I'll do my best. He and Monika must have had one hell of a brawl, huh?"

Neidler frowned. "I do not think we should discuss that."

Eagle nodded and grinned. "I'm with you on that. See you, Klaus."

As he came to a turning in the path he glanced back. Neidler was still seated on the bench, staring after him.

He did not waste time trying to figure it. Not that important and anyway he knew the general outline. Toller couldn't get it up, if you believed Monika, but he must have gone to her room last night to give it a try. Eagle shook his head. He could almost feel sympathy for Toller. Monika was no doubt a mean bitch when she chose to be, and last night she had been

114

tired and satiated. Toller wouldn't have gotten much of a reception. He was a fool for sticking his neck out. Monika had probably taunted him about his membership in the limp phallus club. Women could be cruel that way, especially with an old lover for whom they had no further use.

He could see the miradors of the big house. From somewhere, mixed with a faint sea breeze, came the smell of breakfast. Eagle quickened his pace.

He shortcut along a gravel path that led through a garden and past a one-story building of buff-colored stucco. The windows were covered with wire grating and the heavy steel door was open. From the interior came the sound of a light bag being punched rapidly and expertly—the staccato rattle of a leather machine gun.

Eagle stopped to peer into the open door. Powerful yellow lights glowed in inverted wire baskets on the ceiling. The familiar smell of a gym came to Eagle— sweat and old socks and oiled leather and dirty canvas.

Helmuth Toller was busy at the punching bag. He gave it a final blow that disengaged the hook and sent the little bladder bouncing across the hardwood floor. He turned, wiped sweat from his face with a glove, and saw Eagle standing there. He beckoned. "Come and have a workout with me, Richard. Exchange a few blows. I am in a mood for violence."

Eagle shook his head. Klaus Neidler had been right. This was a Helmuth Toller he had not seen before.

"Not before breakfast," he said. "I never fight on an empty stomach."

Toller put his gloved hands on his hips. He wore shorts and boxing shoes and the gray furze on his big chest was streaked with sweat. He had the sloping shoulders and the over-developed biceps of a boxer. He had to be near fifty but at the moment he looked like a formidable thirty.

Eagle was tempted. He did not like the man and to land a few punches on that bony German face would give him pleasure. In the center of the gym a crude boxing ring was set up. Beyond it was a rack of fencing equipment—foils and masks and pads. And sabers. Eagle noticed the sabers just before his attention was diverted by Toller's words.

"I doubt," said Toller with a sneer, "that you ever fight, Richard. Even on a full stomach. I doubt that you have *any* stomach for fighting at any time. Like Jews. Like the dirty sheep who let themselves be led to slaughter without even bleating."

Something had gone wrong. Somewhere, back along the trail, things had gotten fouled up. Everything had changed. He was in a brand-new ball game. Eagle knew this. But it was all he knew. He was not going to worry about it now. At the moment he was on the verge of doing something rash, something he really could not afford to do. Losing his temper.

Eagle stared hard at Toller, unsmiling. He made a step to turn, to leave the gym.

Toller said, "A report has come through from Scotland. Your story is true and Franz is satisfied. You are not a newspaper man. You are not even a Jew, a matter which I checked personally."

Eagle knew that he could not leave. Not until he had messed the arrogant face, planted a few rights between the manic blue eyes. The genial Herr Toller had vanished. This was the real man. The inner man. Unmasked. *Todfeind*. A natural and deadly enemy.

Eagle walked toward the ring. "I'll be happy to oblige you with a few rounds, Helmuth. Even before breakfast. It is always a pleasure to punch an arrogant bastard in the mouth."

Toller snickered as he tossed a pair of four ounce gloves to Eagle. "So you do have a temper, Richard? A breaking point? Good. I was beginning to think you were, as the Yanks say, chicken all the way through."

Eagle took off his sport shirt. Toller watched as he tied on the gloves, using his teeth to knot the strings. Toller leaped into the ring and made a formal little

116

bow. "Be my guest, Mr. Brookson. I will perhaps teach you some things. But I am a fair man—you know something of boxing? I myself was once an amateur champion."

Eagle was not happy with the lacing, it was a sloppy job, but he did not care. He moved toward the center of the ring where Toller waited.

"I know something of boxing," he said. "I hope you really do. I've got at least twenty years on you. And it is not a breaking point I have, Toller, it is a boiling point."

Toller went into an experienced crouch, circling slowly to his right, his left high and his chin hiding behind his shoulder. He grinned at Eagle. *"Ja—ja—Gut—gut*—never mind about the years, Brookson. I do not."

Eagle went after him, pressing, trying to work him into a corner. "I hope you can fight better than you can fuck. Monika tells me you're not much good at that."

Toller leaped at him with a snarl. He jabbed three times with his left and crossed with a right. Eagle blocked two of the jabs. The third cut him above the right eye. The right bounced off his shoulder. He put a left into Toller's mouth and crossed with his own right, missing.

Toller slipped out of the corner and sidled artfully across the ring, evading and slipping punches. He was a clever boxer. Eagle pursued him, keeping the pressure on. Toller was in superb condition for a man his age. Eagle smiled tauntingly and scored with a couple of light lefts. Toller, instead of retreating, came back with a flurry of punches. He got in a hard right that shook Eagle. He landed again on the cut over Eagle's eye.

Eagle bided his time. Boxing is a cruel torment for the lungs. He was feeling no strain. Toller was beginning to puff a bit.

Toller went into a classic straight-up stance, left extended, and danced away. Eagle plodded after him.

Blood from the cut dribbled into his right eye, clouding his vision, and he swiped it away with a glove.

Toller flicked a couple of lefts into Eagle's face and pranced away. "Shall we time the rounds, Mr. Brookson? Your pleasure. It is of no matter to me."

Eagle shook his head. "Me either, Mr. Toller. I am going to beat the shit out of you and I don't much care how I do it. Rounds or no rounds."

Toller leaped in with a cry of rage, windmilling punches at Eagle. Eagle rode most of them, catching them on his gloves and elbows. One right landed on his nose, bringing numbness and a trickle of blood. He bulled Toller away from him and hit him twice with hard rights. Toller's knees buckled, but he recovered and skipped out of danger. Eagle did not pursue for the moment. He had Toller now. He could take him out any time. He decided to enjoy it. Eagle brushed the blood from his nose and eye and went back to his relentless pursuit.

Toller was breathing hard, his lungs laboring, fighting not to show it, using all the little boxing tricks. Dancing on his toes and sneering, keeping up a line of chatter. Eagle made no effort to end it—he could do that any time. He had his temper under control again and knew he had made a fool of himself. So that only proved he was human. Not too much damage done yet. And still he had a feeling that there was more to all this than he knew. Toller had not told him everything.

He spared Toller, exerting just enough pressure to make the man move constantly. He worked him into a corner, feinted his guard down, had him set up for the crusher and then did not throw the punch. He pulled it and stepped away with a tantalizing grin. Toller knew that he had been spared, that Eagle was playing with him, and his face writhed with fury. He rushed at Eagle. Eagle cuffed him lightly and slipped to one side. Toller fell to his knees. Eagle helped him up.

"Not breathing so good? The old legs going?"

Toller cursed and swung at him. Eagle blocked the

118

punch and deliberately, with insult, roughed Toller in the face with the heel of his glove. The dangling laces scratched Toller's nose and mouth. Eagle laughed and pushed him away.

"You're not exactly Super Kraut, are you? I think a Jewish little old lady could take you."

Toller moved away, gasping. His eyes were wild, blue slits, killer's eyes. "I did not like you from the first," he said. "Or trust you. I had to pretend, but now I think Franz was right. There is something about you. Something I cannot find or prove, but something wrong. You are not a newspaperman and Franz is satisfied of that—but I am not."

Eagle lanced him with a long left hand. "Stop talking so much, superman, and fight. I still want my breakfast."

Toller rushed him. "Jew lover!"

Eagle stabbed him with a left and right and retreated. "Wrong again, Mr. Toller. Girl lover. Monika lover. What happened last night when you went to see her? I bet she turned you down, eh? Threw you out. You really shouldn't blame the lady. She was tired. She had a hard day and night sucking my cock."

Toller stopped in the center of the ring. His arms dangled like leaden weights. He glared at Eagle through a mask of sweat and blood, his chest pumping like a bellows.

"*Schwein*," he gasped. "I am going to kill you!"

Eagle prepared to move in for the kill. "I thought the word was *schweinhund*. I always saw it that way in the comic books, when the German officer was kicking the prisoners around."

Toller screamed. "Lousy Jew-loving pig!"

"That's better," said Eagle. "What was your rank in the Hitler Youth, Helmuth? *Oberstleutnant*? Higher than that? Colonel, General? How many old Jews did you kill when you were a teenager?"

Eagle watched it happen. He saw all light of reason flicker and fade from Toller's eyes. Mania took over.

119

The eyes became opaque steel balls, bulging from a death's-head face as Toller rushed screaming at him.

Eagle was human. More than that he was an Apache, when he chose to be, in all but blood. He was cruel.

He stopped Toller with a hard left and crossed a right, careful to avoid the jaw. He did not want to finish Toller too soon. He punched viciously, twisting his wrists so the leather would cut, pounding the face but avoiding a knockout blow.

Toller tried to fight back. Eagle gave him A for guts. But it was like a winded child against a man. Eagle punched him around and around the ring. Toller tried to fall and Eagle held him up and kept hitting him. Toller attempted to knee him and Eagle hit him with a terrible right that spun him across the ring. He lolled over the ropes, arms dangling and legs twitching, blood dripping from his battered face.

Enough. Eagle didn't want to kill him. He already regretted his flash of cruel temper. For a time there he had not been much better than Toller. He picked up Toller's heels and dumped him over the ropes. The man fell like a sack of old guts, moaning and twitching, by the rack of fencing equipment.

"Bravo," said Monika Altekruse. "I liked that. But I think you are too merciful."

Eagle vaulted the ropes and set about untying the gloves as she came toward him. She was wearing tight-fitting pants and a white leather jacket with gold military buttons.

He eyed her as he bit at the tangled laces. "How long have you been there?"

Monika looked across the ring at the body of Toller. He no longer twitched. A snoring sound came from him. Monika's wide mouth worked moistly and her gray eyes narrowed on Eagle. She was breathing hard, her small tight breasts pumping at him.

"Long enough," she said. "Long enough to hear you say terrible things about me."

120

Eagle shook his head. "No. I didn't say anything that you didn't do."

Monika stared at him, her mouth open, a round wet hole edged in scarlet. "This is a serious thing, what you have done. Helmuth deserved it. He is a cruel and crazy bastard. But when Franz Six hears there will be trouble. And when Helmuth recovers—I think you had better leave the island as quickly as possible, Richard."

Eagle tossed the bloody gloves away. "I've been thinking that myself. But first I want some answers out of you. Something has happened that I don't know about. Yesterday everything was fine. Today everything blows up. What the hell goes on?"

The cut over his eye had stopped bleeding. He probed his tender nose with his fingers, watching her face. He knew her well enough by now to know when she lied.

He was sure she was speaking the truth when she said, "Your employer is dead. Franz and Helmuth got the report by radio early this morning."

"Mr. F is dead? When and how?"

Monika shrugged. "They did not tell me all the details. They had a man in Scotland, double-checking on you, and he sent a radiogram to Quito. You are genuine, not a newspaper imposter, and your employer died of a heart attack. Very suddenly. They did not tell me this, but I heard Franz and Helmuth discussing it—your Mr. F was in the local village at the time, with his chauffeur, and the attack came suddenly. Our man, their man, was at the village inn and it appears that he actually saw it happen."

"Very convenient." Eagle understood now. His cover had held up under a second scrutiny—probably one of the Seven Sleepers had flown to Scotland in person—but now the cover was worthless.

Monika made the point. "You see how it changes matters?"

Eagle saw. "I am not a billionaire and I don't need a new set of balls. Where I was a pest before now I'm a menace—nosey and skeptical. Okay. I'll go quietly. The gruesome twosome, Franz and Helmuth, should be happy to see the last of me."

Monika took a man's handkerchief from her jacket pocket and stepped close to him. She wiped at the sweat and blood on his chest. Her lips brushed his face. "You must take me with you. I am frightened to remain here. There is no time to explain now. Later. When we are away from this place and alone."

Eagle nodded. He had been wondering what her angle was, why she had made such a play for him. He still didn't know, but she must have her reasons and it couldn't do any harm to listen to her.

"Okay," he told her. "It's a deal. You got the keys to the helicopter?"

"Yes. I—"

She screamed and pushed at him. "Richard! Behind you!"

Eagle ducked. The saber made a humming sound as it swooshed past him. Monika ran. Eagle rolled like a ball and came to his feet facing Toller.

The man's loose mouth drooled blood. His nose was smashed and his face puffed and lumped, but from the ruin the cold blue eyes glinted death at Eagle.

"Now we see," Toller said. "Now we see in the end who wins. I am going to slice you, Jew lover."

Eagle could have run for it, could have made it to the door. Instead he moved sideways and back toward the ring. Beyond it was the rack of sabers. Toller moved between Eagle and Monika and the door. His puffed lips tried to smile and he spat out a piece of tooth.

"I have you now. Both. I heard you, Monika. I have been too easy with you. I admit it. You have made a fool of me too long. But that is over now. Go ahead, Richard. Choose a saber. There is time. You cannot get away."

Neither of them could get away. Toller had the angle

on them. There was one door and gratings over the windows. Toller's saber guarded the way out.

Eagle reached behind him. His fingers touched cold steel. He did not want to fight the bastard with a saber. Toller must know all about sabers. Eagle had fenced in his time, but the cut and slash of sabers was another matter. And there was Monika.

He yelled at her. "Over here. By me."

She paid him no attention. She stood wide-legged, hands in the pockets of the leather jacket, staring at Toller. "You are crazy, Helmuth. Stark raving mad. You know this is true. It is like before, when I helped you. And I will help you now. Put down the saber, Helmuth, and listen to me. It will be all right. There is still time to make it all right. I will help you. I swear it. I will explain everything to Franz."

Eagle hefted the saber. When he went in it would have to be fast. He would have to kill Toller. Or Toller would kill him.

"Bitch," said Toller. "Lying bitch. Cocksucking whore."

Eagle moved forward. Toller leaped at Monika, the saber flashing in the yellow ceiling lights. He knew Eagle would not run, knew he had time to kill the woman and still meet Eagle's charge.

Monika took a little automatic out of her jacket pocket and pointed it at Toller. She shot him four times in the chest. Pop-pop-pop-pop-

Toller went to his knees. He put both hands to his chest and squeezed at it. Blood rolled from his open mouth. He gave Eagle a last stare, eyes wild with agony and despair, then slid down on the gym floor. A noise seeped from his throat. "Bit—"

Eagle dropped the saber with a clang. "God damn it!" he shouted at her. "You didn't have to kill him. I would have managed him someway. Now our ass is in a real sling. You goddamned stupid bitch!"

Monika smiled at him. She was wiping the little automatic with a clean handkerchief. "Do not talk to me like that, Richard. I did only what I had to do. You saw. And you could not have handled him. Helmuth was a champion with sabers. The Hitler Youth champion of all Germany."

She tossed the pistol at him. Instinctively Eagle caught it.

"Now your prints are on it," she said. "If we are caught I will say you killed him. It will be your word against mine and I have many friends among the Ecuadorian police. I do not think you have any, Richard. Have you ever been in a South American prison?"

For the moment she had him. Eagle shoved the automatic in his hip pocket. It was a Walther .25 and fit snugly. He nodded at her. "Okay, boss lady. Have it your way. What do we do now?"

"In a moment."

She ran to the door and peered out, then pulled it shut and locked it. She came back to where Eagle stood looking at Toller's body. He did not regret the man's death. But a body was a body and murder was murder and things could get pretty tacky if the Ecuadorian police got into the act. He was mindful of his contract with Merlin. No help. No way.

"I think no one heard the shots," Monika said. "It is not a very loud gun."

Eagle touched the corpse with his foot. "Not loud, but effective."

He added, "What about the guards? They have any kind of a patrol schedule? I don't know a damned thing about anything."

Monika smiled. "That is why you will need me, *liebling*. Do not worry about the guards. They are mostly for show. To reassure the old men who come here, and to keep curious people away from the island. And to guard the women, of course. The guards are no problem."

Eagle had flung his sport shirt over a gym horse. As he reached for it Monika said, "Do not touch it. You are all over blood and sweat. Wait until we have finished with the body and then you can take a shower."

Eagle studied her. "You think we've got all that much time? You've got the helicopter keys. Why don't we just take off?"

She made an impatient gesture. "That would be wrong. Come. Let us get to work. I will explain as we go along. You take his shoulders and I will carry his feet. Into the locker room."

If she had the keys to the helicopter she might also have keys to the boathouse and the hydrofoil. And there might be other keys in Toller's clothes.

She took Toller's feet and led the way through a side door into a small shower and locker room. Toller's clothes were on a bench before a row of tall green lockers. As soon as they put the body down Eagle went through the clothes. Monika watched with a cool half smile. No keys. Not even a wallet,

"Helmuth was not a pilot," she told him. "There is only one set of keys for the hydrofoil and Franz Six keeps them. We are wasting time. Let us get him into a locker."

Eagle started opening lockers. Most were empty. "I thought you weren't worried about time."

She tapped his chin with her fingers. "I am not. It is a matter of routine. If we do not break the routine and call attention all should go well. But that is no reason to waste time. Come. Do you think he will fit into this one?"

"They're all the same," Eagle said. "You take his feet and get them in—then get back out of the way. I'll do the rest."

She picked up the feet and shoved them into a locker. "Like so?"

"Like so. Stand back."

Toller's feet were in the locker. Eagle had him beneath the armpits. He raised and grunted and shoved. Toller was big and floppy, resisting everywhere. Eagle swore. It was like trying to get three pounds of shit into a two-pound bag. Feet and hands, arms, kept popping out,

Eagle began to sweat again. "Stuff his hands in, for Christ's sake!"

She worked beside him, pushing and shoving, her body against his, her breath and sweat mingling with his. To his amazement Eagle began to get an erection.

He slammed the locker door on Helmuth Toller. Monika handed him a padlock. "Lock it. If we have luck he will not be found for a long time. Perhaps we will be in Scotland by then."

She seemed to know what she was doing. Eagle had to concede that. He started to strip off his clothes. "We're going to Scotland?"

Monika sat on a bench and watched him undress. Her eyes caressed his body. She nodded. "That is the agreement, no? I help you and you help me. I will get us safely off the island, with no police, and you will take me to Scotland with you. You will give me some money and you will make love to me. I do not ask you to marry me."

Eagle stepped out of his shorts. "That's damned decent of you." He carried the little pistol into the shower stall with him and put it on the soap dish. "No offense," he told her, "but I've seen what you can do with this peashooter and I don't want to end up in a locker."

Monika smiled. She watched his groin and ran her tongue around her lips. "*Liebling*. Do not say such things. I am mad for you. But you are right—we must be sensible and not trust each other too much."

Eagle began to soap up. "I'll go along with that. But to get back to Scotland—why do you want to go there? I don't think you'll like it. They don't like Germans much and you won't find any Nazi underground. As for the money, we might be able to work something out. We'll see. You realize that I am now unemployed?"

Monika smiled and nodded. She crossed her long

126

slim legs. "Scotland will be fine for me. The farther away from them the better. That is the truth you must understand about me, *liebling*. I swear it. I am German, yes, but I was never Nazi. I got into this thing for money. For money so I could get away from them, though I could not tell them that."

She pointed at the locker. "He was Nazi all through. A Hitler Youth leader. He told me many wild stories when he was drunk and crazy. He told me too much and regretted it and watched me as a hawk watches a rabbit. I became very afraid of Helmuth."

Eagle began to rinse. She was talking and he thought she was mostly telling the truth. He nudged her along, trying not to break the flow.

In a casual tone he said, "And the good Doctor? Were you afraid of him, too?"

Monika made a shivering motion and crossed her arms over her breasts. "Franz Six is a horror. An abomination. Helmuth told me terrible things about him. He was himself frightened of Six. As is Klaus Neidler."

Eagle turned off the shower and stepped out. "Speaking of Neidler, what do we do about him, if anything? He might be trouble. Six is an old man and a cripple. No sweat. But Klaus Neidler might—"

Monika handed him a towel—and a knowing smile —then stooped to give his penis a quick fluttery kiss. She straightened and patted his cheek. "You are a beautiful man, Richard, but there is much you do not understand."

She could say that again, Eagle told himself as he began to dress.

"You have got it absolutely backward," she explained. "Klaus will not be trouble if I handle him correctly. Six is the one I am afraid of. That is why we must be so careful to stick to routine. Why we cannot run for it now. Everything must go on as planned. We will have lunch. Then Klaus and I must take some movies of the girls in the villa. At lunch I will persuade you to come with us and you will agree. Six will not like it but he will not forbid it. At least I think not. Later I will take off for Quito, as I am already scheduled to do, and you will be with me. As is natural—your work is over here and you must return to Scotland for the funeral of your employer."

She buttoned Eagle's shirt and tapped his nose with a finger. "We will not, of course, mention that I am returning to Scotland with you."

He slipped the pistol into his pocket. He nodded at the locker. "What about Superman there? Won't he be missed at lunch? If old Six is all that sharp won't he want to know where Toller is?"

Monika nodded. "That is maybe a problem. I think I can handle it. Leave it to me and play along. Now come. We had better go. Six spends most of the day in his lab, but when he comes out he likes matters to be punctual. He will not like it if we are late to lunch."

Eagle's stomach growled. "I haven't had any breakfast yet." It had been a busy morning. Rewarding too, he supposed.

He gave the locker room a final check. Nothing belonging to Toller was lying about. It was all in the locker with his body. Eagle tested the padlock. It would take a bar to break it.

He checked the gym, wiping up blood with the wet towel and tossing it into a basket. Not really important. People got hurt in gyms and used towels.

Monika waited near the door. "The guards are lazy and incompetent," she said. "I do not think they will find anything. They do not care much for us."

Eagle joined her at the door. "He'll start to smell in a couple of days. The dogs will find him then, if somebody doesn't do it before."

Monika shook her head. "I do not think we will have two days. One, with luck. But it will be enough. We can be on our way to Scotland by then. This is true, *liebling*? We have the agreement? You will take me with you?"

He grinned at her as he unlocked the door. "Yes. We have an agreement. You've got me over a barrel."

"Over a barrel? I do not understand that, quite. I think—it is good?"

"Depends on the barrel, Monika." He winked at her. "But you've got a deal. You get us out of this, with no mess and no jail, and I'll take you to Scotland. And give you some money."

She pressed against him. "And make love to me? Every day?"

"As long as my strength holds out."

He would have opened the door but she stayed his hand. They kissed a long time. She groaned and thrust her tongue into his mouth and reached to grab his hard buttocks.

Eagle had the thought that she would do it atop a corpse if she had to.

He broke it off and opened the door. "Let's go to lunch."

The day was as pleasant as he remembered. Birds sang and there was a smell of gardens. Eagle padlocked the gym door. "Might as well make it as tough for them as we can."

As they strolled toward the big house she took his arm. Eagle decided to run a test.

"Part of our deal," he said, "is that you answer some questions. Okay?"

He did not expect her to balk. She was as deep in it as he was. She was afraid of Six and that had been a lot of crap about being buddies with the police. High connections, maybe, but it would be Six that had them. Maybe Toller. It did not matter now. She had been waiting for an opportunity to get away from them, for whatever reasons, and had killed Toller without a second thought. All in all, at least for the moment, he was calling the shots.

She was even more acquiescent than he had hoped.

"I thought there would be questions, Richard. I expect them. Many questions. I will answer them if I can.

I will not even ask you why you ask them. But all this I will do in Scotland—not before."

Eagle almost said *shit* aloud. Cagey kid. It looked like he was going to have to take her to Scotland, or send her, and spend a lot of Merlin's money doing it. Probably worth it.

He shrugged. "Have it your way. One thing that I've been wondering, though, that you might know. Not important. Just idle curiosity, but it's been bugging me. Where does Six get the testicles for his transplants?"

Monika laughed. The sound rang high and silvery in the failing morning. A frightened bird skittered from a bush.

"I suppose I can tell you *that*," she said. She did not break step. She squeezed his arm. "Indians."

"Indians?"

"Yes, *liebling*. Jungle Indians. Savages. Barbarians."

Eagle stared at her. "Six pays Indians to donate their balls?"

She gave him a look of contempt. "You are being stupid, no? Six pays hunters, bounty hunters, to go into the jungle and bring back the testicles of young Indians. It is bad, I know, but they are only savages. Six has invented—he is very clever—a refrigeration box which the hunters use."

XI

HERR DOKTOR FRANZ SIX was in the cold room counting out the testicles. They had done well this time, the hunters, and as he injected each shriveled scrotum with an analeptic fluid of his own devising—it had taken him forty years and a hundred thousand experiments to perfect the operation—he was thinking that he was, for the time being, overstocked. He would pay the hunters off, a thousand dollars a pair, and send them back to the village.

He continued to putter about the lab, pausing to take a pain pill now and then, and finally admitting that neither his brain nor his heart was in the work today. He was depressed and uneasy. Had he not been a scientist, and therefore a scoffer at such matters, he would have said that he had a premonition. Of just what he did not know. He could not put his finger on it. Of evil, of misfortune? Bah. That was gypsy thinking—another inferior race—and any intelligent person knew that men made their own fortune and misfortune. He was living proof of the theory. Nearly eighty and still going strong, working for the sacred cause and bringing it nearer to victory. Not tomorrow, perhaps, nor even the day after tomorrow. But someday. If only he could live to see it.

None of the others had. All his *Kameraden*, the fine lusty fellows from the past, all dead and gone. Killed in battle for the Fuehrer. Suicides. Natural deaths. Hanged.

The old man rubbed his throat. Never mind all that. Let the past bury its dead—the fools had had the world in their grasp, in their very hands, and had let it slip away. Forget the past, but for the mistakes. Be sure they were not made again. Oil politics was not his field, but that was in capable hands.

He glanced at the lab clock. Nearly an hour since lunch and still Helmuth Toller had not called. Drunk last night and making a terrible scene with that bitch of a Monika. Toller was still in his bed, no doubt, sulking in his room with a hangover. Or so the woman had said at lunch and he saw no reason to disbelieve her. Klaus Neidler had also said that Toller was in a murderous temper and better left alone.

Six—not since he had disappeared in the spring of 1945 had he thought of himself as Sechs—sat in his especially constructed chair and smoked and thought, seeking some easement of the pain in his back. Just what was bothering him? Bugging him, as the Americans said. Give the Yankee swine that—they were capable of mordant slang.

Was his mind failing after all these years?

No. His body was a disaster but his brain was still good. As sharp and clear and cold as ever. He had no emotional troubles. No ghosts haunted him. No regrets. He was not so soft as some of the *Kameraden* had turned out to be. He never wept into his pillow at night and begged forgiveness. He would do it all over again. Every bit of it.

He forced his mind back to present and practical things, trying to isolate the source of his unease. There had been setbacks lately, of course, but none were fatal to the plan. Relatively minor matters. One must expect that.

The Valhalla Club was showing a fine profit. So was

132

the multiple holding concern organized under the name of the Demogorgon Society. The cost of operating was scandalous—high government officials were expensive, even those with German sympathies—but still the profit margin was high enough.

The political moves were going well. This was slow work, and being played down for the moment, but the base was solid and being widened all the time. That would be all right. *Der Tag* was still far off, five or even ten years, but when the time was ripe the fruit would fall into their laps. Realism counseled that he, Franz Six, would not be around to see it and that was a pity. But he would be remembered as the architect. He was sure of that.

There were more immediate and pressing things. He left the chair, even the special construction did not ease the pain for long, and hobbled around the lab, attending to this and that and thinking.

There had been setbacks. He listed them in his mind, seriatim:

The Jew agent, Kleinberg. It had been a serious failure to let him get out of Ecuador alive. He couldn't have known much, but what he did know he must have told his Embassy and possibly others. A trifle, perhaps, and remote, but just one more little fishhook to scratch his mind. The Jew was dead now, of course, but so was Karl. Weighted down in the Potomac. The kidnapping had failed and there had been no answers. Failure.

Hans Rascher was dead. The old man sighed and pressed his crippled fingers to his chalky spine. Poor Hans. Found in a slum with most of his penis cut away.

Another fishhook in his mind. Had poor Hans talked before he died? Why kill him in that particular manner? Was it happenstance or did someone know about the Indians? That could not be kept a secret forever, but in the end it would not matter.

Just now it did matter. Next week a whole wave of new clients would be arriving on the island. At least a

133

dozen, if they all showed. Twelve million right there, at a minimum.

Rudy Bottendorff. Stabbed behind the ear with a long old-fashioned hatpin. In broad daylight, in a narrow *cul-de-sac* in busy downtown Quito.

The doctor raised a trembling hand—for years he had been afflicted with Sydenham's, a minor chorea which did not adversely affect his operating—and stared at his knobby knuckles. He was having trouble marshaling his thoughts in correct and proper order. Most unlike him. He must try harder, organize. There was nothing worse than disorganization—it led to all sorts of trouble. Disorder, especially in thinking, was to be avoided at all costs.

His rigid spine pulsed with new pain. He could not remain quiet. He went into the operating room and turned on a light. Here he felt at home, more comfortable, better able to align his thoughts. The white tile and table, instrument stands, the great lights with their reflectors, the glistening machines, gave him a renewed sense of command. Here he was master. Here it was skill alone that counted and even his enemies had not denied his skill.

Three dead men. All in the past month, all of them belonging to the elite—the Seven Sleepers.

His thin lips twisted in a snarl. How had they failed so badly? Their job was to kill, not to be killed.

Hans Rascher

Rudy Bottendorff

Karl Muller

All Sleepers, all bound by oaths of iron and blood. Sacred oaths to serve and protect.

All dead.

Klaus Neidler must be right. Klaus was a fool and a fumbler in many things, and would never be more than a fair surgeon, but in some things he was astute. And a trusted messenger.

Klaus, on returning from a high council in the

134

village, had passed on the consensus—the Jew Kleinberg had left an agent behind when he fled Ecuador.

Six went to the operating table and stood gazing at it. He felt himself dribbling and wiped his mouth with his fingers. Old men were at times disgusting. He stroked the table, visualizing the Jew on it—he had never seen the man—and his crooked fingers curled as if holding a scalpel.

The theory was feasible. They were probably right. Kleinberg had left a man behind, a capable and bloodthirsty killer who was not bemused or sidetracked by the Bormann myth.

Six cackled aloud. That had been a splendid idea. A bit worn now, even granting the Jews' manic obsession with Martin Bormann, but for a long time the ploy had worked. Rumors of Bormann seen, discovered, betrayed—they had fetched the Jew agents into killing range.

Six laughed again. Poor Martin. Dead all these years, yet his old bones were still killing Jews.

So a Jew agent was still on the loose in Ecuador. He must be found and disposed of. Above all he must not discover the truth about Isla de Pelo.

The question was—how to find him? They had no idea who he was or what he looked like. No clue at all, except three dead Sleepers. If they could be called clues.

The man was a murderer. Also a sadist. Look at what he had done to poor Hans Rascher. The poor fellow's penis carved away inch by inch.

Chances were that the man was a WOG. They were capable of anything. Monsters. An organization of militant Jews calling themselves the Wrath of God. Fanatic. Maniacs. They thought only of revenge. They did not, could not, would not even try to understand that the Germans were not a cruel race—that they only did, at times with great reluctance, what was necessary to purify the human race. Cancer must be cut out. The Germans had been chosen by Divine Power to be the

135

surgeons. A duty they had not asked for, but when it was thrust on them they did not shirk the task. The resultant onus was unfair, but must be borne.

How to stop the Jew agent before he killed again? Before he succeeded in so terrorizing the organization that progress would be stopped. Before he found out about Isla de Pelo and, chilling thought, even the village itself? None of this must be allowed. The Beard must continue to grow.

If only they had some idea of who the man was, what he looked like, knew something of his friends or background. Nothing. No file.

He went back into the lab, hunching between the long tables like a weary old crab, to an office cubicle partitioned off in a corner. He would call Toller. Roust that *tolpel* from his hangover bed. Helmuth Toller was a fool and, what was worse, a German fool. A romantic clown who thought he was still a Youth Leader with the world at his feet. *Dumnkopf!* He could not see that the world had changed, had left him behind.

Six sank into the hard chair with a groan, reaching for the phone and then staying his hand. Let the poor *dummkopf* dream yet a little. Dream of the past, when he had been young and near the Leader. When he could manage an erection six times a day.

The doctor searched his desk until he found a cigar. He lit it, rubbing his back and groaning. This he permitted himself only in private. He eyed the phone but did not pick it up. Toller could wait. Let him grieve over his limp penis and that woman. Monika. There was a whore for you. And old enough to know better. It had not taken her long to latch on to the man Brookson.

Cigar smoke stung his eyes and he brushed it away irritably. He hated his age. Nothing could be enjoyed. Then he grimaced at himself—that was thinking like Toller, the child-man who was mocked by Monika and was a little crazy into the bargain.

He would like to get rid of Toller. Give him to the

136

Sleepers for final disposal. *Unmoglichkeit!* Toller was the nexus, the link and liaison, between the grand plan and he who lived in the village of Zal. Toller was the only one in Ecuador, perhaps in all of South America, who had known the Leader personally. Who had received benediction from Hitler's hand. No. He could not dispose of Toller. Not until *after* Der Tag. Put it out of his mind. Do not be tempted. Think elsewhere.

He had perhaps made a fool of himself over the man Brookson. But one had to take all precautions, especially with this mad Jew agent on the loose. For a time he had thought that Brookson might *be* the agent. Come to kill them all. Toller had accepted the man too readily, Monika was naturally after his cock, and Klaus Neidler lacked imagination. So he had invented his suspicions of a journalist. Unfounded. Brookson double-checked out. He was what he was—a cocky young fool, a smart ass, *gescheitkopf*, an errand boy.

Forget Brookson. Get him off the island as soon as possible. Let Monika find another penis to play with. Six chuckled and rubbed his shriveled gums with a finger. They hurt nearly as much as his back.

He regretted the death of Mr. Frobisher. No surprise, for the man was old and hearts did not last forever, but the death was inopportune. Later would have been better—after they had installed the old man on the island and begun to milk his fortune. Oil. Old Mr. F had controlled most of the oil in Ecuador, one way or another, and if things had gone well they would have controlled Mr. F.

Doctor Six sighed and did not waste time on thoughts of heirs and possible recouping. Let the oil experts worry about that. They would not be happy. As though he, Six, was responsible for the bad luck of a failed heart. Let them go screw themselves. He chuckled again. Or Monika. It was all one to him. All that mattered to him was the cause and his work. There were plenty of rich men in the world and the richer they were the easier they were to indoctrinate. Especially when you kept your promise and gave them renewed youth. An old man, screwing a pretty young woman for the first time in twenty or thirty years, would sign just about anything you handed him.

Pain stabbed his spine. He groaned his way back into the lab. Nothing was solved by all this thinking. That murderous Jew agent was still on the loose and unless he was caught things could go badly wrong. The Beard might stop growing. Three Sleepers had been murdered and—

A hatpin? Rudy Bottendorff had been stabbed with a hatpin!

Herr Doktor Franz Six smote his forehead with an arthritis-clawed hand. *Gott!* He was a fool and he was surrounded by fools. What blunderheads! All of them. None had seen the possibility.

He blamed himself most of all. A hatpin. How stupid he was, to only now see the possible significance of that.

Women no longer used hatpins, or very few did—he was not *au courant* in such matters—but it was the kind of weapon a woman might *think* of. So easy to hide. And with the proper sort of hat, even these days, so natural an article to have on her person.

No wonder poor Rudy Bottendorff had strolled into that *cul de sac* with her. To come out on a stretcher.

The old doctor hobbled to the phone. It was a distinct possibility and, to his knowledge, it had been overlooked until now. Only a guess, a hunch, but it was worth passing on.

He smiled and fingered a brown tooth as he waited for his call to be put through the automatic PBX to the Pedernales exchange. The decadent French had a phrase for it. *Cherchez la femme!*

He would get them started on it at once and send a message in greater detail by Monika Altekruse when she flew the Brookson man out later this afternoon. Toller was going with her, back to Quito, and he could

138

see that immediate action was taken. At least he was good for that.

When the Herr Doktor put the phone down he was smiling. It was underway. It might come to nothing, but anything was better than inaction. It might be, as the stupid Americans said, a whole new ball game.

Suddenly he felt like working. He would have the old Frenchman in and take a look at him. Something wrong there. The transplant was not working well. Not well at all.

Herr Doktor began to whistle. And to think in his orderly manner—where would a woman, a Jew woman agent, a murderess, where would a woman like that try to hide?

XII

LUNCH WENT BETTER than Eagle had expected. He began to think that Monika, with himself tagging along, was going to bring it off. There were four at table: The old doctor, himself, Monika and Klaus Neidler. Six listened to the woman's expert lying and grunted acceptance. He cast a surly glance at Eagle and said, "You know of the death of your employer?"

At Eagle's nod the doctor continued, "I will not offer hypocritical condolences. I did not know the man. The financial loss I regret. Also I was looking forward to meeting Mr. F—as a fellow genius, you might say. Not many men can accumulate a billion dollars."

Eagle went along with that. They must have had very special plans for Mr. F.

"His death changes everything," said Six. "As you will admit. There is nothing for you on the island now. *You* certainly do not need our services and"—with a show of brown teeth—"I regret the rudeness of last night. I had to be sure you were not a journalist."

Eagle murmured that no apology was necessary.

"I do not apologize," snapped Six as he pushed back from the table. "I only explain. And I will say good-bye, Mr. Brookson. Helmuth and Monika are going to

140

Quito this afternoon and they will take you with them. *Auf Wiedersehen.*"

Monika said, "Klaus and I are going to film after lunch—I thought I would take Richard along if you have no objections?"

Six peered from his eternal crouch at Eagle. "Why should I object? If his tastes are so by all means let him watch. But I do not understand, Monika, how with you around the young man needs stimulation. But by all means—those women cost us a fortune to maintain, we may as well have some use of them."

He crept to the door and glanced back. "You might even let Mr. Brookson participate if he is so inclined."

Eagle shook his head and smiled. "No thanks. I'm more the voyeur type."

The old man shrugged his ruined shoulders and left.

Klaus Neidler left a moment later, saying he would meet them at the women's villa in half an hour.

Eagle and Monika were alone at the table. She put a hand under the cloth and squeezed him. Eagle moved her hand.

"Down, girl. For Christ's sake! He bought it for the moment but we're still walking a narrow way. You heard what he said to Neidler—that fast spate of German? I couldn't follow all that."

She laughed. "He is very angry with Toller. He was telling Klaus to haul him out of bed and get him sober and on his feet. A cold shower, whatever. He wants to see Toller before he leaves for Quito."

"That is not so good," Eagle said. "They start looking for Toller and we're in big trouble."

She took his hand. "I know. But Klaus is our cameraman. Only he knows how to get results. He will not go looking for Toller until *after* the filming. So we have time enough. Come now. You must trust me."

That was one thing, Eagle thought, that he couldn't do.

They took one of the golf carts and whirred toward

the villa of women. Monika said, "You have not shown much grief about your employer."

Eagle grinned. "I'm the stoic type. I don't show my feelings."

She gave him a thoughtful look. "I am still not sure of what you are, or how I feel about you. Except that I love you, of course. But there is something peculiar."

"There sure is," he agreed. "A dead man in a locker. Do we have to go through this movie-making stuff?"

They were gliding past the three Nissen hut hangars. He pointed. "You've got the keys. Why don't we just take off and run for it?"

She patted his knee. "I told you. Let Monika handle it. The filming is necessary because it is routine. Expected. If we do not arrive at the villa Klaus will call the old man and a search will begin. The mestizos will be questioned. The doctor will know that we left alone, without Helmuth. How long then until they find the body?"

Eagle shrugged. "We'll have a head start." He had given the flight a lot of thought. Once they were airborne he would lose some degree of control over her. He had little enough now. And he could not fly a chopper.

"Six will not need to find the body," she went on, "to know that something is wrong. The moment he knows that just the two of us left he will radio ahead."

Eagle shrugged again. "So? We're not going back to Quito. I had Esmeraldas in mind. It's only fifty miles from here and I have a friend there. I think."

If Enrique Chulde, Merlin's man in Ecuador, was still in business.

They were skirting the golf course. Her glance narrowed. "That is good. We will need friends. I may as well tell you, I suppose, that after the old man radios ahead we will be sought for—by a great many skilled and unscrupulous people. Six has used them before. On several occasions that I know of they—"

She pulled the cart to a stop a little way from the

villa. She stared hard at him and took his hand in hers. "I told you I was afraid. You do not understand all that goes on. Nor do I, not all of it. But I know too much and I know they will harm me if I remain. That is why, apart from my great love for you, that I am doing this thing."

For once he was near to believing her. She had lost color and her hand was cold in his. Her eyes brimmed with tears and she looked old.

Eagle patted her hand. "Stick with it, kid. Keep your bargain and I'll keep mine. If we can get to Esmeraldas we'll fox them. Their *mordklub* won't get us."

She snatched her hand away. "*Mordklub?* You know about that!"

"I've got big ears," said Eagle. He pointed to the villa, then to the cart's controls. "Let's get on with it. Make the feelthy pictures and stick to that sacred routine of yours. Let's go."

She started the cart. "We still have the deal, no? We help and protect each other and you will take me to Scotland and give me money?"

"The deal is still on."

She eyed him sideways. "And make love to me?"

"Naturally."

As the cart stopped before the villa entrance she said, "Now that your employer is dead you might be a rich man, yes?"

"It is possible. I am probably in his will." A little bait might keep her as honest as she ever could be.

Two guards touched their caps to her as they entered the villa. Monika nodded curtly. They stared with curiosity at Eagle, remembering him.

Monika led him down a long cool hall and into a small bar. Three women were at the bar. All wore loose wrappers and not much beneath. Eagle had never seen a pornographic movie made, even a scientific pornographic movie, and he found the prospect mildly exciting. Had the circumstances been otherwise, with-

143

out a corpse waiting to be found, he could have enjoyed it.

Monika did not introduce the women to Eagle. She spoke briefly, and a bit harshly, in Spanish. Here was a side of her he had not seen. For a moment he imagined her clad in shiny black leather and cracking a whip.

There were bottles and glasses on the bar and a bucket of ice. The three women nursed small drinks as they listened servilely to Monika. Eagle made himself a light scotch and water and listened and watched. One of the whores especially caught his attention.

There was no sign of Klaus Neidler.

"I want this to go quickly," Monika was saying, "and there must be no mistakes. I am in a hurry today. Anyone who does not obey, who makes mistakes, will be punished. Now, before we go into the studio to begin, I will outline to you precisely what I expect—"

Two of the women were obvious types. Pretty little whores of Spanish or Indian descent, possibly with a touch of Negro blood. They listened and nodded, now and then glancing at each other and giggling. The third woman, sitting on a bar stool nearest to Eagle, was of a different type. Jewish, he would have guessed, but if so what in Christ's name was she doing here!

The voice of dead Kleinberg, on the tape, spoke in his brain. Eagle had listened to the tape half a dozen times. *Jews can be just as stupid and evil as anyone in the world.*

So a Jewish whore? Why not?

Eagle puzzled over it. Why not? He could not put his finger on why not. All he knew was that there was something wrong with the picture. He felt that somewhere *der organisation* had fouled up. A wild thought struck him, so wild that he immediately ruled it out. No way.

The woman was watching him. Eagle watched back. She looked Jewish and yet, now that he saw her full face, did not. *Maybe* Jewish. One thing was not maybe—the face had seen a lot of wear. Her skin was sallow, unhealthy looking, and she had black puffs under her eyes. Her hair was dry and lifeless. Deep lines led from her nose to a bitter mouth.

Her eyes did not fully meet Eagle's stare. He had the impression of being sized up, categorized. Professional? A whore's glance?

The woman lost interest in him and turned her attention back to Monika.

"The last films have not been satisfactory." Monika's manner was cold. "We are paying you good wages here and we expect more. If you cannot perform adequately we will get rid of you and bring in new people. You must put more life, more interest, into your performances. If you do not actually enjoy what you are doing then you must pretend just the same. Simulate pleasure and excitement. These films are to stimulate very old and very tired men—this cannot be done if you look as if you are thinking of other things while you perform."

One of the girls, a fluffy blonde with dark roots, giggled and pointed to her companion. "I do my best, Señorita Altekruse. But Marie will not cooperate."

The one called Marie shrugged. "I do not like women that way. I cannot help the way I am made, Señorita. And the taste repels me. But I will try."

Monika glared at her, hands on hips. For the moment she had forgotten Eagle. "You had better try, Marie. Or you will be sent packing back to the mainland. No matter about your personal tastes—you are not here for your own pleasure. If Conchita can pretend so can you. This is understood?"

Marie pouted and nodded sullenly.

Monika turned to the third woman. "You, Stella, have not yet worked with these two morons. I expect you will find it difficult, but I understand that you have had great experience and there should be no difficulty. You, I trust, have no objections on moral grounds? No personal distaste for making love to another woman?"

The woman spoke in a calm and husky voice. "No,

145

Miss Altekruse. I have no objections. You have been very kind to me, bringing me here and letting me rest. I will do anything I am told and I will do my best."

Monika clapped her hands briskly. "Good—good. That is more like it. I expect you can teach these two imbeciles a thing or two. Some tricks they do not know. I will appoint you group leader, then. You will be in charge of the threesome. Now then—first there will be mutual cunnilingus. Then you will use the dildo and—"

Eagle stared into his drink. For a moment he did not dare look at the woman. Stella! Stella Helpern? The woman Kleinberg had left behind in Ecuador.

Impossible. No way. Can't be. That Stella is—was?—whatever, only twenty-seven. This one must be forty going on eighty. And the name? Wouldn't she have changed her name?

Not necessarily. *They* didn't know her name.

Monika was going into details about who was going down on whom and when and how. So forth and so forth. Giving them the script to save time in the actual shooting.

The scotch tasted like piss. Eagle felt eyes on him and looked up to meet the eyes of the woman named Stella. They stared at each other. Her glance carried voltage. And a question. Hope and despair, expectancy and fear, they were all in her glance.

This is a goddamned crazy nightmare, Eagle told himself, but I am not going to wake up. It's real. It is really happening.

What did he do now?

Monika came to touch his arm. She lowered her voice. "Klaus is not here yet."

Eagle nodded. "This I can see."

"It is not like him to be late," she said. Her moist red mouth twisted in worry. "If something has gone wrong—if Klaus has found that Toller is not in his room, if he begins looking for him, then—"

"We are in trouble," finished Eagle.

146

Monika looked over her shoulder. "Keep your voice down. I do not know what to think. Klaus is always punctual."

They heard Neidler's voice. He was speaking to one of the guards. "Take that *verdammen* cart to the shop, Juan, and have a new battery installed. It quit on me. Is the Señorita Altekruse here yet?"

Monika smiled her relief. She patted Eagle's cheek. "It is all right. Some trouble with his cart. I will go with him to the studio and start setting up. Finish your drink, *liebling*. Come when you are ready. A guard will show you the way."

She waved an imperious hand at the three women. "Come, you. We must begin."

Marie and Conchita followed her out of the room. The third woman, the one called Stella, lingered for a moment. Eagle watched her. Their eyes met and she looked afraid and desperate. Eagle gave her a tentative smile. What he was thinking was insane.

For those few seconds they were alone. The woman patted her mouth and smothered a yawn. She smiled at Eagle. "I did not sleep well last night. Now that it is time for work I am sleeper."

He caught it and admired the cleverness. It could be only a slip of the tongue. She could still disown it.

Eagle had an advantage. He could afford to go straight to the point. He said, "There is a joke about that, you know. About sleepers."

She watched him. "A joke? Where did you hear it?"

"A man called Kleinberg told me. He is dead now."

The woman did not so much as blink. She regarded him steadily. "I knew a Kleinberg once."

Eagle nodded. "I think it is the same man."

Monika called from the hall. "Stella! Stella—come at once. We must begin."

The woman slid off the bar stool and gathered her wrapper about her. Her body was still good, the breasts firm and the legs slim and straight. Her heavily painted mouth quirked in a faint smile as she nodded at Eagle.

"Be ready," she told him. "Be ready for anything."

Eagle watched her leave, wondering what the hell now? This was a whole new kettle of fish and he didn't know how to handle it. This Stella—Sleeper—was sitting right in the middle of the lion's den. His own position wasn't much better. If he played along with Monika, stuck to *der routine*, he had a good chance of making it out before they found Toller's body.

Could he do that? Leave the woman in the lurch? It must be a pretty tight lurch. No doubt about the appeal in her eyes. She needed help, had been asking for it.

He repeated Merlin's cable in his head:

```
Serendip —- if million one contact
Stella Helpern code Sleeper could be
friend in need -- K deceased hard
way --
```

The million to one shot had come in. Sleeper, Stella, was a friend in need, all right, but read it the other way. *She* needed *him*. To get out? He doubted that. What then?

Eagle shrugged and left the little bar. Play it by ear, minute by minute. See what happened.

At the door he stopped. A guard was at the front entrance, his back to Eagle. The hall was empty. To his left a stair climbed. Eagle craned his neck and made out the khaki legs of the other guard on the landing. The house was quiet but for a subdued buzz of talk somewhere upstairs. There was an odor of dust and food and women. Eagle stepped back into the room.

He went behind the bar and pretended to mix a drink. It took him thirty seconds to find a sharp paring knife used for slicing fruit. It had a three-inch blade and a bakelite handle. He slipped it into his belt and slid it around to the base of his spine.

The guard on the landing nodded and pointed as

Eagle approached. Eagle followed the brown finger to a leather-padded door and pushed in. It was dark inside except for lights rigged over a huge round bed. On the bed was a coverlet of scarlet cretonne and on the coverlet were the three women in a tangle of limbs. Eagle did not waste time trying to sort it all out. He had no interest in who was doing what to whom.

Klaus Neidler, using a hand-held camera, was moving around the bed. He knelt occasionally, sometimes leaned in for a closeup, speaking to the women in a low coaxing voice.

Eagle's lips curled. *Herr Direktor.*

Monika came out of the shadows and touched Eagle. He had an erection and nothing to do about it. Not a thing you could wish away.

She stood close to him. "It is exciting, yes?"

He admitted that it was.

She caressed him. "*Ja—ja*—even with sluts like this it is exciting. I think I cannot wait until we get to Scotland, *liebling.*"

Eagle muttered something.

Monika released him. She was breathing hard, her voice catching in her throat. "Klaus is good with the camera, I think. It is a hobby, *ein steckenpferd.*"

"Some hobby," Eagle said. "He's probably a better photographer than he is a surgeon."

Monika laughed, then put her hand over her mouth. "We must be quiet. Do not distract. It is hard enough to get these sluts into the mood."

Eagle nodded. "It is easy to understand. When you have to do something for a living it loses a lot of glamor. But they seem to be doing okay. Good enough to get old men stirred up."

Monika put a finger on his lips. "Whisper, *liebling.* We must get this done as quickly as possible. Then, while Klaus goes to the big house to get Helmuth out of bed we will take a cart to the hangar and take the helicopter. We should have fifteen minutes clear. Perhaps a bit more. It will be enough if we do not make mistakes."

"I hope you're right," said Eagle.

Neidler called a halt. He beckoned to Monika, nodding at Eagle without speaking, and began to reload the camera. Eagle hovered in the shadows, watching without expression as Monika handed the woman Conchita a large pink dildo. Eagle tried to catch the eye of Stella. If she knew he was there she made no sign.

For the finale Marie and Conchita did a sixty-nine while Stella used the dildo on herself. When it was over Neidler turned on some lights and the rest of the studio could be seen. It was larger than Eagle had suspected. In one corner were a wicker table and chairs.

The women, with their wrappers on, were lying exhausted on the bed. Klaus Neidler, adjusting his camera, grinned at Eagle. He looked more like a pig than ever. A pink pig rooting in truffles.

"You enjoyed the show, *nein?*"

Eagle smiled at him. "*Ja.* Most educational."

Neidler made a face. "Not the best, of course. The women are of poor quality, I know. The best we can get. But for the old men it is enough, I think. It excites them enough for us to determine if the operation has been a success. But now I could use a drink, *nein?* You, Richard and Monika?"

She assented grudgingly. Eagle also. They dared not hurry Klaus—do anything to make him suspicious.

Monika shot a glance at Eagle. Patience. She clapped her hands at the three women. "Stella! Go to the bar below and fetch us some drinks. Bring bottles and glasses and ice. Marie and Conchita, you may go to your rooms. At once now. Hurry."

The women left. Klaus unstrapped his cameras and meters and put them carefully on the wicker table. "After my drink I must go and roust Helmuth out of bed. You heard the doctor at lunch. Why must I always have the dirty jobs? Helmuth is a fool and half crazy,"—he looked at Eagle—"as I told you this morn-

150

ing. He would be better left alone until his sickness passes. But I suppose I must obey."

He leaned back in a chair and put his feet on the wicker table, scowling. "Then I must go to the darkroom and begin processing. Sometimes I think of telling the old man that I am a surgeon also, not an errand boy."

"We must all bear our crosses," said Eagle piously.

Neidler shot him a suspicious glance. "I suppose so. At least you will soon be going back to civilization. You and Monika and Helmuth—remember, please, what I told you. Do not goad Helmuth, or even try to be friends with him. At such times he is impossible. You must simply ignore him. He will probably try to start a fight if you give him the slightest pretense."

Eagle glanced at Monika. She was staring at the floor. "I won't," promised Eagle, "give him the slightest pretense."

Neidler crossed his booted feet. "Where is that whore with the drinks? Oh, Monika, can I use your cart? The battery failed in mine. You and Richard can walk back—you cannot leave anyway until I have Helmuth on his feet."

Monika nodded. "Take the cart."

Stella came in. She pushed an old-fashioned tea cart before her. On the cart were bottles, glasses, and a thermos jug.

Neidler gave her a sulky glance. "About time, you bitch. What kept you?"

Stella put a tray on the table. She placed a drink before Monika and another glass before Eagle. She was obsequious. "I took the liberty," she said, "of preparing the drink for Miss Altekruse. And for this gentleman. I noticed that before he drank scotch." Her eyes implored Neidler. "I did not know your choice, sir, so I could not—"

Monika gave her a cold stare, but picked up her glass and drank. When she put the glass down she said, "It was not necessary, Stella. You were not hired to

151

serve drinks. Do not hereafter take so much on yourself."

Stella cringed. "I only thought, Miss—"

Monika snapped her fingers. "You may go, Stella."

As the woman turned away she glanced at Eagle. He knew something was going on, without the slightest idea of what it might be.

Stella put an indicating finger to her mouth. One of her eyeteeth was missing. Suddenly gone. She had had all her teeth downstairs. And during the filming. Eagle was sure of it.

Stella nodded, nodded ever so slightly, at Klaus Neidler. Realization came all at once to Eagle. Capped tooth. Monika's drink. The nod at Klaus Neidler.

"GUH—GUH—" said Monika Altekruse. Her face flamed and turned purple. Her eyes bulged. She clawed at her throat as though trying to strangle herself. She struggled from her chair, made it halfway, then fell over the wicker table.

Klaus Neidler was slow in reacting. He stared at Monika, his porcine face working, eyes narrowed. He started to reach for her, to touch Monika, then swung to accuse Stella.

"*Gott innen Himmel!* That drink! You—"

Eagle cut his throat with the paring knife.

He leaped back from the gush of blood, pulling the woman with him. He thrust her away, watching Neidler thresh about and try to scream through the torrent of blood. Eagle picked up a bottle from the tea cart and smashed in the back of Neidler's head.

The woman ran to the door and locked it, then turned to face Eagle. The first thing she said was, "Is it true? Is Kleinberg dead?"

XIII

"HE'S DEAD", SAID Eagle. "And you're the girl he left behind?"

She remained at the door, leaning against it, as though her frail body could bar pursuit.

"I am Stella Helpern," she said. "I worked with Kleinberg. He sent you? You are Israeli Secret Service?"

Eagle shook his head impatiently. "In a way he sent me. I am not Israeli. I cannot tell you anything. There is no time to explain. You will have to trust me, believe that I am one of the good guys."

She left the door and came to the table. She looked down at the bodies of Monika and Klaus Neidler. There was a coldness in her eyes that gave Eagle a chill.

"I believe that," she told him. "The way you used your little knife—you are a professional."

Eagle hardly ever sweated, but he was sweating now. He forced the action. "Help me," he commanded. "We will talk as we go. Not that there is much to talk about—you've screwed us up good this time, woman. Come on, Neidler first. You take his feet."

They carried Klaus Neidler to the bed. Stella gave Eagle a gap-toothed smile. "The pig is heavy. Lard."

"I guess the jogging didn't help much," said Eagle. As they went back for Monika he said, "That was your cyanide tooth?"

"Yes. For myself *in extremis*."

He was searching Monika. He found keys and held them up. "I don't suppose you can fly a chopper?"

"No."

Eagle slipped the keys into his pocket. "You don't plan very far ahead, do you?"

She picked up Monika's feet. "Not of late. Not in my profession. It does not pay."

They arranged the bodies on the bed and covered them with the scarlet cretonne spread. Eagle stared at the mess around the table. He nodded at her. "Go quietly to the door and listen. You might try thinking a little while you're at it. I'll do the same. There has to be some way out of this."

Stella regarded him steadily. "You're afraid?"

"Cautious," said Eagle. "I've gotten used to breathing. And you'll have to admit that we have a problem. I was doing all right until you got into the act. I was on my way out. Now I've got you to worry about. Go watch the door, I said."

As she tiptoed to the door she said, "You mean two is a crowd?"

Eagle did the best he could. He took pillowcases from the bed and mopped up the blood, then thrust the cases under the mattress. He rearranged the table and chairs and put the tea cart in order. All this in less than two minutes. He joined her at the door and looked back. At first glance everything looked normal. Even the two shapes under the coverlet. It was that kind of a house.

Stella touched his arm. He could smell her whore's perfume. She whispered. "We have time. At least an hour or two. Marie and Conchita will mind their own business and the guards will not dare to interrupt. For them it will be simple. They will laugh and make jokes

154

about it. They think we are in here doing queer things to each other."

Her face was close to his. Her complexion was bad and the shadows beneath her eyes looked like bruises. She was haggard, lined, strained and unlovely. But it was her eyes that caught and held his attention. Eagle had never seen eyes that held such torment and despair. And courage. Without knowing why, without even wanting to, he put an arm about her shoulders. She was trembling.

"Take it easy," he told her. "We'll get out of this somehow."

She nodded. She sat down on the floor, cross-legged, and reached to pull him down beside her. They sat with their backs against the wall, holding hands. Eagle put his ear against the wall and listened. He could hear nothing.

Stella clung to his big hand with both of hers. Her hands were small and not very clean and the nails were badly chewed.

"You must get out of this," she said. "That is all that matters. I will stay behind. I have work to finish here."

The look in his eyes warned her. She put a hand over his mouth. "Speak softly. I doubt that the guards are still out there, but speak in a normal soft tone. If we do not attract attention they will not bother us. I have studied them since I arrived here. They are not conscientious and they do not love their employers. I have heard them with the other women, speaking in Spanish which they did not think I understood. If we are careful we will have no trouble with the guards."

Eagle nodded. He was of the same opinion. He said, "Okay. But what is this crap about you staying behind?"

She gave him a level stare. "It is not crap. I mean what I say. I am staying. You must understand that. If you try to force me to leave I will make a scene and attract attention."

He waved a helpless hand. "Okay—okay. Stay if you

want to. Have it your way. You mind telling me why?"

She told him.

When she finished he said, "It figures. I had a feeling he must be someone like that. And you're going to pay him back for your mother and all the others, eh? In a way I can see it—but is it worth the price? Your own life?"

"I died a long time ago," she said. "I died but I did not rest. Now I will welcome sleep. But not before I kill Wolfgang Sechs. Slowly, if possible. On his own operating table, if possible. Have you a weapon, other than the little knife?"

Eagle sighed. "Greater love hath no man." He took the little Walther out of his pocket and handed it to her. "It ain't much, but all I got. With it you might bluff your way to where the big guns are, if any. They're sure to have some kind of arsenal on the island. And the guards are armed. You should do all right."

"I will. The guards are mestizos and they will not want to die for these German swine."

She was lost in thought for a moment, staring at the bed across the room. "They are dead. That leaves Sechs—who will be in his laboratory—and another man called Toller."

"You can forget him."

She raised her eyebrows. "Oh?"

"Yes."

"Good. That leaves—apart from the guards—only the six men who came in last night."

Eagle remembered the sound of a big helicopter and the lights. "Tell me about the six men?"

She related what she had seen. "They carried something to the labs. Two white boxes. They looked like portable freezers, something of the sort. I—"

Eagle told her what was in the white boxes.

Stella did not turn a hair. She only nodded. "Yes. It all fits. The six men, after they delivered the boxes,

156

went to the far end of the island. There must be some kind of barracks there."

Eagle said, "Let's hope we don't find out. Rough characters, you say, and armed?"

"Heavily armed. Rifles and pistols."

Eagle frowned. "We sure as hell have to avoid them. Can't fight six with a popgun and a paring knife. Of course I can disarm a couple of the guards and—"

"You are forgetting," she said softly. "You will run for it. I am staying. I will handle the six men. If I must. I do not think they will be much in the way of what I plan to do—they are just back from the jungle."

That figured. Men just back from a long trek in bad jungle—dangerous enough at best and much more so when you were cutting the balls off young Indians— men like that would be sleeping and drinking, bathing, thinking about their own affairs. Thinking about women!

"Hell," said Eagle. He told her what he was thinking.

"Yes. I suppose they will be here sooner or later. That may even be good. We will be gone. You to your task and I to mine. And now I must give you something. It may be worthless and it may be priceless. I do not know. There is no time to tell you. But you must take it out, give it to your people, whoever they are, and let them see what they can make of it. I have written it all down. It is in micro-writing, in a code of sorts, but you will be able to figure it out."

Stella had been holding his hand. Now she let go and slouched down beside him and spread her legs. Her wrapper fell away. She had black pubic hair that grew in a thin line nearly to her navel. She thrust the first two fingers of her right hand into her vagina.

Eagle watched without any change of expression. Stella, her face tense, said, "Not really a secret place, not in my life, but the best I could think of. Damn it! It has slipped up. I cannot get my fingers on it. Oh, damn!"

157

She had three fingers in her vagina now. She shook her head. "You will have to help me."

Eagle looked at his hands. "I'm not exactly clean."

"For God's sake, do you think that matters now!"

He grinned at her. "Guess not." As he put his fingers in her he said, "You haven't got any bombs or anything in there?"

She did not smile. "It is possible that it is a bomb of sorts. I hope so. Do you feel it? A little tube?"

"Got it."

He handed the tube to her. She wiped it on her wrapper and handed it back to him.

"Get it out. It could be very precious."

"Or worthless?"

"Yes. But now we must go. Do you have a plan yet?"

Eagle did. She listened and objected and together they agreed on alterations. At the very last he tried again to change her mind about remaining.

"Revenge isn't all that satisfying," he told her. "The old bastard is dying of slow torture now. Falling apart. Why not leave him to it? Kleinberg said you were only twenty-seven."

Her face told him it was no good. Her ravaged flesh turned to sallow concrete. "Save your advice," she told him. "You cannot possibly understand. It did not happen to you. You are like Kleinberg and the others. They do not understand the joy of killing these brutes. But I am WOG and I understand."

Eagle nodded. "I thought that might be it. Wrath of God?"

"Yes. We infiltrate the regular Israeli Secret Service. To use their apparatus and equipment. They are not fools, or soft men, but they want to do everything legally and for propaganda value. A fair trial and a public hanging. We of the WOG kill the rats where we find them."

Eagle knew when he was licked. He got up from the floor and put the aluminum tube carefully in his pocket. "Okay. I wish you good hunting. Give me about twenty minutes before you start."

"Don't worry. I will make plenty of diversion for you."

She accompanied him to the door. Eagle glanced at his watch and realized that only twenty minutes had passed since he cut Neidler's throat.

Stella held up a finger. She ran to the table and came back with a bottle of whisky. "You are a man who has just had his fill of sex and alcohol."

Eagle gargled some of the whisky and spat it on the carpet, careful to spill a bit on his shirt front. "That should do it."

They looked at each other. He said, "You're absolutely sure you won't—"

"Go! For God's sake just go!"

She leaned to kiss him on the cheek. Her mouth was cold and dry. She gave him a little push.

"Goodbye."

XIV

NIGHT HAD FALLEN. Polly Perkins listened to Merlin's Churchillian prose. Unlike Molière's character, *Gentilhomme,* Merlin was fully aware that he was speaking prose, and magnificent prose at that. He was pleased and in an expansive mood. Polly was being honored with his confidence and, a rarity, his secret thoughts.

The glass room turned on its hydraulic axis. Makaluha suspired, exhaling bright sparks to float and die.

"From the very first," said Merlin, "I had the thought that there would be a *tertium quid,* a third thing of importance. Quite apart from the testicular racket. Which turned out to be no racket after all. Quite a remarkable man, Doctor Six. Or Wolfgang Sechs, whatever. A pity, in a way, that he had to leave us. In a few more years I might have had recourse to him—to his services—myself."

Polly smiled gently and did not laugh. Merlin enjoyed his triumphs as much as lesser men. Let him. It was not her province to remind him that at times he was a boastful old man, given to arrogance that approached hubris. Nor to remind him that the most difficult part of Operation Gaul still lay ahead and that John Eagle, in exactly six minutes, would be dropping by parachute into deadly peril. Merlin *knew* all that.

"The murder club, the Seven Sleepers," he continued, "is still extant. Though in shock and badly shaken. They will regroup, of course. No matter. Except to future victims and I am sorry for that, but it is not a factor in our thinking now. The *mordklub* was never more than an adjunct, security and bullyboys, to the first part of this triangular puzzle. What is the time, Polly?"

She knew what he meant. "If all has gone well, and we have had no negative reports, he will be dropped in about three minutes."

Merlin powered his wheelchair to the great window and peered out over the darkling sea. "I do not understand it," he told Polly. "I am not usually so nervous. We have taken every precaution. We have all worked day and night for a week to ensure the success of this operation. Nothing can go wrong. I know that. Yet I am nervous."

Polly had once loved this man physically and loved him still. She was not a *yes* woman. She said, "You know better than that. Something can always go wrong. He has to get through three hundred miles of the worst jungle on earth. He has to find a small village that may or may not be there."

"The village is there," said Merlin. "Zal exists."

"It isn't on any map."

Merlin snorted. "I know that. And I know why. Purposely left off. A favor, paid for naturally, done by certain high officials. Why not? They couldn't have thought that it mattered—a tiny German enclave in the Andes. A bit of the Old Country transported to the new. How could they know it mattered? Such little national backwaters are found all over the world. The Little Italys, the Chinatowns, Yorkville in New York—why not a minor Bavaria in the Andes? Innocuous. In most cases."

"Apparently not in this case."

"Remains to be seen, Polly. This thing may be all a lie. A legend. A myth."

161

On the Venetian desk a phone rang. Polly answered it, listened a moment, made a soft acknowledgement and turned to Merlin.

"The drop was made on schedule."

Merlin rolled to the humidor and took out a thick Cuban cigar. Polly lit it. "This is one of the times," he told her, "when I wish I had my legs and my youth again. I am always sending my people into danger."

The woman touched his white hair for a moment, then dropped her hand. She picked up a notebook from the desk. "There is nothing you can do now but wait—and try not to fret yourself into a breakdown. Do you want me to go or stay?"

The old man stared out at the night. Not particularly friendly, he thought, and remembered the storm warnings.

"Stay awhile," he told her. "Put up with me. Be a good listener."

Polly nodded and found a chair, arranging the loose-flowing muumuu about her good legs. She smiled at him. "You were being very latinate," she reminded him.

"I was being what?"

"The *tertium quid* bit?"

"Oh, yes. That." Merlin inclined his massive head and regarded her with a jocular look. When he did that, though lacking the cigarette holder, he reminded Polly of a dead President of the United States. One of the few hard facts she knew about her employer, and former lover, was that he had been a college chum of that past President.

"The second facet, I exclude minor matters, is the scale of the organization, of which the Valhalla Club and the Demogorgon Society were only a part. Important parts, but *only* parts. They, and the late lamented medics, Six or Sechs, and Klaus Neidler, were important cogs but only cogs. They will be replaced. As will people like Monika Altekruse and Helmuth Toller.

And, for that matter, the man Kleinberg and the woman Stella Helpern."

"So much death," said Polly.

Merlin puffed on his cigar. "There will be more death, and nastier, if this thing is not nipped in the bud. Provided, of course, that it is not just another myth."

"You don't have any *proof*," said Polly impatiently.

He waved his cigar at her like an admonitory wand. "Nearly proof. Logical premise. Five hundred people all over the world working for a week. And the computers—they produced a model."

"I know. I suppose it *must* be true. It just seems incredible. Impossible."

"The Germans," said Merlin, "are an incredible people. And, at times, an impossible people."

His cigar glowed red, mimicking the sparks of Makaluha.

"Our second facet," said Merlin, "is more important than the first and less important than the third, if there is a third. A vast conglomeration of schemes to raise money. Huge sums of money. Mostly, I would guess, by legitimate means. Business. Even Isla de Pelo was legitimate in a sense—according to our reports they *did* rejuvenate old men. Give them new testicles. Hard on the donors, of course."

Polly was silent. She knew that part of the story. It was, she thought, somewhere on her list of the ten most appalling things she knew about the world.

"Big money," Merlin continued. "Oil. Many other things, but mostly oil. I am not being too florid when I say that in the near future Ecuadorian oil will flow like a river of black gold. They want to control that oil. And they don't mind waiting a few years. It took me a little time to grasp that point—in this matter the urgency is all on our side, not on theirs. They are not going to insist on having the world tomorrow. The day after tomorrow will do."

The room continued its slow silent revolutions. Merlin lit a fresh cigar. Polly crossed her tanned, satin-smooth legs.

"That is why they went after Mr. F," Merlin said. "He owns, did own, a large part of the oil in Ecuador. His death must have come as quite a shock."

It had also come as a shock to Merlin. He did not exactly grieve for the man in Scotland. The actor had had a long and full life, had been well paid, and had lived in luxury. He had lived and died using Merlin's real name, keeping the bargain to the end. Merlin had not even been inconvenienced or endangered by the death. If anything it was fortuity welded to serendipity—a favorite word of Merlin's—and his cover was still unbroken. He was dead and in a grave. He supposed that his enemies would find him again in time, but for the moment he was ahead of them.

Polly did not know the truth about the man in Scotland. She had sent a cable and flowers and had engaged a clipping service to supply obits. There had been a sheaf from papers all around the globe. Merlin read them with a strange melancholy, mindful of the dualism, with a feeling that his twin had died.

Polly said, "He should be well into the jungle by now. If all went well."

Merlin powered his wheelchair around the room in tight circles. They expressed his mood. "No reason why things shouldn't go well. I don't send boys to do men's work. Eagle is an Apache in everything but blood. He's half Apache all the time and when he gets into the jungle he will be *all* Apache. I am not worried about John Eagle."

Polly accepted the lie. She talked for a little time and then left. "Sleep," she told him. She smiled. "It knits up the raveled sleave. And you have been pretty raveled of late. Goodnight."

Of course he did not sleep. He sat in the wheelchair and stared at the moon balanced on the crater of Makaluha. Had he thought of everything? Since Eagle's return he had spent close to a million dollars and tapped his human resources to the limit. Was it enough?

The test was still to come. If Eagle lived, if he found what he sought, if he followed orders and his own conscience and judgment, then they would know.

He ran it through his mind for the thousandth time. The village of Zal existed. The Valley of Vultures existed. A breeding place, a sanctuary for condors.

Valle de Buitre.

Geier das Tal—in German.

That far the dead Stella Helpern's story checked out. That weird mishmash of Hebrew-Yiddish code—in micro—that Eagle had brought back. Merlin's code people had worked on it for three days and in the end broken it. He had secretly checked it with Tel Aviv, carefully holding back certain facts. He did not want the Israelis in on this. Too many cooks. Besides they were still obsessed with Bormann.

So far the story checked. Zal was there. The condors were there. The village a piece of Bavaria set down in the Andes, full of cows and pretty girls in dirndls and brawny men in *lederhosen.*

Brawny men. Merlin nodded at the moon. The *mordklub*, the Seven Sleepers, would be recruited from the village.

Go in the back door, Eagle had suggested. The only way. They'll be alerted now, warned and frightened by the mess on Isla de Pelo, and the front door will be impossible. They'll feel safe with the jungle at their backs. They *know* that no lone white man can survive in that jungle. They won't be watching the back door.

Merlin nodded again at the moon. Eagle was right. It was the only way to get at them in secret, and secret it must be.

Merlin watched the moon fall down the sky. Now that the thing was done, that Eagle was on his way in, he felt a certain peace. He had taken a great deal on himself. If he was wrong he would pay for it. You always paid for wrong decisions. As the French had paid,

165

and the Czechs and the British. As the world had paid.

For a time Merlin had wavered. He did not like to think of himself as a murderer. Before he gave the order he must be very sure.

All during the week that John Eagle spent on Maui, never leaving the tubes beneath the volcano, readying himself for the ordeal ahead, Merlin had struggled with himself. To give the order for that ordeal. Or not to give it. He was about, as Polly put it, to play God again. Not for the first time. But always before he had been sure, surer than he was now, or the circumstances had been different.

In the end he focused his thoughts—he remembered a date. March 13, 1936. Hitler had sent his troops into the Rhineland. A gigantic bluff. Call it and Hitler would run like a rabbit.

Not a telephone was lifted to give the order. Not a French general or politician had the guts to send in the three divisions that could easily have done the job. In that hour France lost the war.

On the fifth day of the week, as Eagle completed his rebriefing and training, his equipping, Merlin made his decision. He gave Eagle his orders.

And now they would see. Myth? Legend? Lies?

Was there an avatar? Could such a secret be kept so long and so well?

Did Hitler live again in his son?

Was that son, the monster's own flesh and blood, alive and well in the village of Zal in the Valley of Vultures?

Waiting?

XV

As THE PLANE vanished with a diminishing mosquito drone, Eagle floated down beneath the green chute, out of the last rays of sun into jungle twilight. But for the abandoned airstrip the jungle stretched unbroken to all horizons. Green quicksand.

The timing was right. There were eyes in the jungle and they would see him. He was counting on that. The Indians in this sector of Amazonas were mostly Yuna and Jivaro, though even the Indian population would be scant in this Godforsaken green hell. As he approached the Andes from the east he could expect to encounter more Jivaro. Head-hunters. Shrinking and preserving heads, *tsantsa*, was an art with them.

Eagle hit the strip and rolled, spilling the air from his chute. From the air the deserted strip had been clearly delineated, but now he stood in tangled creeper and masses of bamboo snarled together with a web of liana. He shook off the harness and dove into waist-high grass and began to crawl on his belly. They would not come at once. They would be puzzled and afraid. They would wait until it was fully dark. It might be hours yet. But they would come.

The single hangar was of galvanized iron. The roof had tumbled in. One sagging wall still bore the letters:

TRANS-AMAZONAS MINING, INC. A long-failed venture. Diamonds, rubber, gold? Eagle did not know or care. Merlin's men had found the site and it was perfect for him.

He left the pack he had been dragging and moved as silently as a snake through the tall grass. He was wearing a suit of dull white plastic molded to his wide shoulders and slim hips. The reverse was black, for use on moonlit nights. There were many unseen pockets in the suit and it was bulletproof and would turn back anything but the highest powered rifle. As he landed he had turned a little knob and the suit was now phased for chameleon effect. The reagents in the plastic took a little time to act and now Eagle watched his plastic skin turn to an exact matching green. He wriggled along on his belly, silent and unseen, passing within six feet of a grass snake without disturbing it.

He circled the derelict hangar. A tattered wind sock still drooped from a pole like a defeated flag. A flock of scarlet ibis passed overhead, flying in echelon with legs dangling like undercarriages. Homing for the Igara River thirty miles south.

Eagle turned noiselessly on his belly and studied the strip of sky over the little *campo*. Purple turning to gunmetal soon to be black. One lonely star winked down at him. Somewhere off in the jungle a toucan screeched. A pigeon cooed. In a moment another pigeon answered. Eagle smiled. They were out there. He wriggled back to where he had left the pack.

From the pack he took a helmet of clear plastic with a locking ring that fitted into the collar of the suit. This he put aside. Next he took from the pack an odd-looking pistol, long-snouted, Lugeresque in style. He slipped a gas cartridge into the pistol and loaded it with flechettes—steel darts vaned for accurate shooting. The kill upcoming must be made in absolute silence. Stealthy and fast, then he must be on his way before the body was found.

The jungle night set in. Eagle lay without moving,

breathing easily through his mouth, suffering the insects that fed on his exposed face. He dare not cough or slap. He could only guess at their number—probably not more than a dozen or so—but this was home country to them. They would move as easily and warily as the animals they hunted.

Two hours passed. Eagle did not move. His Apache discipline helped him ignore the insects even though, by now, his face was swollen and lumpy and itchy. Patiently he waited.

They were puzzled. They knew a white man had fallen into the clearing—who else would drop from an engine bird?—and now he had vanished. Gone. This was not the way white men acted.

Eagle's lips twitched in a grim smile. Jungle Indians had one failing in common with Plains Indians—an insatiable curiosity.

He smelled them before he heard them. Grease, mud, body sweat. What little breeze there was came from the south and brought the odor of unwashed Indian. Stronger now. Moving toward him.

Three Indians, silhouettes in dimmest starshine, passed within six feet of Eagle. No good. He wanted a loner. If possible he wanted a headman or chief.

The three moved toward the hangar. One of them made a soft bird-like sound. It was answered from the far side of the hangar.

Eagle waited. It would have to be soon. They thought he was hiding in the hangar. When they discovered he was not they would start yelling and stomping around, drawing together, and his chance would be gone.

There!

The solitary Indian came skulking in at an oblique angle. Eagle grinned. A smart bastard. Sensing something wrong, coming back to double-check the tall grass. Maybe he smelled Eagle. The plastic suit was odorless but the insect bites were exuding poison.

Eagle let the man get to within three feet of him.

169

The Indian towered over him, in silhouette, and Eagle shot upward at an angle calculated to put the steel fletchette through the throat.

The pistol hissed softly in a near silent, exhaling sound. The Indian stopped in mid-stride, amazed at death as the slim steel needle tore out his voice box. Eagle, moving soundlessly, had six inches of blade in him before the man could fall.

Eagle eased him down and lay beside the dead man, feeling him over, stripping him of some kind of battered hat with feathers in it, knife and belt, two pouches, a cheap store hatchet. The real prize was a long bow and a quiver. The length of the bow, at least six feet, spoke Yuna. Eagle nodded. He'd hoped for that. A lot of jungle Indians used toy bows or blowguns. He was proficient with neither.

The man was barefoot, but wearing beaded anklets. Eagle took them. He also took a skimpy breechclout of bark. He arranged everything in a neat pack, not hurrying and not making a sound, and when he finished he lay on his back and listened.

By now the Indians were beginning to realize they had been had. They were being audible about it. From the hangar came chirruping and hissing, grunts and more bird calls and animal sounds. Eagle decided it was time to make his goodbyes. They would be taking roll call soon.

He tucked the pistol away and, still on his back, balancing the two packs on his belly, began to inch his way toward the edge of the jungle. He stopped several times to let Indians pass him. They were no longer so stealthy and he heard sounds of anger from the hangar. Sooner or later they would stumble over their dead brother and then the shit would hit the fan.

When he left the clearing he got to his feet. He needed a little room now, not much but a little, and he stood silently, seeking orientation and the glimmer of a star. He had no need of the little compass he carried. He knew which way the hangar stood in relation to

170

north and he was headed south. He studied the over-growing mass of trees until he at last found a silver pin, a star, and moved cautiously in that direction. The fact that he could see the star at all meant the foliage was a little less dense in that direction. He felt his way along, inch by inch and foot by foot. It took all his skill, all his Apache upbringing, but at the end of two hours he had put a few hundred yards between himself and the airstrip. It should be enough.

Eagle was no novice in the jungle. One of his survival tests, before being accepted as an Expeditor, consisted of being dropped into a British Guiana rain forest with only a knife. The nearest white settlement was two hundred miles away.*

He had lost the solitary star now. The jungle was Stygian, humid and oppressive, and though the plastic suit kept his body cool the sweat dripped on his lumpy face. He did not fear malaria or yellow fever—contrary to belief *Stegomyia fasciata* still survived in the para-Andean jungles—for Merlin's medics had pincushioned his ass before departure. He found a tree bole and decided it was home for the time being. He fumbled in his pack and applied an odorless salve to his badly bitten face.

Somewhere to the west a jaguar coughed sullenly. Fireflies and click beetles glimmered in the ropy lianas. Far off a band of howler monkeys went into insane outcry, then as abruptly hushed. Eagle settled himself—composed, patient. He could hear the Indians as they moved around the hangar. They sounded defeated and querulous. Eagle grinned and thumbed his nose. Poor disappointed bastards—no white man to skin alive or roast over a slow fire.

A vine near him moved, slowly detached itself from a tree and slithered off. Tree snake. Eagle watched it and debated whether or not to sleep. He decided against it. Too chancy. He might snore or, worse, oversleep. He must be well hidden in a tree before the sun came up,

* NEEDLES OF DEATH—Expeditor Book #1

As the first faint gray light permeated the jungle he went up the tree, having lashed all his gear fast with cut liana. He carried the bow and slung the quiver. He went cautiously, making sure the branches did not move before he grasped them, and in a few minutes was high and secure in a leafy fork. Around him the jungle came alive with sound and flutter as brightly plumaged birds swooped and small monkeys prowled and chittered. A wide-eyed capuchin stared at him resentfully, then decided to yield the territory. Eagle thanked him silently and settled in for the day.

He killed the long hours by sleeping fitfully, Apache fashion, dozing with his eyes open. He chewed a dozen water and food pills, concocted by Merlin's chemists and tasting like pellets of horse dung. He saw no Indians, though he heard them when they discovered the dead man. There was quite a to-do about that, screams of outrage and fear, and after a time only silence. He guessed they had gone home, to a village somewhere on the Igara River to the south, and taken the body with them.

The long tropical day droned past. His only visitors were wild pigs that rooted and grunted about his tree without suspecting his presence. Eagle debated whether to descend and get started west, then decided to play it absolutely safe. He couldn't afford any mistakes. One was too many. Indians were canny. They might have left a man or two behind in hiding, waiting for just the mistake he did not intend to make.

He had plenty of time—within reasonable limits. If the tale was true, the weird story deciphered from Stella Helpern's cryptic message, the man Merlin called the avatar would still be there. Waiting in the village of Zal. For if the story *was* true, about which Eagle had serious private doubts, that man could have no existence outside of Zal. The village was camouflage and natural habitat to the man. Beyond Zal he had nowhere to go and no reason for being.

Eagle dozed, came awake, dozed again and thought back.

Getting off Isla de Pelo had been no sweat. One of those ridiculously easy things that you can never quite believe. He took a golf cart across the island to the boathouse. He saw no guards and the few mestizo laborers paid no attention to him.

The boathouse door was locked and the windows barred. Eagle jumped in and swam under the water gate, unbarring it before he inspected the hydrofoil. It was a gleaming blue and white job with reconditioned Rolls Royce engines and full tanks. None of the keys he had taken from Monika Altekruse fitted. He jumped the wires and in five minutes had the engines purring. Still no company. It was uncanny.

Eagle unlocked the land-side door and peered out, half hoping he would see the Helpern woman running toward the boathouse. Instead he saw a thick column of greasy black smoke rising from the villa of women. The diversion she had promised him.

He listened for gunfire and did not hear it. Only the roil of smoke against the sky and a babble of voices from the villa. Then a muted siren and what sounded like a jeep or small truck. They would have some kind of fire-fighting equipment on the island.

Eagle lingered, against all reason, hating to leave her, knowing that in the end he must. Stella Helpern had meant what she said. At the moment she must be on her way to the labs where the old doctor, Six or Sechs, was at work. She meant to kill him. He remembered her words.

"Slowly, if possible. On his own operating table, if possible."

Eagle whetted the paring knife, all the weapon he had, against his leg and waited. The villa fire was out of control, the smoke spreading into a dark mini-atomic cloud. He could see flames and hear them crackling.

173

Behind him the engines of the hydrofoil idled, rumbling contentedly. He had never piloted a hydrofoil but saw no great trick to it.

He waited. Come on, you crazy little bitch! I can still get you out of this.

In his head he plotted a course. Only fifty some miles to Esmeraldas, dead northeast, impossible for even an amateur to miss. He did not worry about Ecuadorian patrol boats. There would be a lot of confusion and it might be hours before any sort of alarm was sent out.

A sound of shots drifted to him. First the raw cracking of rifles, then what sounded like the faint popping of Monika's little gun. That was that, then. She was not coming. She was never coming.

Eagle saw the dogs. Great brute Dobermans bounding toward the boathouse. Eagle shrugged, slammed the door and locked it, and vaulted into the cockpit of the hydrofoil.

He beached the hydrofoil in a cove ten miles south of Esmeraldas and walked north until he found a paved road. All his luggage was on the island, but he had his wallet and a good supply of *sucres*. After several hours a decrepit bus hauled him into town. After discreet inquiries he located Señor Enrique Chulde at a motel called The Yellow Monkey. Señor Chulde owned it. Señor Chulde gave him a room and ignored him until that night, when he took Eagle to an outlying house where, concealed in the attic, was a transceiver.

It was an updated Hallicrafter S 40 B, a single sidebank setup, and Eagle was through to Merlin's communications center in a matter of seconds. While he waited for a reply, Señor Chulde explained why he was never bothered by officialdom.

"Money makes the burro move," he said. And twiddled his fingers.

Merlin's answer came zinging in.

"Return at once."

Señor Chulde continued to be obliging. When a tanker left Esmeraldas that night Eagle was on it. As crew.

XVI

EAGLE SPENT A silent day in the tree, a dreary night, and with the next dawn he descended. By now the birds and monkeys accepted him and made no disturbance. He had a raging thirst. The pills prevented dehydration but they did not satisfy the craving.

He had the airstrip to himself. The body was gone. He began to look for the well or spring that must be there. He found it oozing in a clump of tree fern and, after watching it for half an hour, quenched his thirst and bathed in the tepid brackish water. Avoiding the hangar, he found a clearing in the tall-growing bamboo and began to sort out his equipment.

He stripped out of the plastic suit, emptied the pockets of various small articles which he put into his musette bag, and buried the suit. If he made it through the jungle it would have to be as an Indian.

He put on the dead man's breechclout and anklets, then twisted the bark belt around his own solid waist. One of the pouches contained a small clay pot of dark brownish red substance. Probably *curare. Strychnos toxifera.* He treated it with great respect. The other pouch contained a stubby pipe—the bowl carved from sandstone—with a reed stem, and a mixture of Spanish tobacco and rubbed weed of some sort.

The hat was the real prize. It and the bow and quiver of bamboo arrows tipped with piranha teeth. Eagle pulled the bow experimentally and grunted in pleased surprise—the dead Indian had been brawny.

The hat was an ancient derby plumed with parrot feathers. He regarded it with some awe. It was anywhere between ten and fifty years old and the letters REGE STR LON could still be seen on the sweat band. The rim was cracked all around and the crown was punctured in a dozen places. It must have been the pride and joy of the dead man, no doubt passed on from father to son.

The hatchet was cheap trade goods, but honed to a fine edge. Most Indians carried spears or lances of bamboo. The dead man had been rich by Indian standards.

Eagle put on the hat and tipped it to a proper rakish angle. He regretted the lack of a mirror. The hat was important. The feathers indicated some kind of chief, or at least a sub-chief, and that was also important.

He left the musette bag and the hatchet and, taking the bow and quiver, worked his way back to the spring. He covered himself with cool brown mud, face and all, a quarter-inch thick from feet to forehead. Protection against insects and jungle thorn and bramble.

You have to proof a new bow just as you have to proof a new gun, and he plucked a long bamboo arrow from the quiver, careful not to touch the stained piranha barb, and fitted it to the bowstring. He waited. There was a plethora of life all about him, the jungle teemed, but for five minutes he saw nothing. Then a monkey peered at him from a high limb. Eagle, after wasting a few seconds adjusting to the strange weapon, released an arrow. The monkey fell, squealing and thrashing about, a poor shot through the hind quarters. Eagle broke its neck and took it back to his nest in the bamboo. He was starving and the pills didn't do much for a hungry man except keep him alive.

With the hatchet he chopped up the monkey,

177

cleaned it, and ate most of one quarter raw. Licking his fingers he admitted that, while not his favorite, it was not bad. There was far worse food than monkey meat. Near the bamboo he found wild plantain and ate one of the outsize bananas for dessert, wrapping the remainder of the monkey meat in the thick leaves. He noticed a dangling three-toed sloth and prodded it with the bow, causing it to unhook one clawed toe.

"You'll never get anywhere in life," Eagle told it.

Back in the bamboo he set about killing the white man. To survive the upcoming days and weeks he had to be all Indian, one hundred percent Apache, no white blood allowed. He had been through it before, this shedding of one persona to adopt another, but it was never easy. And it took a little time. The sooner he started the better.

From the musette bag he took three sections of aluminum tubing. He uncapped them and assembled the sniper rifle. It had been made in Merlin's machine shops, a lightweight skeleton with a telescopic sight and a sniperscope for night shooting. Eagle assembled it, snapped the trigger a couple of times, and counted out his ammo. Fifty rounds of 303. Forty standard ball and ten rounds of explosive.

Satisfied, he repacked it in the aluminum tubes and stored it in the bottom of the musette bag. As he worked he updated and reviewed his cover story as it had been worked out by Merlin and his advisors. There were gaps, and Eagle would have to invent as he went along, but generally he was content with the story. He was a loner Indian, of mixed bloods, say Auca and Yuna, and he was more than a little crazy and one mean sonofabitch. A killer and renegade even among his own people.

"Banished by your tribe," Merlin had suggested. "Possibly for murder, adultery, incest or all three."

Eagle had grinned at the time. "You're not giving me much of a character. Suppose I run into some missionary Indians?"

178

"The chances of that are remote. Half a dozen missionaries have vanished in that region in the past three years. Presumed to be dead. Probably eaten."

Eagle did not pursue the subject. He remembered a certain most sacred ceremony—he had been thirteen—when he and some other "wild ones" had been inducted into dark and bloody mysteries. Even White Deer, who knew everything about him, did not know about *that*.

"You may have to explain your equipment," Merlin had pointed out. "Certain possessions that an ordinary Indian would not have. The simple way is that you murdered for them."

Reasonable enough. Jungle Indians were poor and always stripped their victims.

Eagle took a pair of high-powered binoculars from the musette bag. They were tinted to avoid sun flash. He took out a machete in three parts and bolted it together. The edge was like a razor. An Indian didn't need a machete to travel in the jungle. He could make ten to twelve miles a day where a white man would make one. With the machete and reasonable luck Eagle hoped for fifteen to twenty miles a day.

He studied a much crinkled and very dirty map, presumbly the property of an unfortunate Portuguese oil prospector. In one tattered margin was the prospector's name—Alberto Da Costa. Eagle moved away from a nest of stinging ants and spread the map, weighting it with small stones. Atop it he placed his combination watch and compass. The watch was old-fashioned, of gold with a hunter case, with an engraving: *To Bill Hunter from all the boys*. Merlin was meticulous. Just the kind of watch an Indian would treasure.

Eagle oriented compass and map. At the moment he was in Colombia. Three hundred miles due west, as the condor flew, was Ecuador and the valley he sought. To reach it he would have to cross a part of the Peruvian panhandle that tipped north and west. Borders did not mean much in this sort of country. Ecuador and Peru

179

still clashed occasionally over large tracts of jungle which neither had wanted until the discovery of oil.

Eagle squatted on his haunches and studied the map. On his return from Isla de Pelo he had spent two days in the South American Room with a mock-up of the terrain he must now cross. Jungle, five rivers, countless small streams that would become the Amazon, then into the foothills of the Andes guarded by forests and deep gorges.

Eagle hummed to himself as he squatted, mud-covered and derby-hatted, tracing another map with the point of the machete. The ideal—perfection—would be to avoid everybody until he came to the Valley of Vultures. No one to see him come or go. He could not count on that. Even in a jungle you could stumble on people.

It should be easy to avoid the oil and gold prospectors. They were few and stuck close to base, supplied by helicopters. Roving Indians were another matter. He was going to cross Jivaro country and they were mean Indians. The mud cracked around Eagle's lip as he smiled—maybe even as mean as Apaches.

He traced with the point of the machete. Since he was not a condor he could not go due west—he would swing south to the Igara and steal a canoe, or make one if he had to, and paddle as near as he dared to the settlement of Palermo. Then cut across a stretch of jungle to the Yubineta and follow it to the source, stealing or making another canoe. From the headwaters of the Yubineta he could cross into Ecuador and head for the Tiputini, a tributary of the Napo River. Both rivers sourced in the eastern Andes and somewhere in a valley between them he should find the condor sanctuary and the village of Zal.

He ran a mud-covered finger down the trace of the Napo on the map and then drew the same line in the dirt. The Napo was a big river, even so near its source, flanked by matted jungle and mangrove swamps. Alive with crocs and snakes. There were a lot of people

180

about, villages and oil-drilling installations, small towns where there were sure to be soldiers and police. Eagle grunted. He must try to skirt the Napo, parallel it, but not get too close to it. The fewer people he encountered the better.

He stored his gear and adjusted the straps of the musette for backpacking. He carried everything to the spring. There he scooped out a shallow hole and let it fill with water until he had a crude mirror. He found a variety of berries and roots, some flowers, and made a paste of mud and dye. Using a tuft of grass as a brush he painted himself over the now hard-caked mud. He had studied, briefly, how jungle Indians painted themselves but he did not attempt to emulate them. He used Apache colors and patterns and painted himself not for war, but in the designs of the Terror Dance, the way his foster mother's ancestors had painted themselves before dancing around a captive who was to die of torture.

Black across the forehead. Vermilion circles about the eyes. Yellow streaks radiating from the mouth. Ribs outlined in vermilion. Legs black and knees and femurs outlined in yellow.

Eagle studied his image in the quiet pool. He nodded. He damned near scared himself.

As he made a last check of his goods he unwrapped and gnawed on a piece of monkey meat. Time to go. At a rough estimate, if all went well, he should reach the valley in three weeks. Maybe a few days more, depending on his luck. And on his survival.

Eagle heard it before he saw it. And didn't believe it. A chopper. He went into the bamboo and flattened, then wormed his way toward the old hangar. If it was a helicopter, and it sure as hell was, they would have to land on the strip if they landed at all. Eagle's thoughts were not pleasant, his language even less so. He muttered in Apache and good old Anglo-Saxon. Who, what miserable, misbegotten, moronic kind of fuckups had chosen this particular time to come screwing around in a chopper?

It would bring the Indians back.

He watched from cover as the big chopper came *whopping—whop—whop—whopping* over the clearing. Twice it circled the strip, low, tilting and banking. Eagle slid into a mass of cool fern and let it spring back over him. The miserable bastards!

The chopper landed and the rotors flapped into silence.

XVII

THE HELICOPTER WAS painted bright red with yellow lettering: ANGLO OIL, LTD. A new outfit getting in on the gravy, the oil strike. Gulf-Texaco had most of the Ecuadorian rights, which explained why these prospectors were working so far east.

Eagle snaked to the edge of the strip and watched. One thing he realized—he should have grasped it before—choppers used this strip with some frequency, otherwise the jungle would have entirely reclaimed it. It would be dangerous at any time. Why now? Why choose this particular time to land?

Eagle hesitated. He could fade into the jungle and be on his way. The smart thing to do. Indians were heading this way, right now, and they would be in a nasty mood. None of this was any of his concern.

Two white men climbed out of the chopper. Both big men. Both a little drunk. One of them, not the pilot, carried a bottle of whisky in his hand. Eagle shook his head. God made all kinds of fools. Drinking and flying over Indian jungle. These clowns were asking for it.

The girl was so small he did not see her until one of the men yanked her roughly out of the chopper. An Indian woman. Eagle began to get the picture. These two characters were taking a break from work—with a little drinking and gang-banging thrown in. And eating. One man held the girl while the other lifted down a box of provisions.

The man holding the girl was bald and bearded. The pilot wore an Aussie hat. He tossed down a chain and a hunk of iron and told the bald man, "Get her chained. We'll ball her after a bit. Heh-heh—"

The bald man looked pained. He snapped one end of the chain around the girl's ankle and fastened the other end to the iron, a rusty chunk that had once been part of a well valve. When the girl was chained the bald man gave her a little push. "*Estou com fome.*" He rubbed his stomach. "Fire. *iIncendio!* Food. *Alimento.* Hurry up. *Pronto.*"

"You're a riot," the pilot said. "You and your goddamned pidgin Spanish, or Portuguese or Indian, whatever the hell it is."

The bald man laughed and swigged from the bottle. "She gets the idea. Look at her shake her ass. We'll have a fire and hot food before you know it."

The pilot reached for the bottle. "You got a lien on that? Give me some."

Eagle still debated. Go or stay? He had the picture now and it was still none of his business. Two men cheating on company time. Taking turns with an Indian girl they had picked up God knew where and were holding prisoner until they finished with her.

He watched as the girl came back with an armful of sticks and some punk gouged from the dry hollow of a fallen tree. She walked painfully, dragging the chunk of iron. There were open sores on her free ankle. Nice of the bastards to switch the chain.

Eagle made up his mind. Against his better judgment. Indians were forever getting the shitty end of the stick, the same here as in the United States, and here was a chance to hit back. Eagle smiled. Merlin would have a stroke if he knew what Eagle was contemplating. Endangering the mission for a dirty little Indian girl.

184

The girl made a small fire and began to cook in an assortment of blackened pots and pans. The two men watched her and passed the bottle back and forth. Eagle had their number—roughnecks, probably good oil men, but not very junglewise. He could take them any time. But it might be better to leave them to the Indians.

He dismissed the thought. No. He couldn't do that. Not even to filth like this.

He got closer and watched the girl. Under the dirty calico dress she was a nubile little thing. Small-breasted, tight-waisted, a little over four feet tall. Bare filthy feet. Her black hair was cut short and banged over her eyes. Eagle could not get a good view of her face. She worked steadily and skillfully, frying some kind of meat and using a can opener with ease.

Obviously she had been around white men enough to pick up a little English. When the food was hot she filled two tin plates and thrust them at the men, saying "Chow now—you eat."

The bald man laughed and put his plate on the ground. He pushed a hand into her loose dress and squeezed one of the little breasts. "You're so damned right, Chikka. Eat first and then fucky-fuck, huh?"

The girl stood immobile, her flat face impassive as the man's hand toyed with her. When he released her she said, "Not fucky-fuck now. Fucky-fuck after eat."

She filled a plate for herself and squatted by the fire, arranging the chunk of iron so it would not interfere with her movements.

The pilot pushed back his Aussie hat and looked at his companion. "You know, Pete, you're a degenerate sonofabitch."

The bald man laughed. "Ain't it the truth, though. But I notice you fuck her same as me."

The pilot picked his teeth. He took a drink from the bottle and regarded the girl. "Yeah. Beats whacking your meat. You know how long since I seen a white woman? I mean one I could stand going to bed with?"

The bald one took the bottle back and drank. He scratched his pate and examined the scurf under his nails. "Sure I know—about nine months now. Same as me. But we could do a lot worse. At least she's clean."

"I sure as hell hope so," said the pilot. "Not that we got any guarantees about that."

"Pretty much," said the bald man. "We had her going on a month now and our cocks ain't dripping. What more you want?"

The pilot laughed. "I'll tell you—when we get back to the town I want a Wassermann. That's what I want. I'll admit she's not clapped up, but about the old syph I worry."

The girl finished eating. She took the plates from the men and began to clean them with dirt and sand. The men took out cigars and lit up. Eagle moved closer, right to the edge of the bamboo. He was within thirty feet of the fire and he wondered if the girl knew he was there. She made no sign.

Eagle listened for a moment, concentrating. Sniffing. He could smell pig somewhere near, over the cooking and whisky odors, and he heard two macaws calling. Then a fox. Another fox. A third fox.

That was it. The foxes. Not foxes.

Eagle began assembling the rifle. It was hard to be accurate with a bow while lying down.

The girl squatted on her haunches, silent, staring at the ground. The pilot shifted his hat over his eyes. The bald man drank and wiped the bottle neck with his hand and passed it over.

Eagle moved a stalk of bamboo. The girl was staring directly at him. Her expression did not change. She knew and she was not going to warn them. Eagle understood that, understood hate that would make her die rather than warn them. She thought he was an Indian.

There was time. They had lost one man and would not come rushing in. They would surely attack, but in their own time.

He weighed the situation. He would have to kill the two men. If he didn't the Indians would. But only after a long time. Indians were good at prolonging life while skinning and roasting their captives. Eagle would be doing them a favor.

The bald man stretched and groaned. "Sure beats working, don't it, Clay?"

The pilot reached for the bottle. "I reckon it does. I feel a little guilty, though."

"Guilty? You?"

The pilot nodded. "Sure I do. Some. Not enough to change my ways, though."

Both men laughed.

Pete and Clay. Enough for a headstone. Not that there would be any headstones.

"One thing bothers me," said the pilot.

The bald man, Pete, yawned. "What's that?"

Clay looked at the girl, then lowered his voice. Eagle barely made out the words. "I don't much like the idea of pushing her out of the chopper."

Pete, the bald one, gave him a look. "I figured that was bothering you. Now you listen to me—don't go chicken shit on me! What the hell you think we can do with her? Take her back to the camp and turn her loose? Let her tell her people what happened? Or go squeal to the missionaries? No way we can do that, Clay. We do and it's our ass. We'll be up to our neck in legal shit. So stop worrying about it. When we're finished with her we push her out at five thousand. You don't have to do it. I will."

The pilot shook his head. "I still don't like it. I wish we could just let her go. Suppose someone sees us and—"

The bald man cut him short. "We do it at night. No chance of anyone seeing it."

Eagle had the rifle assembled. The special magazine held three shots. He slipped in two ball cartridges, regular 303, and one explosive. He waited until the

187

bald man laughed again, harsh as a curassow, and closed the bolt with an oily *snuck*.

The pilot was saying, "Laugh if you want to, but that story has got the Indians plenty riled up. I don't feel real comfortable sitting here."

The bald man drank. "A crazy rumor. Nothing to it. Some witch doctor probably started it. It don't make sense, Clay. Why would white men go around cutting the balls off Indian boys?"

The man named Clay glanced around uneasily. His glance passed the patch of bamboo where Eagle lay.

"I don't know why. And I agree it don't make no sense. But I heard the story enough—where there's smoke there's gotta be fire, you know. A party of white hunters has been killing young Indians and cutting off their balls. I even heard the government was sending in an investigator and some troops."

Baldy laughed. "Some good that will do. Some spic shavetail that can't find his ass with both hands. Come on, Clay. Drink up and stop worrying. We been here before and never had any trouble. Besides I know these parts pretty good—there ain't an Indian north of the Igara."

A fox barked to the south. From the east came an answer. Eagle's mouth twitched. Famous last words.

The bald man stood up. "But since you're such a nervous nelly let's get it done and be on our way. Who goes first this time?"

"Me. You went first last time. And you leave a damn sticky trail, I'll tell you."

The Indian girl watched the pilot approach. Her expression did not change as he unzipped himself and stood before her. He was half tumescent, his penis a drooping arc of veined purple-white flesh. She still squatted. He seized her hair and pulled her forward. "You sucky-suck."

Baldy farted with his mouth. "You are nervous, man. You can't even get it—"

The bamboo arrow made a *zzzzzzz* sound. It

188

slashed through the bald man's throat. *ZZZZ ZZZZ ZZZZ* Three in the chest. The bald man was a feathered pincushion.

The pilot ran for the helicopter, his penis still hanging out. The bald man screamed. He was flopping about. Eagle put a hand out of the bamboo and crooked a finger at the girl. She hobbled toward him, carrying the piece of iron.

The pilot was half into the helicopter when an arrow pierced his back. He clung to the door, making sounds, looking down at the six inches of arrow protruding from his chest. He did not believe it.

Eagle had not yet seen an Indian. The girl slid into the bamboo beside him. Eagle made a shushing motion and pushed her down. Her eyes, narrow and black in the flat face, glinted with understanding. She lay silently beside him.

The pilot lay half in and half out of the helicopter. The bald man no longer flopped. Eagle waited. Surely they had seen the girl.

Four arrows *zzzzzzed* in and plunked into the pilot's back. He made noises. His body tilted and fell back out of the chopper.

Silence. Nothing moved. Big green flies were already gathering on the bodies.

Five minutes passed. The girl lay unmoving beside Eagle, her body touching his, her breathing as silent as his.

Across the clearing there was movement in the brush. An Indian stepped out of the bamboo. He was tall and wore a headdress of scarlet macaw feathers. He carried a long bamboo spear. He stood for a moment looking at the helicopter and the dead men. Eagle figured it out. They knew about the girl but were in no hurry to find her. They knew she was an Indian. They would expect her to come to them when her fear passed.

The chief raised a hand. A dozen Indians came filtering out of the jungle edge, most of them armed with long bows. As the chief spoke, they listened and answered, glancing at the helicopter now and then but keeping their distance. The chief made a circular motion with a bangled arm. He was telling them to start looking for the girl.

Eagle felt honest regret as he fingered the two ball cartridges out of the magazine, leaving only the explosive cartridge. It had to be done. Once they spread out to look for the girl it would be too late. They would be all around them. If he made the kill now, and made it spectacular enough, the others wouldn't stop running until they reached the Igara River.

He glanced at the girl. She still wore the chain and chunk of iron. Eagle motioned for her to pick up the weight and be ready to run. She nodded, her obsidian eyes bright and intelligent. They might have been the eyes of an Apache child, as dark, and as hard as flint. Eagle gave a nod of reassurance. He could not know what she made of him and did not care. She had cast her lot with him.

He knew the rifle, having proved and zeroed it in Merlin's underground range. He laid the cross-hairs on the chief's forehead, between the eyes, let out half a breath and squeezed gently.

The head exploded, a balloon of blood and brains. Blood spurted high from the torn neck and the body walked upright a few steps before it tottered and crashed down. By that time the Indians were in full retreat. They knew guns, and feared them, but none had ever seen a devil gun that took a chief's head away. They pelted into the jungle, screaming and wailing, in a panic that would not wear off for hours.

Eagle examined the girl's ankle. The chain was held by a small padlock. Eagle looked at the body of the bald man and decided against searching for the key. The Indians were running. Most of them. It only took one, braver and smarter than the others, to foul up everything.

There was a little play in the chain. He took a piece of monkey meat and rubbed it on her ankle until it was well greased. She sat unmoving, watching him without expression. Eagle got his fingers between the chain and her ankle and tugged. The chain would come off. He looked at her and smiled, knowing how he must look in his Apache paint. He put pressure on the chain, holding her ankle in one hand and pulling with the other.

"Maybe hurt," he told her. "Not bad. Not long."

She shook her head. "Not hurt. You do."

He gave the chain a sudden downward wrench, at the same time pushing her foot upward. She watched him. Tears formed in the corners of her eyes but she made no sound.

The chain came off with a scrape of flesh. Eagle smiled at her and indicated the jungle around them.

"You can go. Free."

She watched him with a dark unblinking stare. She showed good teeth in not quite a smile and shook her head.

"Not go. Afraid."

She pointed to herself. "Jivaro."

Eagle nodded understanding.

She pointed to the headless body of the chief. "Yuna. No good. Much kill. Me. I go you."

Eagle did not argue the point. She might come in handy. There was no time to think about it now.

He studied the airstrip intently. Touch nothing, he decided. It told its own story. The headless Indian would puzzle the search party, when and if they came, but they wouldn't be able to figure it out. Or care much. They would bury the remains, what was left by that time, and salvage the chopper unless the Indians came back to burn it. Even if they talked to the Yuna they wouldn't get much sense out of them.

There was nothing here that could tie him into the thing, or in any way warn of his presence in the jungle.

It was time to start. He set about gathering his possessions. When he was packed to his satisfaction the girl reached for the musette bag.

"I carry."

XVIII

HER NAME WAS Chikka. Thrust your tongue against the front teeth for the "chik" and open your mouth wide for the explosive "ka." She was like a little cockroach with flexible bones that could slip through any narrow crack. One day with her taught Eagle enough to repay any trouble she might be or cause. She slipped through the jungle like a wraith, finding passage where there was none, leading him through tangled creeper and liana and close-growing ironwood as though they were strolling on a sidewalk. At times he was hard put to keep up with her. Despite a late start they made ten miles that first day.

As darkness began to usurp the eternal green gloom of the jungle they came to a pool. Chikka looked at Eagle. "Eat here. Sleep. Good."

He gave assent. It would be a cold camp. He did not want to risk a fire so soon. Chikka put the musette bag down and disappeared into the brush. She did not attend to her natural functions before a man. Eagle had noted this and took it as evidence that a good part of her young life had been spent around white men. He did not think missionaries were the answer. She did not appear to be a church Indian. Her language, for one thing. She used foul language without much idea of what it meant. As a child would use swear words it had overheard.

She came back with fruit and nuts. These and the cold monkey meat made an adequate supper. As she set about preparing the meal Eagle headed for the pool. To his amazement he was feeling very weary. The girl had set a rugged pace and she was far more jungle-wise than he. More than that, he wanted to wash off the mud and paint and let her see him in the living flesh. She seemed to have adopted him, for now, but she did not know he was a white man. They had spoken very little and Eagle had confined himself to broken English and Apache. The latter caused Chikka to roll her eyes and shake her head. She took it for an Indian dialect she had never encountered before.

Eagle wanted her to accept him as a white man. She was a treasure and could be useful to him. What he did not want was misunderstanding or treachery. There would be times, and sleeping was only one of them, when he would be at her mercy. He had to know he could trust her.

He studied the pool, stripping down as he did so. It looked cool and inviting.

"No yet," the girl called to him. "No big-assed Buick good." She pushed him aside and began to toss stones into the pool. She found a long stick and stirred the water, at the same time staring at him in reproof and shaking her head. "Big-ass Buick bad."

He had given up trying to puzzle *that* out. Somewhere she had picked up the phrase, big-ass Buick, and she used it to full potential and a bit beyond.

Chikka stirred the pool with the stick until two snaky heads popped above the surface. Eels. Probably electric, with a charge that would knock a man out. Eagle joined her in hurling stones. They routed a small stingray and two more eels. Chikka nodded. "Now okay. No big-ass Buick."

Eagle washed away the mud and paint. When he emerged, clean and dripping, she made a long inspec-

194

tion of his naked body. Her narrow black eyes gave nothing away. At last she grunted and nodded, showing small clean teeth in what he took as approval. She handed him meat and fruit wrapped in a leaf.

"Eat."

After they ate she went into the pool. She splashed for a long time and came back carrying the calico dress. She wrung it out and hung it over a liana. Eagle saw that she had made herself a necklace out of bright-colored nuts. Eternal feminine wiles, he thought with a chuckle. Even in the jungle.

He arranged his defenses for the night. The rifle and the bow and quiver, the hatchet, were near to his hand. The musette bag made a pillow for both of them. She lay in his embrace, her short hair still damp from the pool, her body relaxed against his and smelling of some vague jungle scent.

For a little time Eagle allowed the white man to return. The educated man who had read W. H. Hudson and knew of Rima—the worldly sophisticated man who could not survive for an hour in this jungle.

Rima. *Green Mansions*. Bird girl. He listened to a band of howler monkeys, heard something slither, noted the hunting sound of a jaguar. He wondered if Hudson had really ever been in a jungle.

Chikka said, "You want fucky-fuck?"

Eagle was limp. Tired. When he did not answer she took his soft member in both hands and rubbed it briskly between her palms like a fire stick.

"Chikka want fucky-fuck. You want?"

She rubbed her nose against his.

Eagle said, "How come fucky-fuck with me? You not like it with other white men."

"They bad. Bad-ass Buick. You good."

Eagle had to chuckle. "I am good-ass Buick?"

"Yes. Good. They steal Chikka. You save. You want fucky-fuck Chikka?"

She put his penis in her mouth and laved it with her

195

tongue. Eagle came tense and erect, pulsating. After a moment she slid up to straddle him.

"I do."

When she slept against him, her head pillowed on his chest, Eagle thought that it was like making love to a wild animal. Sweet and violent. Dangerous. He could not peg the danger, but the thought occurred.

Before they left the next morning he drew a map in the soft mud near the pool. He drew in the main rivers and indicated the directions. Chikka squatted in her ragged calico dress and squinted as she tried to understand. At first he did not think he was getting through, but when he pointed out the Ecuadorian border and the Napo River she shook her head.

"Bad. Bad-ass Buick. Secoya people. Bad—bad. Me Jivaro." She pointed to the south of a cross he had drawn in the mud.

"There me. There Jivaro. Me you take there. No Secoya. Bad. Hate Jivaro. Hate *apaci* too. Kill."

Eagle smiled. It was a coincidence, and one she did not understand, but the Jivaro name for whites was *apaci*. Pronounced Apache

It was the first inkling that she expected him to take her back to her people. It explained her ready adoption of him. Maybe it explained fucky-fuck. Why did not matter. He was lucky to have her. He did not intend going out of his way, but he would take her as close to her tribe as possible. The least he could do. She was going to save him a lot of time.

So it proved. They made two hundred miles in twelve days, a great deal of it on the rivers. She was a better canoe thief than he was and held her own with the paddle. They ate well. Eagle killed wild pigs and one capybara, a sixty-pound creature resembling a rat with a flat nose. Chikka mixed new paint for him and made him a new headdress of scarlet cock-of-the-rock feathers. She washed herself and her dress at every opportunity and every night they slept together. During

196

the day she would sometimes reach to touch him for a moment, to stroke his arm or his face, or touch his hair. She seldom smiled. But she talked. How she talked. At times serious, at times with a droll humor, sometimes chattering like a manic monkey, at times sad and with moist eyes.

Eagle was touched by the pains she took to make herself desirable to him. She cleaned her teeth morning and night with a twig shaved to a brush end. She plucked her body hair. She scrubbed the calico dress until it was all but falling apart. Once when she did not know he was watching she cut a small wooden plug and fitted it into a hole in her lower lip. He had thought it a scar. He said nothing, but she threw the plug away. Instead she made herself earrings and a new necklace of stones and shells.

One night, after they had made love, she was restless and could not fall immediately to sleep. A jaguar had made a kill nearby and the jungle was uneasy. Chikka told him how the men, Pete and Clay, had stolen her. Bit by bit, piece by piece, Eagle figured it out.

For some years the Ecuadorian government had been building a road from the eastern slopes of the Andes into the jungle. Eventually it would link with the trans-Amazon highway now under construction. Indian labor was used whenever possible. Jivaro men who worked on the road sometimes took their women with them.

Eagle, because of his briefing, was fairly well informed about the Jivaro. They were fierce warriors— among the most warlike tribes in the Americas. Much given to shamans and witchcraft, bitter blood-feuders, and skillful in taking and preserving heads. *Tsantsa.*

His guess was that they made poor workers. Chikka said no. The men worked hard and bought shotguns with their wages. When they had enough money they walked off the job.

Chikka had been living with some other Jivaro

women near the construction. Some of the women were whores.

"Me not," she told him. "Me good girl. Not bad. Not fucky-fuck for pay. Very bad-ass Buick business. Husband catch, kill."

Eagle had to agree that getting caught was pretty bad-ass Buick. "Men in flapping machine come," she said. "Stay for time. Much go to women. Drink much bad-ass Buick."

She put her thumb in her mouth, tilted her hand and made a gurgling sound. "Drink all time. See me one time. That night steal me to flapping machine."

Eagle smoothed her hair. "You fight? Scream?"

She nodded. "I do. They hit. Hurt much. I not know what happen. I dream. I wake up, am in flapping machine. Much afraid. They take me many places, tell me kill if I do not do them what they say. I do. Not want die."

A not uncommon occurrence, Eagle thought. Men who looked for oil and gold in the jungle—men who built roads through it—were rough types. They usually regarded Indians as vermin—the men to be exterminated, the women to be used. He believed her. It must have happened exactly as she told it.

"We will come near to your country soon," he told her. "You can return to your people."

She did not answer. Her silence puzzled him a bit. Chikka usually had an opinion about everything.

They left the worst of the jungle behind. It was no longer a near solid lattice of liana and creeper tying the massive *jatoba* and *sepupemba* together. Eagle had less use for the machete. Fewer leeches sucked at them. Deer were plentiful and he made a fresh kill every day, leaving behind what they did not eat. Once, as they were about to leave a camp, they watched a sixteen-foot boa, too lazy to hunt for its dinner, slide in and engorge most of a deer they had left.

On the thirteenth day, crossing a long savanna where parched grass grew waist high, Eagle caught a glimmer of silver-topped hills in the distance. Nearer to them, where the jungle set in again, low growing and scrubby, a buzzard wheeled in lazy circles. Not a condor. Eagle would know a condor when he saw it. Saw them. Saw many condors whirling and planing over the nests of their young.

He was pleased. He reckoned to be within a hundred miles of his objective. The land had a gentle uptilt and the nights were cool, the terrain still easy but with a hint of gorges, cliffs and mountains to come. He took a sun reading, with the aid of his compass and sticks; that night was clear and he checked his figures with a star reading, hoping for accuracy within fifty miles. By guessing at the distance covered since the confluence of the Tiputini with the Napo he reckoned they were well inside Ecuador. So far they had encountered no one, and he had no sense of being watched. Eagle, as sharp as he was, depended on Chikka for that—she would know before he did. It was her country.

A little too much her country, as he found when he had finished his computations. It was dead reckoning, using crude instruments, but he had an Apache's sense of direction and would have bet that he was within fifty to seventy-five miles of where he thought he was.

Where he was, was too far to the south. Too close to Jivaro country. When he pointed this out to Chikka she gave him a flat black stare and said nothing. The next morning, when Eagle set a course to the northwest, she was still silent. You could, he thought, even call her mood sullen. He said nothing and by noon she was smiling and chattering again.

During the day they quietly bypassed two villages. Eagle studied them with binoculars from a crag. They were ramshackle affairs, stone and tile houses flung into a valley and forgotten, capsuled, sealed off from time and progress. Wheat grew on the valley terraces and there was a scattering of lofty eucalyptus trees. Men and women worked in the fields with horses and donkeys. Dogs ran and barked. Eagle was always wary of dogs, great either as guards or betrayers, but none of the animals caught their scent.

In late afternoon they threaded their way down steep gullies into more jungle. In this last bastion they found a long-dead rubber plantation. Eagle thought it too far west for rubber, but he had to believe his eyes. The jungle had long ago reconquered the plantation, but the mansion house was still there. Eagle decided they would spend the night among ghosts.

The rubber trees had long ago gone wild. Bamboo, twined with liana and creeper, had taken over the *campo*. Overgrowth covered the stables and outbuildings, the labor shacks and smoking sheds, like a green scab. Only the mansion, rotting away in its clearing, retained a hint of prideful configuration, of glory past. It reminded Eagle of an antebellum mansion that might once have stood in Alabama or Mississippi.

It had been gutted long ago. Floors rotted away and staircases fallen, the windows open green sores where vine and weed flourished. Chikka did not want to enter at first.

She scowled. "Bad-ass Buick place."

It had been wuthering all day, coming on to rain, and now thin sheets of moisture gusted over the *campo*. Eagle grinned at her.

"Not bad-ass Buick. Good-ass Buick. We camp here. If you want to sleep in rain, or in jungle by yourself, plenty okay with me."

She gave him a resentful look. "No like sleep alone. No can have fucky-fuck alone."

Eagle patted her behind. "All right, then. Into the library. After you, madam."

Only one corner of the library had fallen in. They made camp where the flooring was still sound and Chikka set about preparing supper. Eagle checked over his gear, laying it out on bookshelves still clinging to the wall. The shelves were covered with green fungus, but still solid. Eagle wondered briefly about the house —the rubber boom had collapsed in 1912—then winked at Chikka, who scowled at him, and went to stand near the gaping entrance. The door had fallen years before.

There was a stillness in the matted surround of jungle that Eagle did not understand or like. He watched a big cat, probably an ocelot, streak across the far end of the *campo* and vanish. He listened for monkeys and heard none. This was not real jungle, they had left that behind, but it was jungle enough, even if isolated from the main, to contain more sounds than he could hear. It was too quiet. For a minute he stood unmoving, hardly breathing, listening to the silence. Nothing. No foxes, no macaws. Nothing.

Suddenly they were there. Six of them, painted on the face and chest, their hair slicked into war knots with red paste. They must have been lying in the tall grass near the *campo*, as unseen and silent as death. Eagle did not bat an eye. He did not call to Chikka or look in her direction. The rifle was in its tubing in the musette bag and the bow and quiver was standing against the wall inside. He carried the hatchet twisted into his G string and the machete were in his hand. The machete was no help. Two of the Indians—one who must be the leader—carried shotguns. Ancient weapons, rusty and pitted, with percussion locks. They were probably loaded with buckshot, or round pebbles —either one could degut a man at close range.

Eagle smiled. He held up his right hand, palm out, and spoke to them in Apache. "Welcome, my brothers. I am glad you come in peace. I am a peaceful man myself. I would be greatly honored if my brothers would stay and share food with me."

None of the Indians spoke. They stared at him, then at each other, then at him again. One of the shotgun carriers cocked his piece. It was leveled at Eagle. He ignored it. A lot depended on Chikka. These were nervous Indians. Two shotguns and four bamboo arrows were pointed at him. One wrong move, or word, and they were both dead.

Chikka spoke from behind him. Eagle did not turn.

201

He kept smiling and looking at the Indian he thought must be the leader. The Indian, his face painted and wearing a feathered crown, stared back. His eyes were the color of strong tea. Cold tea.

Chikka was still speaking, softly and rapidly, in something that Eagle thought could only be Quechua, a kind of lingua franca used in the eastern Andes. But for a rare word he could not follow it.

It seemed to be working. The leader lowered his shotgun and took it off cock. The other shotgunner followed suit.

Chikka was at Eagle's elbow. Without looking at him she said, "Be much careful. This very big bad-ass Buick. Maybe they kill."

He smiled at the chief. "Who are they? What do they want?"

"Achuara. Bad men. Enemy of Jivaro. I think come south look for Jivaro girl, maybe big-ass Buick war with Jivaro people."

The chief said something to Chikka. The six Indians moved in to form a ring about them. They made no move to take the machete or the hatchet. This puzzled Eagle. He did not at the moment see a way out. The trouble was as bad as it could be.

The chief, a squat man with stumpy muscular legs, pointed to Eagle's head and spoke to Chikka. She explained to Eagle.

"He want your hat. Thinks big-ass Buick hat fine. Wants."

Eagle took off the tattered, crushed and befeathered derby and handed it to the chief. "Tell him I make him a present and wish nothing in return. Say I am happy that he is happy."

The Achuara chief paid no attention to Eagle. He turned the derby over in his hands, grunting and hissing with delight. The other Indians gathered around. One of them reached to touch the derby and the chief let out a cry of rage and slapped the hand away. For the moment the Indians appeared to have forgotten

202

Eagle and the girl. So Eagle thought until he made a tentative move to get nearer the weapons in the library. Two of the Indians moved between him and the entrance.

Chikka touched Eagle's hand. "You do good. Not spoil. I think maybe now they not kill. Take me but not kill."

"What will they do to you?"

Her eyes, blank as black buttons, met his. She shrugged. "Not know. Think maybe much fucky-fuck. Not kill. Maybe take me Jivaro country, let me go."

Eagle did not think so. He did not think they would kill her, she was young and strong and, by Indian standards, beautiful. They would not kill her. Neither would they let her go back to her own people.

The chief, having discarded his feathers and placed the derby on his red-plastered hair, spoke sharply to Chikka. He pointed at Eagle, then at two of his men. The two Indians went into the house. In a moment they came back carrying the musette bag and Eagle's bow and quiver.

Eagle did not show his frustration and anger. Only coolness could get him out of this.

The chief was still pointing at Eagle and speaking in Quechua. Eagle allowed himself a luxury. "What does the sonofabitch want now?"

Chikka did not understand the word—to her it made as much sense as big-ass Buick—but she caught his tone. Her eyes warned him.

"Not talk bad. They kill quick. They say you sit down, they tie. Take me. Take all yours. Leave you. No trouble and not kill."

Eagle nodded. "Tell them I do. I do not want trouble. Do you want to go with them?"

She blinked. "Not want. Want stay you. No can. No want them kill you. Kill me. I go. I go goodbye big-ass Buick. Much goodbye."

They slashed lianas into convenient lengths and bound Eagle well. He was puzzled, though grateful, that they did not simply kill him and have it over with. His Apache mind could not account for it. An Apache *would* have killed him.

He did not have to watch them having sex with Chikka. The Indians ignored her except to feel her legs and examine her teeth. There was nothing sexual about it. They examined her as they would a work animal, any beast of burden. From what he could put together Eagle got the idea that Chikka would be community property, with the chief being number one in the saddle.

Okush, the chief, went through the musette bag with much interest and care. He could not figure out the aluminum tubes and tossed them to one side. Eagle breathed a trifle easier. If they left him the rifle he still might be in business. He did not doubt his ability to survive, but without the rifle he could not do his job.

A heavy rain fell as the Indians prepared to leave. Having bound Eagle securely they ignored him. Okush kept admiring the derby and trying it on. He did not seem to care when Chikka spoke to Eagle.

"You maybe okay now," she told him. She squatted beside him and touched his face. "I tell them you white man sick in head, live in jungle. So they not kill. Not like kill white man. All much big-ass Buick afraid of soldiers come."

Eagle nodded understanding. She had saved his life.

Chikka touched his cheek. "You not come me. I okay maybe. Do much fucky-fuck and be okay. You not come me. They kill."

Eagle nodded again. "I will not come after you, Chikka. I have things to do. There is not much time. You understand?"

She rubbed her nose against his and whispered, "Okay. Understand; I go now. Have much big-ass Buick love for you."

Okush, tired of preening with the derby, spoke sharply. The Indians began to load Chikka with various gear. Okush came to stare down at Eagle. There was a glint of mockery in his tea-colored eyes. He pointed to

204

his chest, then to Eagle, and spoke in Quechua. Eagle caught the word *soldier* now and then. He guessed that Okush was taking credit for sparing his life and wanted the fact passed on if the soldiers came.

Eagle nodded and smiled. It came hard. What he wanted was the chief's guts all over the *campo*.

Chikka was not permitted to speak to him again. One of the Indians went back to the scattered aluminum tubes, examined them, was baffled by the tight-fitting caps and with sudden rage flung them far into the bamboo. Eagle kept his face impassive.

They took everything but his breechclout. One of them pulled off the anklets Eagle had taken from the dead Yuna. They left him lying bound in the rain. As they filed south into the jungle Chikka glanced back at Eagle. The Indian behind her cuffed her hard about the face.

For a time he lay unmoving. It was raining harder and soon the lianas binding him would give a little. In an hour, maybe half that, he would be free. Free to get on with the mission. Without food or weapons—unless he could find the tubes—and with no compass or map. It was, he admitted, going to make things a lot tougher than he had reckoned on.

Eagle began to laugh. He was a poor bare-ass Indian if there ever was one! He laughed again. Merlin and company, any of his friends in the white world, would have thought he was a sure candidate for the funny farm, but Eagle knew better. And it *was* funny. Talk about a poor-ass Indian—he didn't even have any pants. All he had was a strip of bark twisted into a crude, rough G string. You couldn't get any poorer than that.

The humor faded and Eagle got to work. It took him half an hour to writhe out of his bonds. He did not waste time searching for the tubes. That must wait until morning. He skirted the house and went back where the labor shacks and curing sheds lay in moldering ruin. Slowly, with infinite patience, he began to sift through rotted wood, crumbled brick and stone, sawdust and debris of every sort. For hours he worked without result. The rain stopped but low-hanging clouds shrouded the *campo*. A chill mist engulfed him. Eagle moved from shack to shack, squatting in the ruined foundations and sifting detritus through his fingers.

Shortly before morning he found it. A rubber knife. Really nothing more than a farrier's knife, with a curving blade to slash the trees. Eagle settled back on his heels with a sigh of relief. This piece of rust-eaten steel was a treasure. He went back to the house and slept.

XIX

IN FIRST LIGHT he searched for the tubes. He found the rifle tubes easily enough but the smaller tube with the ammo eluded him. When at last he spotted it a thin green snake was guarding it. Eagle cursed. *Ferde-lance*. A five-minute death. He didn't even know if they *had* a vaccine for it.

He retreated and searched for a rock. By the time he got back to the tube, the snake had disappeared. Eagle snatched up the tube.

He had any number of things to do. The snake, along with the chill night mist, reminded him that a twist of bark around his butt was not enough. His feet were in bad shape. Every inch of his hide was bitten and bumpy. He had read of great plans, grandiose schemes to exploit the jungles, but he had news for them. Get rid of the insects first! The biters and stingers were more of a menace than all the crocs and snakes and Indians put together.

Mud was no good in this clime, and as he got farther into the Andes it would get colder. He knew that rubber trees would survive, at poor yield, as high as two thousand feet. He was about at that altitude now.

He left the *campo*. Okush might have second thoughts. He found a brook and some proper stones and began to whet the knife blade. There was enough tang left to take a hilt and after an hour's hard work he had a passable blade, precariously thin in spots and with no point, but it would serve. He needed an edge more than a point. There would be gouges back there, he supposed, or even a long-buried grindstone, but he did not succumb to temptation. He wanted to forget the *campo*. It had been a defeat. Eagle knew you couldn't win them all, but he did not like defeat. He did not allow himself to think about Chikka. The episode was over.

When the knife was as sharp as he could make it he slashed a strip of bark from a rubber tree and made a temporary haft, binding it tightly with thin liana. He cut two bamboo spears and sharpened them. Lacking a fire he could not harden the points, but they would serve.

From a rubber tree he carved great slabs of cork-like bark. Working with this, and with lianas cut to length, he made himself crude sandals and leggings, a kilt, and a sort of breast and back plate that he wore like a sandwich board. He bathed in the icy brook, its water colored with Andean silt, and donned his new gear. He made a carrying satchel, sort of a knapsack, of bark and put the gun and ammo tubes in it. By this time he was starving.

Eagle followed the brook until he found a broad pool. He lay by it, spears ready, and caught butterflies and tossed them into the pool. No bites. Too deep anyway. His stomach gnawing, Eagle gave up in disgust and moved downstream. There, in minor rapids, he saw the biggest catfish he had ever seen in his life, a monster that could have swallowed a small child. Eagle did not know that it was a *pirarucu* and did not care. It was there, trying to get up the rapids for reasons of its own, and it was food. He put both his spears in it and after a long and bloody struggle got it to the bank.

He did not waste time in finding tinder and making rubbing sticks. He slashed off strips of the still-quivering fish and ate. He thought of Monika Altekruse and her exact words came back: "I hope you like raw fish, Mr. Brookson."

Eagle nodded. He stuffed another strip of fish into his mouth and gobbled. Mr. Brookson was dead. As was Monika Altekruse and Klaus Neidler and Franz Six. Herr Doktor Wolfgang Sechs. *Schutzstaffel.* SS doctor. Once Merlin had the name it did not take long to turn up the facts. Sechs had been a pioneer in sex transplants and during the war he had no shortage of subjects.

The overcast persisted. Eagle found a dry hole under tall leaning rocks and waited for the sun. Until he could draw a quadrant in the mud and take a shadow reading he was lost. Not totally lost. He knew the way out—all preparations had been made—but he was still on his way in. Still had to do his job. Still had to find the valley and the village of Zal. This he could not do without the sun. In that sense he was lost.

It started to rain again. Eagle, dry in his hole, killed time by taking the rifle out of the tubes and assembling it. He wondered what he would have done if the Indians had taken the rifle. Made a bow and arrow and tried to do the job with them? Stolen a gun? Gone right into the village and strangled the man?

He counted out the cartridges, shining them with a piece of bark, and let his mind slip back. How much more he understood now.

The Ecuadorian authorities did a good job of suppressing the story. No newspaper, anywhere in the world, carried the facts. No paper knew the facts. But Merlin knew. Being Merlin, he had ways. It took a few days, but by the time Eagle left for the jungle he knew, or almost knew, as much as Merlin did.

The police, summoned by a terrified mestizo who swam to the mainland, found a shambles. Bodies. Herr Doktor on his own operating table with a scalpel in his chest. Stella Helpern riddled with rifle fire. Two dead

209

men, brawny outdoor types, and four similar types who weren't talking. Two dead. Stella had used the little gun well.

Out of the welter of misinformation and lies and coverup emerged the fact that the police were looking for a mystery man. One Mr. Richard Brookson. A passport check revealed that Brookson had arrived in Quito and had called the office of Helmuth Toller. Phone checks and Toller's secretary confirmed this. Servants at the Villa Vilcabamba, Toller's house near Quito, also confirmed that a man named Brookson had come to dinner. Later that same night the man had flown to Isla de Pelo with Toller and the Altekruse woman.

Eagle broke the rifle down and repacked it. As he poured the burnished cartridges back into their container he wondered how long it had taken them to find Toller. There had been no mention of Toller in any of the reports, other than as missing along with the Brookson person. Eagle smiled as he put the tubes back in his makeshift knapsack—surely the dogs would have nosed out Toller in the locker. After three or four days a man with a head cold would have smelled him.

All that day the sun sulked behind a low-hanging overcast. Eagle remained in his hole and ate cold raw fish. During the night the rain stopped and a chill wind swept down from the *cordillera*. Eagle could have used a blanket, yet he slept well enough. The morning was bright and clear. He made a fire, roasted the rest of his fish and packed it in damp leaves in his knapsack. When he guessed ten by the sun he drew a quadrant in the dirt and took a reading with a stick. He knew his approximate latitude, and longitude did not matter. Nor was he worried about degrees, minutes and seconds. There must be a thousand hidden valleys in the eastern Andes and he could not explore them all.

When he had his bearings he destroyed all traces of his camp and took off, running now, loping at an effortless and mile-consuming pace. Always he climbed, the inclination slight, but always upward. Three times he saw smoke and avoided it. He traveled all day to the west and a bit to the south, crossing two ruts that were supposedly roads and skirting around another desolate village. The terrain roughened. Gorges yawned and he refreshed himself at a waterfall that plunged two thousand feet into jungle. It would be humid down there. Where he stood he could scent snow in the air.

After a day of slogging through murderous country he came, as night fell, to a plateau lying between two soaring vegetation-clad hills. The higher foothills of the Andes.

From cover he scouted the plateau. On the far side, where the rim swooped into a deep *barranca*, was a stone hut. Part of the roof had fallen in. Eagle lay in his rocks for half an hour before he crossed the plateau and entered the hut. It had a smell of men and dogs and in one corner of the dirt floor was an earthen pot with traces of moldy food. Eagle tested it with his fingers. Rice.

The treasure was a sheepskin coat hanging on a wooden peg. Though ancient and smelly, torn in places, to Eagle it was a boon. Coat and blanket in one. He pulled it over his bark vest and went to inspect what lay beyond the ravine.

The light was nearly gone. As he stared to the southwest, through a slot formed by the two foothills, he saw a flare of color. It vanished even as he realized what it was—sunset on high ice and snow. The Andes.

He was close. The valley he sought must lie between this plateau and the first range. All of Merlin's data pointed to that—the valley was isolated, with only an airstrip for small planes and helicopters, but there was a village there, a bit of old Germany, and the climate would be livable. Pleasant in fact. They would not have built a village on a glacier.

For a time he stood there searching the sky, knowing

it was useless. It was too dark to see condors. They would be nesting.

But he would find the condors. Tomorrow or the next day or the day after. They were all the beacon he needed. When he saw the majestic birds wheeling and planing, riding the thermals, he would have come to the Valley of Vultures.

To the Ecuadorian government it was a bird sanctuary—*Valle de Buitre*. To be left alone. Entry forbidden. For years the villagers had acted as wardens for the birds. As recompense the government allowed them to live alone and in peace. They were few and did no harm, made no trouble. Cozy in their valley—*Geier das Tal*.

How very convenient for them, Eagle thought as he went back to the hut.

XX

HE DECIDED TO use the stone hut as a base. That night and half the morning he lay in rock cover at the edge of the plateau and watched the hut. No one came near it. He could read no human sign in the vicinity. When the sun was directly overhead he felt secure enough to move into the hut. He went to the ravine and sighted through the slot in the hills. Shielding his eyes with both hands he stared for a long time and turned away satisfied. There was a glimmer of snow line and occasionally, against the snow and rock, a spiral scroll of wings. Condors?

For the first time he really missed the binoculars. His eyes were superb—what he was seeing was forty miles distant—but the glasses would have been of tremendous help. Eagle grinned. Instead of crying over stolen binoculars he had better get his ass in gear.

He was damned tired of fish. As he was thinking this he cursed himself for a fool. He loped to the hut and got the telescopic gun sight and trained it through the slot. They *were* condors. Five of them swooping and whirling, riding the currents. Eagle searched about and picked up three more of the giant birds. *Vultur gryphus*. He was convinced. Where there were so many of them there had to be a breeding ground, a sanctuary.

For a while longer he watched the birds carve the sky with their ten-foot pinions, searching for carrion.

As he went back to the hut he thought that he and the condors were much alike in that respect—they were both searching for carrion. The condors were not so particular as he, they would eat anything, so long as it was dead.

Eagle's case was different. He was there to make something dead, if at the last moment he so decided. Merlin had left the issue in his hands. It was not a cop-out. Merlin could not be there. Eagle was his proxy. Doing jobs for Merlin was Eagle's business, why he was paid such enormous sums, why he received rich fringe benefits. But he and he alone must make the final decision.

"Your heart and your mind must tell you," Merlin said, "and they must agree. You have been briefed to saturation. You know all that I know. I could tell you what to do, or what I would do in your stead, but I will not. I leave it to you."

Eagle spent the afternoon preparing for tomorrow's journey. He would leave at first dawn and be somewhere near the valley at dusk. Beyond that he had no ideas. This must be done by guess and God, catch as catch can, using the tactics of the moment. Eagle did not mind working that way. Plenty of flexibility.

In the meantime he did not intend to starve. For a time he considered stealing a sheep or lamb—there must be sheep, and shepherds within twenty miles; his plateau was well cropped and the hut built for shelter—but he decided it was too risky. So far he had not seen or heard anyone or any domestic animals. Back a few miles he had seen droppings, either llama or alpaca, but no beasts. This was desolate country. Which did not mean that he could not blunder into a shepherd or a farmer or hunter. Best play it safe and eat what the country offered.

The country did not offer much. He was above ten thousand feet and though there were plenty of trees and scrubby brush there was no fruit for the plucking. He wanted something more nourishing than pine seeds. He was not familiar enough with the local berries and roots to risk eating them. As he studied the plateau and gnarled rock formations—mostly gneiss, mica schist and other ancient crystallines—his stomach growled and he considered how to fill it. He dared not light a fire. The shepherd who had left the coat in the hut might not come this way for weeks and Eagle did not want to hurry him. Water was also a problem—it would be a dry as well as a cold camp.

Just as he decided he must starve a little longer—either that or eat more of the goddamned fish—he heard the squeal. Some small animal in terror of death. Eagle loped toward the sound, into a maze of broken and leaning boulders, in time to see a mountain fox vanishing. All he saw was a glint of silver fur with something dangling from its mouth.

Eagle dropped to his hands and knees, his bamboo spear at the ready, and prowled the rocks where the fox had been. The fox spoor was strong, but the underscent was there and very near him. In a few minutes he spotted the nest beneath the overhang of a boulder. Cavies. Plump tailless little rodents. The mother guarded them dauntlessly. There was no sign of Dad. Eagle speared the mother and the litter. He skinned them then and there and cut them into bite size. He ate until his belly protruded, then wiped his bloody hands and mouth on the coat and went back to the hut. He thirsted but there was no water on the plateau. He could wait. Once he had endured three days without water. When he started for the valley he would find water.

It would be a day of hard and fast travel, for he must be near the village of Zal when night came. That would give him darkness in which to prowl and lay out the careful design of the assassination. If he went through with it.

ZAL.

How myth-loving the bastards were. RESEARCH had come up with the background. The concept of Zal was worthy of Goebbels himself. Zal was a divinity of Persian myth. Purest Aryan. Also, as Merlin had permitted himself to say, purest horseshit.

But it fitted, it all fitted. Blood myth. The Valhalla Club. The Demogorgon Society. Barbarossa and the Seven Sleepers. How it all interlocked and dovetailed. It was all there.

But was *he* there?

Eagle curled up in a sheltered corner of the broken hut, wrapped in the smelly sheepskin coat, and dozed. Thinking back.

He had given Stella Helpern's micro-message in its tube to Merlin's code people. The next day he and Merlin had spoken over the closed-circuit TV.

Merlin said, "Do you have any idea of what was in that tube?"

"No, sir. She said it might be very precious. Or worthless."

"That is the rub," said Merlin.

"I'm going to gamble that she had something," Merlin continued. "That it's precious. You're going back in. Through the back door this time, where they won't expect you. Because *if* the Helpern woman was right you would never get in the front door. They are murderous people and worse when they're frightened. They'll be frightened now. And alert. You have no objection to going back in so soon?"

Eagle shook his head. White Deer was convalescing well—a report had been waiting for him—and Ruth Lame Wolf was inured to his long unexplained absences.

"Very well," Merlin said. "We've proved our first point—there is a neo-Nazi setup in Ecuador. It goes deep, Isla de Pelo seems to have been only the tip of the iceberg, and we cannot cope with all of the

216

ramifications at once. But if the information in the tube is correct we had better act on *that* at once.

"The gist of the tube notes is this—Adolf Hitler had a son."

A rising wind swept across the barren plateau. A few flakes of snow drifted into the shattered hut. Eagle pulled the coat tighter around him and remembered how startled he had been, how he must have looked on Merlin's screen. Not much cracked Eagle's stolidity, but that had. He repeated, parroting, "Hitler had a son?"

"So the tube states," said Merlin. "I will condense.

"Eva Braun could not have children. Both she and Hitler had known this for years. So long as the Thousand-Year Reich endured it did not matter. But the Reich was dying after twelve years and both Hitler and Eva would die with it.

"We know what romantics they were. It makes the tale very nearly credible. Hitler decided he could not die without issue. He must have an heir, a son, to carry on. To grow to manhood and re-establish the Reich. But he had waited until the last moment, it was nearly too late. Operation Phoenix was established ten months to the day before Hitler killed himself and Eva in the *Fuehrerbunker*.

"Operation Phoenix had two parts. One—the getting of a man child. Of the purest and best Aryan blood. Ten such women were procured, I believe the word is well chosen, and the task set about.

"Part two—a thousand youngsters, the best of the Hitler Youth, were chosen. Five hundred boys and five hundred girls. All that remained of the purest strain.

"Four submarines were assigned the task of moving the teen-agers to South America. I am inclined to accept this part of the story. We know the village of Zal exists. One submarine was loaded with gold—plunder, I have no doubt. A check-back reveals that the Ecuadorian government at that time had many strong proGerman elements. Politicians are politicians anywhere in the world and most of them have sticky fingers. Combine a natural sympathy with millions in gold and no prospect of trouble—all the immigrants wanted was a secret place in the Andes where they could be alone and live in peace. And you get the creation of the sanctuary, Zal."

The wind, rising and colder now, moaned across the plateau. It flung a fusillade of hailstones at the hut. Eagle moved to dig a softer place for his hips in the dirt floor, then wrapped himself again in the coat. Freak weather did not bother him. If it snowed he could have a drink. He closed his eyes and went back to remembering.

"Did Hitler get his son? And if he did, was the infant smuggled out of Germany by submarine and taken to South America, to the village of Zal?"

Merlin had hestitated then, had not spoken for a long time. Then he said, "Since your return with the tube, John, I have devoted all my efforts and time and resources to this. As you know they are not inconsiderable. But I do not have a definitive answer. The thing is absurd and impossible on the face of it, and yet it is not that at all. Hitler and the men around him in those last days were capable of imagining it, and perhaps capable of bringing it off.

"One thing points strongly to the possibility—one of Hitler's favorites was a man named Helmuth Toller. He was still in his teens at the time and was a leader of the Hitler Youth with high rank. He disappeared after the war. Nothing was seen or known of him until a few years ago, when he suddenly appeared in Quito using his real name. Where was he for all those years? In Zal?"

At that point Eagle had interrupted. "As important as where, sir, is *why* he showed up at that particular time. It couldn't have been in expectation of a new *Tag*. They aren't strong enough to take over now, and they certainly couldn't have been then."

"I think that was the beginning," Merlin said. "The very beginning. The thin edge of the wedge. Their village, Zal, was safe. Secure and established. A thousand little supermen growing and procreating. And not so secretly — RESEARCH tells me that fifteen years ago the *National Geographic* did an article on the village. A Bavarian enclave in the Andes. Photos and everything. *Lederhosen* and yodeling. The *Jagers*, huntsmen, as guards and keepers of the condor sanctuary. It was all there in the pages of the magazine. No one paid much attention to it."

Eagle stirred under the sheepskin and opened his eyes. Snow was blowing in through the roof. He scooped a handful into his parched mouth.

He remembered saying, "No one knew about Hitler's son then—if he exists."

"That," said Merlin, "is what you are going to have to find out. For if he does exist our time is running short. He would be twenty-seven now. If this thing is not a hoax, and the child was not an imbecile, they have used every one of those years to train him, to prepare him for his task. The Fourth Reich. It could begin in Ecuador as easily as in Germany. Easier. Ecuador has mineral wealth that has never been tapped. Gold and, above all, oil. Oil at this particular time, when the world is running short. They are on their way, whether this man exists or not, and the condor as a symbol of conquest is as valid as the eagle. The world is in trouble. A great many people have lost faith in democracy. Our own country is torn by dissension. We are losing the battle of the dollar. The time is ripe for them. They have been very patient. They will still be patient. It is up to us to see that their patience is not rewarded. When your briefing is completed, John, I will have a last word with you."

After a moment Merlin added, "I will not have the world go down into the darkness again for lack of a stitch in time."

Someone was coming across the plateau. Eagle rolled

219

to his feet and peered from a window, gripping one of the bamboo spears. He did not want to use the rifle. A single gunshot could ruin everything.

She came toward the hut, the wind patterning the ragged calico dress to her body, plastering her dark hair with snow. Chikka.

XXI

SHE CARRIED HIS musette bag and the machete. When she saw Eagle standing in the door of the hut she stopped and gave him a tentative smile. She shivered and her skin was goose-pimpled. Her feet were bare.

"I find," she said. "Have big-ass Buick love for you. I find."

He motioned her in and put the coat about her. He was amazed but not surprised. She was an Indian.

She handed him the machete and the musette bag, her dark button eyes searching his face. "You glad I find?"

Only another Indian could have read his face so well. He was not glad. He was glad about the musette bag, especially about the binoculars—everything but the hatchet was there—but he was not glad about her. She would be in the way.

He gave her the rest of the roasted fish. "I'm glad," he lied. "How did you get away from the Achuara?"

Her thin shoulders moved beneath the sheepskin coat. Her bright dark eyes remained intent on his. Eagle had the impression that she was waiting for him to do, or say, a certain thing. Some one thing which would make all the difference.

Chikka explained that the Achuara had encountered

221

a small party from a friendly tribe and bartered game for drink. She made a sign of drinking.

"All get big-ass Buick drunk. Much fucky-fuck me. Much fight them. Much sleep. I take all and go. Come back you. We fucky-fuck now?"

Eagle shook his head. He was going through the musette bag. It was all there. Something had been added, a brown beer bottle stoppered with a rolled leaf.

He lapsed into the pidgin he used with her. "No time for fucky-fuck. Not time now. Maybe later we do."

He sniffed the bottle. "This make Achuara big-ass drunk?"

Chikka nodded. She looked sulky. "Is yes. I bring you. I think maybe I find we have big-ass marriage drink."

He put the bottle down. Some concoction made from jungle cactus. Thick ropy stuff, it smelled like the mescal Apaches sometimes used.

He smiled at her. "It is good you thought of me. I will drink maybe later. We share it. Now what is this of big-ass marriage?"

Chikka squatted on her heels, pulling the filthy coat about her to cover her bare feet. She nibbled on the last of the fish.

"I want make big-ass marriage you. Love much. Much good fucky-fuck all you want. I not dumb-ass Indian like other. I see, learn. Can do. Have big-ass Buick marriage with you. You take me your tribe."

Eagle shook his head. "No can do that, Chikka. I go soon. Not come back. I have job, work, to do here. A task—you understand? Important task. Big-ass Buick important."

She nodded at him. "I think this. You kill someone maybe. I help."

He kept his face straight, wondering how he could get out of this. He couldn't let her tag along. Not so close to the village. Two people were twice as easy to spot as one. And when he did the job, if he did it, he would be running hard for his life along a preplanned route where split-second timing was all-important. He could not afford excess baggage.

Patiently he sought to explain. The wind howled, blowing snow through the hut, crystals that sparkled as the sun came out and shafted through a window.

When he had finished she said, "You not make marriage Chikka? Not want? Not love?"

He decided against trying to explain. He wasn't getting through to her. He grinned and patted her shoulder.

"I like. Much like. For friend. But no marriage. No can. Job. Work. Then much go fast. Run."

"I run too. Marriage you. Take care you. Be big-ass Buick good wife you."

No use. Eagle made himself look stern. "No! Not marriage talk any more!"

Still she stared at him. Her eyes never left his face. She did not smile or cry or frown. Her face was immobile, her mouth greasy from the fish. At last she nodded.

"Chikka understand. Marriage no good."

Eagle smiled at her. "That's my girl. Marriage me no good. Much run away. Leave wife, leave baby, leave home—marriage me no big-ass Buick good. You plenty smart girl." He tapped his head. "You smart girl. Not marriage me."

She appeared to accept that. She reached for the beer bottle and pulled the leaf stopper out. She handed it to him with a hint of a smile.

"Is okay. Chikka understand. Be much friend, drink."

He raised the bottle and drank. The stuff was like a thick gruel, cold to the taste and warm to his belly. Sour tasting and smelling and, if you had too much, probably dynamite. He drank half the contents and handed the bottle to her.

Chikka did not drink. She held the bottle in both hands and stared at Eagle. A dark unblinking stare. He pointed at the bottle. "You drink."

She put the bottle down. "Not drink. Save maybe for go. Long time walk to my people."

He felt better about matters. She was going to be sensible. He looked at the musette bag. She had brought his compass and binoculars, invaluable from now on, and he owed her for that.

He pointed to himself and then to her. "We always be much good friend. I fix you presents someday. Not now. Come back maybe. Maybe send. Money. Presents. All much big-ass Buick good. Okay?"

A pleasant flame drowsed in his belly. That cactus juice did the trick in a hurry.

Chikka shook her head. "Not want. Want marriage you."

Eagle laughed and shook his head. "No big-ass Buick deal. Not talk of that."

He could not move. He could breathe, barely with a great sense of constriction, but he could not move. Could not talk. He could see and he could hear, but with all his great strength and will power he could not move his little finger.

Chikka stood up and came toward him. She picked up the machete.

Eagle could not move his eyes. He saw her only when she stood directly in front of him.

Chikka swung the machete. "I big-ass Buick sorry you and me. Not want do. Want marriage you and all time fucky-fuck. Want you take me your people. You not want. Bad."

Eagle could still think. Nothing wrong with his head—yet. She'd mixed some jungle poison and put it in the drink.

The machete moved. Chikka said, "I want marriage you, can not have. You go. I not want that. I much love for you. Take head for remember. Have much love for head. Keep it all time in my house."

Had Eagle not been paralyzed by the poison he would have laughed. As bitter as the irony was, it was funny. Big man! Big Apache warrior. He'd walked

224

right into it. Stupid little Indian girl was going to win. Have the last laugh.

"I do when you big-ass Buick dead," she told him. "Not hurt. No want hurt you. Much love. Keep head always my house. My people know how make small, save head. Not spoil. I keep my house for look at always."

She was out of his line of vision. Eagle closed his eyes. No way out of this. She was Jivaro and she knew, or would have kin that knew, all about shrinking and preserving heads. The thought came—how would he look with a head the size of an orange? Dangling in some Jivaro hut. Would she, when she was a withered crone, fondle the head and remember fucky-fuck?

If Merlin had said it once he had said it a thousand times—you can never think of everything. Something unexpected will always turn up.

Merlin had been right.

Something cold was filling his nose and mouth, suffocating him. Eagle strangled and spat. Snow. He was lying with his face in snow. A mountain of snow. Two inches high. He was alive, lying on the floor of the hut, and the blowing snow had drifted against his face. He moved an arm. A leg. Feeling was back and his body tingled. Chikka had underestimated the dosage and—

Chikka! He rolled over. Only then did he notice that the sheepskin coat had been draped over him. A last-minute change in her primitive heart. She had intended to kill him and take his head for a love remembrance—Eagle did not doubt this—but she had been unable to carry it out. For reasons of her own, reasons he would never know or understand.

She had left the coat to shield him against the cold.

He called out, "Chikka?"

No answer. He had expected none.

He groaned and sat up. His body was coming back to normal. A glance out the window told him that several hours had passed. It had stopped snowing and a westing sun was transmuting the two-inch fall of white

225

into gold. Eagle stood up, rubbing his eyes and temples with snow. He wondered what in the hell she had put in that drink.

Everything was just as it had been when he passed out. She had taken nothing.

He followed her prints across the plateau to the east. Bare feet in the snow. The tracks led down the slope of the plateau and vanished in a wilderness of rocks. Eagle stood for a moment looking at the prints, small and wide-toed, then went back to the hut.

He checked the musette bag and took a compass reading. He was all right for distance and direction and, as he counted back on his mental calendar, he still had two days. Today was the 28th of January.

Eagle was due in the village of Zal on the 30th of January.

"I cannot think," Merlin had said, "that they will let the date pass without at least some celebration. In 1933, on January 30th, Adolf Hitler came to power in Germany. If the man we seek exists, if he is in Zal, they will mark the day."

Eagle scanned the sky. There would be a bright moon, near the full. He might as well take advantage of it. He packed his gear and removed all traces of his stay in the hut.

All that night he traveled, running and walking, the moon silvering his way. When dawn came he was on a ledge high over the valley entrance. There was a shallow cave for shelter and he was protected on three sides by towering rock formations. Beneath his ledge a long slope of scree fell sharply to a cliff overlooking a road twining through the valley entrance.

As Eagle settled in he heard the whine of wind in pinions. He glanced up. A condor glided over him, its shadow enlarged by the rising sun, feet down for a landing. Eagle lifted the binoculars from the musette bag and trained them on the giant bird.

The bird was resting. It was a hundred yards to Eagle's right and slightly above him. If it knew of his presence it did not appear disturbed. The powerful glasses brought the image within hand's reach, the cruel beak and naked head, the red neck over a ruff of white. It must have been feeding, for now it cleaned its beak and head on the scree and sand around the perch, rubbing first one side of its head, then the other. Then it began to pluck at its black body feathers, preening itself.

Eagle put the binoculars away and lay on his back. He counted a dozen condors circling in the sky. There would be nests in the little caves pocking the cliffs, some with a single egg, some with the chick, some barren. Eagle did not know all that much about condors. Except that they made an excellent homing signal. They had led him to this valley.

The condors had their prey. Now he must find his.

With his gear he crawled back into the little cave and slept. Just before he dropped off he heard it. Doubting at first, waking just enough to make sure, then dropping back into sleep with a smile.

Far down there, somewhere in the valley, someone was yodeling.

XXII

EAGLE SPENT THE 29th of January in his eyrie. His fellow birds of prey, the condors, took no notice of him. There was a nest somewhere in the cliff face above him and at times he heard the hungry complaints of a chick. After a time Eagle was satisfied that he was not noticeably disturbing the condors. This was important, for they were taking security measures in the village.

The binoculars were tinted and he did not have to worry about sun flashes. He lay all day at a loophole in the rocks, scrutinizing and remembering and planning. He was meticulous. He would have one chance. The magazine held three cartridges. Three shots, all explosive 303s, was all he would get. By the time the echoes faded he must be on his way out.

Zal was a picture postcard from Bavaria. It could have been any little village near Ulm or Innsbruck. Steeply pitched snow roofs, balconies and half-timbering, a narrow main street that ended in a little square before the *Burghaus*. Cultivated land terraced up from the village and cattle and horses grazed in the meadows. Frequently through the long day he heard the sound of yodeling. Happy villagers at play. *Gruss Gott!*

His hunger and thirst must be endured. He dared not stir by day and when night came he would be too busy to worry about food or drink. Neither hunger nor thirst would kill him. The good people of Zal would.

Halfway through the morning a helicopter came chopping in from the west. It landed on an airstrip in a meadow beyond the far end of the town from where Eagle lay. A car from the village went to meet it. Eagle's view was partially blocked by a line of eucalyptus trees, but when he picked up the car again it had five people in it. Four must have come in. The distance, he reckoned it five miles, was too far for detail.

The arrival of the helicopter cheered him. So far the village had shown no signs of activity, of any festive spirit. It lay somnolent, slow to wake, with only an occasional man or woman moving in the streets. It occurred to Eagle that today, the 29th, might be devoted to fasting and prayer. The day before THE DAY. *Der Tag.*

Sure enough, around noon, a bell tolled and he saw people leave their houses and head for a *kirche* on the square, catty-corner from the *Burghaus*. Today was Monday. Not regular services. Eagle smiled.

As the day passed and more helicopters and light planes came in his satisfaction grew. Merlin's great fear had been that the man they sought did not move abroad, that he would be, as Merlin had put it, "perpetually *in camera.*" Eagle could not hang about and wait. It was in and out fast or the deal was off.

At the moment it looked as though the deal was on. The last plane, a small Cessna, came in at about four in the afternoon. Eagle, who had been keeping a rough tally, figured that about a hundred men and women had come into Zal. They were gathering for something.

Their security measures did not worry him. There was a half-hearted quality about them that bespoke confidence. A light truck with five men in it came from the village to set up a roadblock a thousand yards below Eagle, where the scree slope ended at the cliff.

They parked the truck at the base of the cliff and built a fire. He could not see them because they were in defilade, but the smell of roasting meat came to him and he could hear singing. The singing he did not mind.

To forget his hunger he placed the compass on a rock and began memorizing his directions for the night. The one road entered the village from the east, the direction from which he had come. It must loop back to the west, following the natural grades. Apart from the airstrip—there were guards there—they did not seem concerned with anything but the road to the west. The only road in and out of Zal. They trusted the wild terrain. They did not think it possible for anyone to come in from the jungle side.

Eagle went back to studying the village, especially the square. He surveyed and calculated distances. After half an hour he put down the glasses, satisfied. It could be done. A shot was possible. If he could get there.

He watched the sun set over the jagged peaks of the true Andes in the far distance. A glacier mirrored the sun, heliographing it, then smashing it into bits of spectrum lost along the lonely peaks. Three condors soared in eminent domain over the nearest peak. Eagle looked away. The sight of snow made him thirstier, if that was possible.

The light was going fast. He made a final check of his gear. For a last time he put the rifle together, checked it out and disassembled it. He checked out the sniperscope. He might use it or might not. He had no way of knowing if it was to be a day shot or a night shot. He hoped for the latter, for before the gunshot echoes died he would be running for his life. That did not greatly worry him. There would be a riot of confusion and it is not easy to source a shot immediately. He would have a head start and that was all he needed. Once he was into the canyons and rock formations they would never catch him and he did not think they would follow him into the jungle. There he would have Merlin's men to interdict and cover his trail.

The mountains vanished in an empurpling shroud. The air chilled and Eagle huddled in the sheepskin coat. Down at the roadblock they were singing *Lilli Marlene* loudly if not well, and with a great deal of shouting. Beered up. Eagle was not old enough to have a sense of *déjà vu,* but it occurred to him that Merlin would have experienced it.

His own thoughts, as he listened to the rowdy singing, were along the lines of—*don't the dumb bastards ever learn!*

He drowsed, using Apache tricks to forget his hunger and thirst, and let his mind wander.

He had spent long hours looking at old pictures of Adolf Hitler. Merlin had an extensive film and clip library. Eagle had studied sketches made of Hitler as a young man, the rare photos of him made before and during World War I, and the profusion of pictures and movies made after he came to power. Eagle concentrated most of all on the old newsreel clips. He studied the body and facial characteristics of Hitler, prepared by a Bertillin expert. He listened to the ranting speeches over and over again.

"You will have a very few minutes to make your decision," Merlin told him. "They will not expose him for long. You must be very sure in your own mind, one way or the other. If you think it is a hoax you will not fire. We do not have to murder a hoax."

Eagle slept until midnight. He awoke easily, at the exact time he had set himself, and listened. All quiet down at the roadblock. The moon was high over foothills to the east. Eagle slung the musette bag into his backpack and left.

He waited until just before dawn, that time of false promise, before he moved into his final position. The village slept, but for a solitary light burning in the *kirche.* Possibly an altar light.

He came in from the west, circling in the rocky hills,

231

and approached along the rim of a high cliff overlooking the square and the *kirche* and *Burghaus*. The edge of the cliff—he had studied every detail carefully through the glasses—was lined with large boulders that formed a rough parapet. The boulders lay in a crazy scatter along the rim and for a time he had toyed with the thought of seeking concealment in them. From this position he would have a clear side shot at the front of the *Burghaus*.

He decided against that. Too risky. The cliff overlooked the neat little municipal building and was perfect for his purpose; it might also be perfect for more innocent sightseers or for lovers. More careful study of the cliff top revealed a path twisting along the edge. There was the possibility that they would post guards there during the ceremony, as lax as their security measures appeared to be. He could not chance it. He would have to get down on the cliff face. With that in mind he had searched and committed to memory, as best he could, the cliff façade.

It was not sheer, which was a blessing. What was not a blessing was that he needed the faint light of false dawn to find the narrow chimney he had spotted with the binoculars. It was the time of greatest risk. For as long as it took him to get down the chimney and out on the ledge that led to the dark opening in the cliff, for that long he would be in plain view of anyone who happend to be awake and abroad, and who happened to glance upward in the direction of the cliff.

Eagle did it as quickly as he could without noise. One stone clattering down could betray him. When he reached the cover of an abandoned condor's nest he let out a long and audible sigh of relief. He settled down to wait. If he had been seen he would know of it soon enough.

The sun came up. Eagle, breathing easier, crept back as far as he could into the shallow cave. There was still evidence, after all the years, that condors had once nested here. A scatter of rotted twigs and small branches and, most discernible of all to his nose, the smell. Most men could not have caught it.

He had chosen the cliff face precisely because of the condor's nest. The cliff was dotted with the cave openings. Eagle had counted more than a dozen. The birds would have gone years ago, the moment the immigrants arrived. Condors would never nest so near to human beings.

The villagers had been seeing those caves for years now. Chances were that they no longer really saw them. Eagle thought himself secure unless he made a mistake, did something to draw attention.

As the sun rose it slanted into the little cave at an angle. Eagle retreated to a dark corner. For the rest of the day, until dark, he would be able to hear but not see. He could stretch and relax his muscles so long as he did not approach the front of the cave. Motion was not a good idea in any case. Motion catches the eye.

His line of vision ran out of the cave and past the church steeple across the square, ending in a thicket on a hillside. There was no cultivated land nearby and no reason why anyone should spy him from the hillside. The weathercock on the steeple could see him—it was a little golden horse—but Eagle reckoned that he would just have to trust the horse.

For a long time he lay and watched the sun creep past the mouth of the cave, layering the floor with liquid butter. It would not reach him in his dark corner. He was very hungry and his thirst had become a torment, even for an Apache. Nothing to be done about it.

All day he lay there, sleeping now and then, waking to listen to the sounds in the village. A pounding of hammers below and to the right suggested they were building a speaker's stand before the *Burghaus*. Eagle smiled and went back to sleep. He awoke again to hear singing and a band playing and remembered the little bandstand near the well in the square. He went back to sleep.

233

When he woke again it was getting dark. He stifled a groan and set about loosening his muscles. He found three pebbles and chewed on them but they did nothing to allay his thirst. There was celebration in the square, songs and the band playing—they must be dancing—and he groaned again as he thought of all that good German beer. Foaming, frothy and cold.

He did not move from his corner until it was totally dark. He stretched and made himself relax and for a moment thought again of those Hitler films. One big shot would not be present out there tonight. One of the films had shown Hitler shaking hands with a tall lad in the uniform of the Hitler Youth. Helmuth Toller had been in his teens, his face like a hatchet, a stringbean of a boy, all legs and clumsy elbows that the well-cut uniform could not disguise. Eagle, when he spotted Toller, had stopped the film and had the shot blown up. Toller gazed at the Fuehrer with doglike devotion.

Eagle squirmed toward the front of the cave. He wondered how long it had taken them to find Toller in the locker.

One glance told him that there was time enough. They were still dancing and singing. As the time approached they would begin to grow quiet.

Eagle began fitting the rifle together. He regretted not being able to use a silencer—it would give him a few more minutes' start—but the muzzle velocity was too high for a silencer. He selected three explosive bullets and slid them into the magazine, then pumped one into the chamber. One up the spout left two. He should need only one.

For the first time he rigged the rifle sling. He would use an elbow hitch to steady it, as he would be firing from prone, and when he ran he could sling it back out of the way. And he would be running.

He did not need the binoculars. He had night lenses for them but he did not take them from the musette bag. Nor did he fit the sniperscope to the rifle. He debated for a moment about that, before tossing the scope back into the bag, then decided not. It was not dark enough out there to benefit from the infrared device. The speaker's platform would be well lighted and the crowd and background would be in shadow. All he needed was the telescopic lens and a steady hand.

Eagle lay on the edge of the little cave and watched, the rifle sling twined around his left elbow, the barrel of the piece resting in his left palm. He had taken off the coat for easier movement. The cave was a little tomb. Cold. Eagle did not mind the cold, or think about it. He thought about food and drink and then, as the moment approached, the decision he must make. He had come a long far hard way for this few seconds.

The square below him was thronged. People were packed elbow to elbow. The crowd spilled into the side streets. Hundreds of torches guttered in the slight breeze, elongated oily flambeaus making the night garish with an undercurrent of threat. Eagle felt it. Medieval. *Walpurgisnacht.* Even the costumes. A great many of the dancers wore *lederhosen* and *dirndls*, the men bronzed and brawny, the *hausfraus* plump and merry, the blonde girls jouncing white breasts in low-cut peasant blouses.

The crowd sound flowed up to Eagle in his niche, was baffled by the cliff and rose skyward. He watched the speaker's stand.

Torches gleamed on the stand. It was decorated with banners and there were three rows of chairs. At the front of the stand was a lectern. The stand had been so erected that it was reached through a window from the *Burghaus.* A drape had been arranged about the window. Eagle studied the arrangement. It was through there he would come. When the crowd was quiet, waiting, he would step through the window and the drapes would part and he would approach the lectern.

He studied the banners and flags decking the speaker's stand. He nodded and smiled. Smart of them. The Ecuadorian flag was above the Nazi flag in every case. They were good citizens of their new country.

235

The swastika was only for remembering. The good old days. Nostalgia. Who could deny them that?

Yeah.

Well-dressed men and women were taking their places on the speaking platform now. No peasant costumes here. They were well turned out and they all wore swastika armbands.

The dance music stopped abruptly. From somewhere powerful spotlights were trained on the speaker's platform. A microphone was being set up on the platform. The crowd gradually hushed. The breeze fell off and the torches burned straighter and brighter, a lurid yellow light.

The band played the Ecuadorian national anthem. There was a scattering of applause. The band swung into *Deutschland uber alles*. The crowd exploded in a frenzy of cheering and shouting. The band switched to the *Horst Wessel* song. The crowd went insane. They sang with all their hearts and lungs. The song filled the Andean night, old voices mingled with young, the tenors and sopranos clear and sweet and childlike.

The song ended. Hush. Eagle watched the speaker's platform. A short bald man was testing the mike.

Einhundert—Dreihundert—Funfhundert—

The Ecuadorian nationalism was wearing a little thin.

Monika Altekruse flashed into his mind. The way she had laughed in the car and said "von hundert." They had been talking about phonies.

The crowd was waiting. Impatiently, for the first speaker did not take much time. He spoke in German. Eagle used him to sight in. He put the cross-hairs on the man's left temple. He had sideburns that were going gray. It would have to be a side shot, there was no way for a frontal, and it really did not matter. Eagle took a deep breath and relaxed, releasing the tension of the rifle sling.

The speaker held up his hand and said something.

236

He pointed to the drapes covering the window. The crowd roared.

A man stepped through the parted drapes and approached the lectern. The crowd adored him. He held both hands over his head and they hushed. The man held out his arm in the Nazi salute. The crowd held its breath and Eagle found that he was doing likewise.

The man began to speak. Softly, in a sweet and rational voice. *Susse stimme.* The German was that of a well-educated man.

"My father," the man said, "was a born orator. I am not. But if I lack his voice and his talents, I possess something as valuable. As sacred. I have his spirit and his blood. I have his name."

For a minute the crowd roared. The man tried to quiet them with his upraised hands.

Eagle kept the binoculars glued on the man. He was of medium height and strongly made. He wore the *lederhosen* and thick wool half-stockings to just below his knees. His shirt was black, as was his tie, and on his left arm he wore the swastika.

At first all Eagle could see was the profile and that was not enough. The chin was right, and the blunt nose, but something was missing. When the man turned and Eagle saw him full-face he realized what it was. No mustache. The comic little mustache was missing—the Chaplinesque fluff of hair that fools had laughed at until it was too late.

The man turned away. Eagle laid the cross-hairs on the temple, then let the sling go loose and picked up the binoculars again. So no mustache. Bad public relations? No matter. He could always grow one.

The speaker's voice changed. Coarsened. No more sweet talk. He began to swing his arms about and thump on the lectern with every other word. Sweat sparkled on his face. Eagle wondered about the chest under the black shirt. Pigeon-breasted? Or—

That was it. The bulge under the black shirt was a bulletproof vest. Eagle smiled. They didn't even trust their own crowd. Or were they expecting company? If so they had made a mistake—they had given him the head shot.

Again and again, as the man turned, Eagle studied the face. The bone structure was right. If only he could see the eyes up close. He would know for sure.

The speaker was shouting now—sweating and shouting and waving his arms about and pounding on the lectern. His hair, which had been neatly combed to the side, parted to the left, now dangled in dank strands over his forehead.

The man stopped and drank from a carafe. The crowd shouted until he raised his hands again.

Certainty came to Eagle. He did not know exactly when he knew, when he was sure, he could not pin the moment, but suddenly it was there. This was the son of Adolf Hitler. This was no hoax, no dummy tricked up for devious purpose. This was the man. *The avatar.* Hitler's blood and flesh come to walk the earth again.

Demogorgon.

The man on the platform was screaming now. Shaking his fist at the world. Eagle nodded slightly to himself. It was all there—the megalomaniac will, the real belief that what he wanted was right and could not be denied him.

The tantrums. Eagle was seeing them now, the frothing gestures of a malign infant who wanted the world. Who demanded the world!

Merlin's words flitted through Eagle's mind.

"I will not have the world go down into the darkness again for lack of a stitch in time."

Eagle tightened the rifle sling. The verdict was in.

For a moment he tightened his muscles, bringing tension to bear on the sling as the cross-hairs slipped into place on the screaming man's head. Lower. A bit lower. More. A little more down.

The ranting man shook his fist at the crowd. He arched his neck and thrust out his jaw. Eagle let out half a breath.

Slowly, gently, softly, he squeezed the trigger.